Praise for the Hamptons Home & Garden Mysteries

"The dazzling houses showcased in the Hamptons Home & Garden mysteries aren't without skeletons in their closets. Fortunately, interior designer Meg Barrett has the golden touch when it comes to solving murders. Cozy mystery fans will adore the characters, stunning setting, and mouthwatering recipes in Kathleen Bridge's delightful series."

—Ellery Adams, *New York Times* bestselling author

"A delightful sneak peek into life in the Hamptons, with intricate plotting and a likeable, down-to-earth protagonist. A promising start to a promising series."

—*Suspense Magazine* on *Better Homes and Corpses*

"*Ghostal Living* is a marvelously entertaining tale of revenge, murder, quirky characters—and disappearing books! With a clever protagonist, wonderful details of life in the Hamptons, and plot twists on top of plot twists, Kathleen Bridge will have mystery readers clamoring for more."

—Kate Carlisle, *New York Times* bestselling author

"An excellent read."

—*RT Book Reviews* on *Hearse and Gardens*

"The descriptions of furniture and other antiques, as well as juicy tidbits on the Hamptons, make for entertaining reading for those who enjoy both antiques and lifestyles of the rich and famous."

—*Booklist* on *Better Homes and Corpses*

Books by Kathleen Bridge

Hamptons Home & Garden Mysteries

Better Homes and Corpses
Hearse and Gardens
Ghostal Living
Manor of Dying
A Design to Die For
A Fatal Feast
The Perfect Staging for Murder
High Style and Homicide

By the Sea Mysteries

Death by the Sea
A Killing by the Sea
Murder by the Sea
Evil by the Sea
Buried by the Sea

High Style
and Homicide

A Hamptons Home & Garden Mystery

Kathleen Bridge

BEYOND THE PAGE
PUBLISHING

High Style and Homicide
Kathleen Bridge
Beyond the Page Books
are published by
Beyond the Page Publishing
www.beyondthepagepub.com

I dedicate this book and all the others we've worked on together over the past eleven years to my late agent, Dawn Dowdle. I picture you, up in heaven, working your puzzles and keeping an eye on all the authors you touched so greatly in your short lifetime. You will be forever missed. XO, Kathy

Acknowledgments

As always, I want to thank my mother for being my first reader and editor. How did I get so lucky! A big shout-out to Cynthia Bogart, former *Better Homes & Gardens* editor, for sharing all the steps a magazine editor goes through before, during, and after going on location. Your insight was a true eye-opener. Ellen "Elle" Broder, thank you for coming through with some great vintage jewelry and clothing tips! Lon Otremba, once again, you delivered amazing recipes. I know we have a cookbook by now! To Maggie Perry, thanks for your support, friendship and sharing your treasured dessert recipe! And to my editor, Bill Harris at Beyond the Page Publishing. I am so grateful for your insight and excellent advice. I'm looking forward to working with you on my next Hamptons Home and Garden Mystery! Last, but not least, thank you to the amazing cozy mystery community of readers and all the cozy authors who support other cozy authors — we're just one big COZY family.

Chapter 1

It's funny, actually hilarious, that I would think an assignment involving everything I loved about interior design would go without a hitch.

I slowed to a stop in front of closed iron gates with a sign that read *Dahlia Lane Farms*. From somewhere in my head, I heard a voice whisper, *Meg, you deluded fool. I give you odds-on another dead body shows up.* I ignored the warning. Nothing could keep the butterflies from exploding in my gut at the thought of meeting home and garden guru Jessica Sterling. My excitement was just a few notches below what I'd experienced last week when I'd glanced into Patrick's gorgeous blue-green eyes and he'd told me he loved me.

You're right. No comparing that one.

But I digress . . .

Lowering my car window, I reached out and pressed a white button on the gate key box. My hearing aids had no problem picking up a loud tinny voice. "Yes? What do you want?"

I couldn't tell if the person at the other end of the intercom was male or female. Whoever they were, they sounded irritated. "It's Meg Barrett. I'm here to meet with Ms. Sterling to prepare for the photo shoot."

Dead silence.

"Uh, Ms. Sterling's publicist, Ashley Margulies, uh, recommended me." Ashley was also Patrick's book publicist. When Ashley heard Jessica was looking for someone in the area with interior design experience to help stage the backdrops for her new coffee table book, *Welcome to Dahlia Lane Windmill Cottage*, she'd thought of me. I owned a local interior design business called Cottages by the Sea and I'd once been editor in chief of a home and garden magazine.

I pressed the intercom again. "Hello, anyone there?"

Rather than a grouchy reply from the person on the other side of the intercom, the gates opened to acres and acres of lush greenery. In the distance I saw a majestic windmill silhouetted against a cloudless blue sky. I put my woody in Drive and inched my way up the blacktop lane.

Soon, I'd be face-to-face with the goddess of cozy home living, not to mention TV celebrity, farm-to-table chef (star of *Jessica's Table*), and master gardener. Jessica also had a line of furniture, home accessories, jewelry, handbags, stylish yet relaxed clothing and Dahlia Lane-logoed merchandise. To top that off, Jessica put out a monthly magazine called *Dahlia Lane Journal*.

What didn't she do?

The only thing missing from my upcoming assignment at Dahlia Lane was Elle Shoner, my best friend and partner in crime when it came to anything having to do with antiques and vintage. Elle was busy fixer-uppering her newly purchased not-so-humble mega-estate in Montauk.

It was a slow period in the Hamptons for interior design. Anyone who had a cottage, whether it needed refurbishing or not, spent their summer taking advantage of the short three-month season. My buddy Elle and I also had side jobs assisting the set designer on a streaming 1930s-era TV mystery series titled *Mr. & Mrs. Winslow* (of which my boyfriend, Patrick, was the screenwriter). Production was on hiatus for the summer, affording me the luxury of accepting the job at Dahlia Lane and allowing Patrick to finish writing his current thriller without me bugging him to come out and play.

I continued toward the windmill. A plethora of sprinklers misted the cool morning air, explaining the emerald vista that surrounded me. Instead of East Hampton, I felt like I was in Ireland. Every plant, tree, and flower flourished, including Jessica's prize-winning dahlias.

My walled cottage garden in the hamlet of Montauk wasn't faring as well. May and June in the Hamptons had been unseasonably dry. To no avail, every morning and afternoon I'd go out onto my deck and scan the horizon over the Atlantic for rain. All I ever found was the sun reflecting diamonds off calm ocean waves and wispy white clouds feathering their way across a periwinkle sky. I yearned for a good Long Island thunderstorm. There was nothing like being cocooned inside, stretched out on my window seat with a view of the Montauk Point Lighthouse, reading a whodunnit and sipping a cup of bookseller Georgia's homemade tea.

At least the influx of summer vacationers who'd trekked to the easternmost tip of Long Island were getting their money's worth of sun and surf. I was just worried about paying my water bill.

When I reached the gravel lot next to the windmill, I parked, got out and walked toward the front steps. The centuries-old windmill was one of Jessica Sterling's most recent projects. On last season's finale of *Dahlia Lane Home Makeover*, the windmill's exterior had received a storybook metamorphosis. The old windmill had been dismantled in Sag Harbor and sent to Dahlia Lane Farms on eight flatbed trucks. How did I know this? Because I was one of the fortunate ones who'd gotten stuck behind them on Highway 114. At the time, I'd been scouring Sag Harbor garage sales for items to furnish twelve small cottages. The cottages were once part of a motel complex in Montauk called the Sea Breeze Motor Lodge. The dilapidated Sea Breeze had been purchased by a wealthy benefactor (my bestie Elle), then renovated to give abused women and children who'd been staying in a shelter in Riverhead a place to call home. My assignment was to furnish all twelve cottages into cozy nests. Did I say I was blessed to have such a caring friend as Elle? Well, if I didn't, I was.

Oh, geez! I thought as I climbed the windmill's front steps. I'd almost forgotten about another one of Jessica Sterling's upcoming projects—Dahlia Lane Shoppes at the Hangar. The grand opening was scheduled for Saturday, July 4th—only four days away.

A few years ago, Jessica and her brother Travis purchased a run-down WWII airport that bordered Dahlia Lane Farms' property. I'd driven by it a few times in the past month, noticing Dahlia Lane's crew had kept the metal exterior of the hangar a rusty army green. In the last issue of *Dahlia Lane Journal*, Jessica had shared a design rendering of the hangar's interior. The center court of the hangar would be filled with indoor trees and seating areas; along the perimeter of the interior there'd be small cottage shops that sold locally sourced Long Island products relating to Dahlia Lane customers' interests.

I stepped onto the small porch and rang the bell, a real bell that was stationed to the right of the windmill's sage green double Dutch doors. I hoped Jessica Sterling turned out to be as personable as she seemed on TV. I even went as far as to fantasize that once we'd gotten to know each other, she would say, "Meg, call me Jessie." Just like her goofy fiancé costar and Dahlia Lane project manager Chris Barnes did on this season's *Dahlia Lane Home Makeover*.

Waiting a good couple minutes, I clanged the bell again. Finally, Jessica opened the door.

Only the person standing in front of me wasn't Jessica. It was the thin-lipped scowl that gave it away. Along with the woman's dark navy eyes.

I wasn't Jessica Sterling's stalker but I did know her eyes weren't blue—they were an espresso brown. This must be her cousin Lauren, whose recent outdoor wedding at Dahlia Lane Farms had been featured on an episode of *Jessica's Table*.

And yes, Jessica had prepared every detail of the wedding, from soup to nuts to decorations. The only thing Jessica didn't do was marry the couple.

On the first season of *Dahlia Lane Home Makeover* Lauren had been Jessica's sidekick. After some kind of scandal, Lauren agreed to a payout from the company business to start her own knockoff version of Dahlia Lane Farms—Lavender Fields Farm. When no network would pick up Lauren's copycat version of Dahlia Lane, she came crawling back on her knees, begging her cousin Jessica to take her back. At least that's the way the tabloids painted it.

During Lauren's two-year absence, Dahlia Lane had grown a hundred-fold. Cut to last fall—when a forgiving Jessica welcomed her cousin back with open arms.

Lauren looked behind me. "Did anyone else follow you through the gates? Did you see anyone lurking around?"

Lurking? "Uh, no," I said.

"I guess come in then."

She guessed?

Lauren opened the door wider, impatiently grabbed my wrist, then pulled me inside. With one last look toward the gates, she closed and locked the door. After a long-drawn-out sigh and an eye roll, she said, "Jessica's upstairs. Tower room." Then she scanned me from head to toe, then toe to head. I was wearing a short-sleeve cotton print ankle-length sundress and flat sandals that I'd purchased on Dahlia Lane's website. Lauren, on the other hand, wore a white T-shirt with a large gold Gucci insignia, skin-tight white capris and two-inch gold strappy sandals. At her neck was a thick gold rope necklace. Each ear was pierced with three diamond studs in descending size. I couldn't believe I'd thought she was her cousin.

"By the time you reach Rapunzel at the top of her latest folly," she added, performing eye roll number two, "you might need a water bottle."

Surveying the space, I immediately swooned at the morning sunshine coming in from a floor-to-ceiling mullioned window at the end of the narrow hallway. Prisms of light made the blue-and-green flowered wallpaper come alive. The wallpaper reminded me of William Morris prints from the late-nineteen-hundreds aesthetic Arts and Crafts period of design. Whitewashed plank floors were covered with a natural sisal runner. The only furniture in the high-ceilinged hallway was a bleached Scandinavian pine bench and console table. A curving wrought iron staircase spiraled up two levels, ending at what I guessed was a small room at the top of the windmill.

"I'm speechless. It's breathtaking. I should have known. I have chill bumps and I'm not cold. The seamless blending of two centuries of interior design was exactly what I'd expected from Ms. Sterling."

Lauren wasn't as enamored as I. Clicking her tongue, she said, "A windmill, for God's sake. I'm claustrophobic just standing here. Another one of her crazy ideas. Thank God she listened to my husband's suggestion of attaching the windmill to the farmhouse. My cousin may come across as the idea woman at Dahlia Lane, but it takes a village—more like a family—to turn her musings into concrete things. Hope the storefronts inside that decrepit airplane hangar turn a profit."

I opened my mouth to defend Jessica, but Lauren had slipped through an open doorway. Near the doorway, hanging over the console table, was a huge pine-framed mirror. It made the windmill's narrow entryway seem light and airy—the *opposite* of claustrophobic.

It appeared Jessica got the sweet family genes and Lauren the sour.

After Lauren disappeared, she made sure to slam the door behind her.

Yikes! Not what I'd envisioned. But that would all change when I met Jessica Sterling.

Glancing down the hallway, I saw four closed doors. Knowing Lauren said her cousin was upstairs, I tiptoed to the bottom of the twisting staircase. Placing my right foot on the first step, I grabbed the banister. *Should I or shouldn't I go up?* What if Jessica was in a compromising position with her fiancé?

Throwing caution to the wind-*mill*, I ascended, making sure my loud footsteps echoed upward to announce my arrival. When I reached the first landing, I called out, "Hello, Ms. Sterling. It's Meg Barrett. Lauren said I should come on up and announce myself." I used poetic license on that one.

"Welcome, Meg. Please come up."

I continued until I reached the top landing. White plaster walls supported by pale wood beams reached up to a peaked ceiling. I glanced around in astonishment. And when I say around, I mean around. Jessica had used every inch of the space surrounding the open stairwell. In front of me was a window seat built into the curve of the tower that looked to the south. Through the windmill's huge fan blades I caught a glimpse of the mighty Atlantic, shimmering in all her majesty. I turned around. One-hundred-eighty degrees ahead of me was a white upholstered chaise with large blue and white pillows. Beside the chaise was a small table and reading lamp. At ninety degrees, a pine drop-front desk and spindle chair stood next to an arched window looking to the east. A sucker for small spaces, give me a kitchen, bathroom and my cat Jo, and I would never leave this tower room.

Jessica Sterling stood with her back to a window that faced west. A small French bulldog and large Olde English bulldog flanked her on either side—their stubby tails wagging in synchronized harmony.

"So happy to meet you, Meg," she said, reaching out her hand. "And obviously, Boo and Ridley are too."

Wow, I knew it. We were kindred spirits. *To Kill a Mockingbird* had been my favorite coming-of-age book. Jessica had named her bulldogs after Scout and Jem's neighbor—Boo Ridley.

I stepped toward her, and she took my hand in hers, its warmth matching her huge smile.

"Welcome to Windmill Cottage," she said.

"Oh, it's my pleasure," I gushed. "I'm completely in awe of how you've decorated the interior of the windmill."

Glancing out the window next to her, I spied a huge red barn and cultivated farmland stretching to the west. The light coming through the window created a halo effect around her.

She was luminous. Just like she came across on TV. Her farmgirl/boho style couldn't be more opposite to Lauren's. She had on a gauzy white cotton ruffled blouse tucked into her jean shorts. Her skin was golden, as if she spent a lot of time outdoors, which I knew she did. Her butterscotch leather belt showed off her narrow hips. On second thought, knowing Jessica's love of animals, I was sure the belt, along with her short cowboy boots, were pleather—not leather. Her long, silky ebony hair was pulled back in a high ponytail, tied with a red bandanna.

"Meg, I'm so thrilled to finally meet you," she said in a lilting voice. "I've heard great things from Ashley. I'm excited to go over what I've planned for us tomorrow," she added. "And please call me Jessie."

It took everything I had not to collapse onto the floor.

Chapter 2

After a tour of the windmill, each small room more impressive than the last, Jessie walked me to the front door. "I'll text you the code to the front and rear gates, then you can come and go as you please. Wish we didn't need a code or all this security. My brother insists."

She opened one of the double Dutch doors and we stepped onto the small covered porch.

Glancing in the direction of the iron gates and speaking almost as if to herself, Jessie said, "Something's going on with Travis. Wish I knew what." She shrugged her shoulders and her fabulous smile returned. Turning to me, she said, "I'm sure everything's okay. With the Shoppes at the Hangar grand opening Saturday, we've both been a little distracted."

Even though Jessie and her fiancé were the spokespeople for Dahlia Lane, Jessie and her brother Travis were co-owners of the umbrella that was Dahlia Lane Enterprises. Travis was a woodworker and had his own series on the Dahlia Lane Network called *Dahlia Lane Woodworks*. The show was a cult favorite with my boyfriend. Woodworking, when Patrick wasn't surfing, writing screenplays or thrillers, was as cathartic for him as revamping old furniture and precious junk was to me.

We said our goodbyes, then I walked with an upbeat spring to my step to where I'd parked my woody. I was delighted to work with Jessie tomorrow, but at the same time a little anxious after what Jessie had just said about her brother. *There doesn't have to be a mystery everywhere you go, Meg Barrett,* I told myself.

Just as I reached for my woody's door handle, I caught movement behind a small white gazebo covered in Wisteria. A man dressed in overalls was watering the Nikko blue hydrangeas that circled the gazebo. I knew who he was. Dahlia Lane's garden expert, Peat Moss Pete. A nickname, of course. I was a huge admirer of his segments on *Jessica's Table* and *Dahlia Lane Home Makeover*. I considered myself a capable herb and flower gardener, but nothing compared to Pete.

I hesitated before getting inside my car, wondering if I shouldn't go over and introduce myself. Before I could decide, Jessie's cousin Lauren came flying across the manicured lawn in her two-inch sandals, straight into Pete's open arms.

What the heck! From watching Pete in his gardening segments on the Dahlia Lane Network, I wouldn't have pegged him as a love interest for *recently* married Lauren. Pete wasn't attractive. But he wasn't unattractive, either. More of a plain Pete. He was shorter than Lauren, thin—almost to the point of being emaciated. He wore nerdy Harry Potter glasses that made him look like an owl. Not a white owl, like Harry Potter's Hedwig, more like a mottled barn owl losing its feathers. Or in Pete's case, the hair above his forehead. On the other hand, when Pete talked about plants, his enthusiasm was contagious, and he had a fabulous smile. I'd learned quite a lot from his sage advice when it came to my own small cottage garden.

I supposed it wasn't out of the realm of possibility that Jessie's cousin Lauren and Pete where lovers. And frankly, it wasn't any of my business. "Rein it in, Meg. This is none of your affair," I said out loud. Lauren and Pete turned in my direction. I must have spoken louder than I thought because of the wind whistling in and out of my hearing aids.

Lauren took a step back. I could tell by her scowl she wasn't happy I'd spotted them. Not knowing what else to do, I grinned, tossed them a quick wave, then scooted inside my car. I started the engine and hightailed it toward the gates. If it wasn't for how slowly the gates were opening, I would have left skid marks. While waiting, a text arrived from Jessie with the gate code, reminding me I could come and go as I pleased. I had a niggling feeling Jessie's cousin might not be so accommodating.

I pulled through the gates. Just as I made a left onto the dirt lane, a white Escalade came hurtling toward me, nearly sideswiping my woody. It was only a flash, but I saw who was behind the wheel. Jessie's brother Travis.

What the heck!

I pulled my car to a stop and watched him in the rearview mirror. The SUV went careening through the still closing gates, leaving a mushroom cloud of dust in its wake.

"Pipe down," I said to my pesky inner voice, as warning bells reverberated in my head. "We're talkin' about working with Jessica, aka Jessie Sterling. I won't be dissuaded from coming back to Dahlia Lane tomorrow."

As I pulled away, there was a distinctive feeling of unease in my gut. As I'd done in the past, to my detriment, I ignored it.

Chapter 3

A few minutes later, I breathed a sigh of relief when I came to Route 27, the Town of East Hampton's main thoroughfare. The quaint New England–style white storefronts housed expensive clothing and jewelry shops, along with restaurants with executive chefs who prepared Michelin-star meals at Michelin-star prices.

The village was decked out in full patriot Fourth of July regalia. American flags swayed from every lamppost and red-white-and-blue buntings hung from storefronts. After all, East Hampton was established in the mid-1600s and had played its part in the Revolutionary War.

Traffic was stop and go because of the tourist season. Even though Montauk was only fourteen miles away, it could take me a good thirty minutes or more to get home.

I continued east on East Hampton's North Main Street, passing the Old Hook Windmill, wondering if Jessie's windmill was as old.

Before showing up at Dahlia Lane Farms, I'd done my research on Long Island wooden smock windmills. Their forty-foot blades were used to power gears that ground corn and grains. The golden age of smock windmills ended when the steam-powered trains from New York City reached the Hamptons with sacks of flour and grains milled in factories upstate.

Between East Hampton and Amagansett, a call came through to my hearing aids.

I knew who it was. Elle. I was surprised she'd waited this long to find out how my meeting went at Dahlia Lane with our idol, Jessica Sterling.

I pressed the small button on my right hearing aid and accepted the call. "Yes," I said. "She's as awesome as you imagined."

"Of course she's awesome," Elle answered. "I so wish I could've been there. Tell me. Tell me. Did you meet anyone else? For instance, her hilarious, adorable fiancé, Chris Barnes?"

"Just her cousin, Lauren. And Jessie's dogs, Boo and Ridley." I left off seeing Pete Moss and Travis Sterling.

"And the Windmill Cottage, how was it? What style is the interior? Scandinavian, I bet."

"Eclectic but definitely leaning toward Scandinavian/Norwegian design."

"Knew it. Did I ever tell you I almost bought a windmill? Before I could put in an offer, a famous celeb stole it away from me."

"Is that so," I said, smiling to myself as I passed through the quaint hamlet of Amagansett.

"It's true. The Edward DeRose Windmill Cottage."

"What were you going to do with it, open an annex of Mabel & Elle's Curiosities? Use it as a big closet for all your vintage clothing and jewelry?"

"Oh, you're a riot," she said. "I love windmills, just like you love lighthouses. I once toured the Shinnecock Mill. It was once part of the campus of Stony Brook Southampton. It was used as a cottage for visiting professors."

"Oh, I read about that. Tennessee Williams stayed there in the late fifties. He wrote a book about his buddy Jackson Pollack, who'd died the year before in an East Hampton car crash."

"Yes, but I bet you didn't know this little fun fact," Elle said. "The Shinnecock Mill is said to be haunted. In the late nineteen-hundreds, Beatrice, the daughter of the owner of the mill, fell down a flight of stairs, broke her neck, and sometimes can be seen peering out the window in the windmill's tower room. Maybe she was Tennessee Williams's muse?"

"Where did you read that? In your *Ghosts of Long Island* book?"

"Stop teasing me, Megan Elizabeth Barrett. You know I don't like to be teased—especially lately."

"I'm sorry, buddy. After seeing Dahlia Lane's windmill-turned-cottage, I wouldn't mind living in one either. Only, I think I'll stick to my oceanfront cottage. And I'm sure once you move into your new home, living in a tiny windmill will be the last thing on your bucket list. By the way, what's the latest name you've given your Montauk estate? Is it still Montaukett Manor?"

"No. That's too pretentious, so I came up with a better one. Heron's Roost. Remember when we first saw the water from the property? A white heron was on the shore, and I told you it was a good omen. The Native Americans were right, my heron is a sign of patience and good luck. I just saw him the other day. His name is Merlyn."

"As in *The Sword and the Stone* by T. H. White?"

"Exactly."

Elle had been a madwoman on a mission the day we stumbled upon the old Willis Estate. It had taken tons of sleuthing to track down the owners. Because the estate had been neglected for so long, there'd been no haggling over the price.

Now, Elle was just as dogged about renovating the decrepit mansion and outbuildings as she had been about searching Montauk for the home of her dreams.

Elle's and Arthur's estate was located on five acres of land with a sunset view of the Block Island Sound. There was a horse stable Elle planned to turn into a three-car garage on one side and our workshop for our fixer-uppers on the other. *Yay!*

The main house was a Queen Anne shingle-style mansion with gables, dormers and wraparound verandas. It rose two and a half stories high and had three brick chimneys. The interior of the house hadn't been inhabited by humans in six decades. The only residents had been mice, racoons and other creatures, including bats.

Any other person would have gutted the entire main house, but not Elle. She planned to repair or replace every crown molding, stair rail, or salvageable architectural piece to bring the house back to its 1900s splendor.

"So, how's it going over there?" I asked. "You sure you're not mad I took on the assignment at Dahlia Lane without you?"

"Of course not," she said. "Just slightly jealous. But there's nothing for you to do here until Duke and Duke Jr. cart off the trio of Dumpsters in front of the house. I won't be sad to see them go. But I'll need you in a couple weeks when I tackle the second floor."

"I'll be all yours. In the meantime, I'll try to get you an invite to Dahlia Lane Farms. Jessie is so sweet. Just like we thought."

"That would be fabulous," she said. I imagined her freckled cheeks turning pink in excitement. "This time don't get involved in any murders. I won't be there to save you."

"Promise. I won't if you won't. Like Shinnecock Windmill, you might have your own things to worry about. Who knows what ghosts have been living in Heron's Roost? They might not be happy you're disturbing their peace."

Elle laughed. "Funny, honey. The only person I want to murder is the subcontractor, who was supposed to show up at eight. Remodeling isn't for the faint of heart."

"Remember your white heron—patience and good luck are your watchwords." I wasn't sure, but I thought I heard Elle growl. She sounded like my fat cat Jo after I relocated her from my reading chair to her kitty bed.

"Yeah, yeah, sure. You try to deal with these subcontractors—it's like herding bees."

"I think you mean cats."

"You know what I mean. Plus, bees would be harder."

"Need anything from the farm stand?" I asked, pulling into the lot of the Montauk Farmer's Market.

"Yes, get me the usual. Haven't had time to shop. If I ever get away from here, why don't you stop over for dinner? Arthur is barbequing bison burgers. Invite Patrick."

I turned off the engine and looked at the line snaking its way to the farm stand's cashier. "I'll be there. Don't know about Patrick. He's in the weeds with his next book."

"OMG!" she screeched. The sound made my hearing aids buzz.

"What? What's wrong?"

"The subcontractor dude finally showed up. Hallelujah!" Then the line went dead.

I had no clue what the "usual" was when it came to Elle's choice of produce. But after being friends for so long, I knew her likes and dislikes. Wild mushrooms being one of her likes. Brussels sprouts being one of her dislikes.

I'd never been a big fan of brussels sprouts, either. But all that changed after Patrick made me his roasted version, using grated parmesan and a balsamic glaze. At the thought of Patrick, I smiled. He'd promised we would have a mini date at my cottage tomorrow night. With his writing schedule, I would take whatever time he would give me.

So there were two things to look forward to tomorrow. My first official day at Dahlia Lane and Patrick.

Little did I know, or perhaps maybe I should have known, one of those things wouldn't go as planned.

Chapter 4

"Meg Barrett!" a male voice called out, almost causing me to drop the Dansk vase I was holding. I placed the vase on the Tulip Room's mantel and turned. Putting my hands on my hips, I said, "Emilio Castillo, as I live and breathe."

He laughed. "I'd often wondered what happened to our fearless leader at *American Home & Garden*. It's like you disappeared off the face of the earth. You should have heard the rumors at the magazine. Naturally," he said with an evil grin, "I was hoping they were all true. Especially the ones involving he-who-shall-not-be-named." Emilio took a few steps toward me. As he walked, dark curly bangs with strands of gray fell in front of hazel eyes that sparked in amusement. "Of all the gin joints and . . ."

I reached out and gave him a bone-crushing hug. I'd no idea my first official day of work would hold such a surprise. Emilio had been our visual director at *American Home & Garden*. After finding my fiancé, who'd also worked at the magazine, in the arms of his ex-wife, I'd left—more like fled—Manhattan and a job I loved. Turned out, moving to the easternmost tip of Long Island was the best thing that ever happened to me. Or at least a close second to meeting Patrick.

"Still as gorgeous as ever, fair maiden," he said. "Same cornflower blue eyes. I see they haven't lost their mischievous twinkle. All you need is a pair of wooden shoes, then I could snap a photo of you clogging up the cobblestones and use it in the windmill book."

I laughed. "Sorry, Emilio, left my wooden shoes at home. I can't believe you're here. What are the chances you'd be the photographer for Ms. Sterling's book?"

"Well, pretty good," he said, laughing. "Like you, I'm no longer at *American Home & Garden*. This is my second year working for Dahlia Lane Enterprises."

"Meg," Jessie called out. "I didn't know you worked at *American Home & Garden*. How lucky for me. And Meg, I told you to call me Jessie. I don't believe in formalities. Right, Emilio?"

"No, you don't, Jessie," he answered with a grin. "Meg was our editor in chief once upon a time. Now here she is."

"Now I have you both!" Jessie was standing at a table near a window overlooking Dahlia Lane's shade garden and was in the process of artfully arranging green tulips in a blue-and-white delft pitcher.

Every windmill needs tulips, I thought.

A short time ago, Jessie had led me to a floor-to-ceiling glass atrium that connected the windmill to the huge farmhouse featured in many episodes of *Dahlia Lane Home Makeover.* Lining both sides of the atrium's glass walls were dozens of tin flower buckets filled with blooms, including tulips in a kaleidoscope of hues.

It was way past tulip season in the Hamptons. However, for the purpose of photographing the book, Jessie shared she'd imported a planeload of flowers from the Netherlands. She'd also told me the windmill's exterior and the surrounding landscape had already been photographed in the months of April and May for the windmill book. Which was a good thing because the Long Island blooming season for tulips, daffodils, hyacinths, freesia, lilacs and peonies was over.

Hopefully, Emilio would share some of the exterior photos before the book went into production. I knew from working at *American Home & Garden* that the time between photo shoot and publication could span six months. Or longer. And that was for a monthly magazine.

"Jessie-ie," I said, a tad awkwardly, wanting to pinch myself that we were on such familiar terms. "I adore how you've furnished and accessorized the windmill. Honestly, are you sure you need me? I wouldn't change a thing for the book. If I'm not mistaken, you're applying the principles of hygge."

"That's why I need you," she said, grinning. "No one else has a clue about what hygge is."

"Sounds like the name of a deodorant or species of plant," Emilio said. "What is it?"

"You or me?" Jessie asked.

I thought back to a cottage I'd worked on for a couple from Denmark and said, "I'll go first. Hygge is a restorative practice that focuses on ten ideals of design—"

"Equality, comfort, pleasure, togetherness, harmony, atmosphere, gratitude, truce, presence, and shelter," Jessie finished for me. "Hygge is like a manifesto for comfy living."

"Well," Emilio said, "if anyone knows about comfy living, it would be you, Jessie."

"I agree," I said. "Everything here is simple and clean with only a few statement pieces, yet at the same time Windmill Cottage is warm and inviting."

"Thanks, Meg," Jessie said as she plucked a tulip from the pitcher, leaving eleven instead of twelve. No doubt sticking to the old interior design golden rule of using odd numbers in staging smalls in a room.

I glanced over at Emilio's puzzled expression and said, "The word in Danish means to give courage, comfort, and joy."

Jessie moved a small table lamp a few inches from the pitcher of tulips, then moved it back again. Now I understood why all her interiors were en pointe—she was a perfectionist.

I gave her a thumbs-up. "Perfect. My friend Elle, owner of Mabel and Elle's Curiosities in Sag Harbor, had a similar lamp in her shop. She told me it was a mid-century Scandinavian Anna something lamp. I learned about hygge from her."

"Ehrner," Jessie said. "Anna Ehrner. Well, I'll be. Guess where I purchased this? I will defiantly have to meet your friend. I love her things. So eclectic. I always find something."

"I'll tell her. Believe me, she'll be so excited to meet you."

"Elle also worked at *American Home & Garden* as our antiques and collectibles editor," Emilio added.

"Then I really have to meet her," Jessie said, taking a step back to assess the tablescape's balance. Satisfied, she turned to us. "I read somewhere hygge is practiced in women's prisons in Denmark. The inmates are allowed to wear their own clothes and decorate their cells as cozy and simple as possible. The study showed an inmate's living environment had a positive effect on their rehabilitation."

"Wow. I never heard about that," I said, thinking about the women and children who would be moving into the cottages at the motel complex Elle bought. They weren't prisoners but in some ways they were. Living in a shelter and fearing their abuser might find them seemed a good reason to provide them with a living space all their own.

Emilio raised an eyebrow. "Why only female inmates? They should try it on men. Real men need to decorate hygge."

Jessie laughed, then, still holding the tulip, she said, "Meg, I do need you to arrange things while I stand next to Emilio and look through his lens so we can frame the perfect shot. Not that I don't trust him. His work has been flawless. That's why Dahlia Lane snatched him away from *American Home & Garden*. Now it seems I have two of you from the magazine. A win-win for me."

I was surprised Emilio would leave the magazine. He'd been there for at least ten years. I'm sure it had something to do with my ex-fiancé, Michael. Whatever the reason, with Emilio's street cred, it was indeed a win-win for Dahlia Lane Enterprises.

A shaft of morning sun pierced the mullioned window, bathing Jessie in golden rays of light. Her long, silky, blue-black hair was pulled back in a headband. Even though I knew she had on makeup, it was understated, her skin healthy and glowing.

After looking her up on Wikipedia (swear I'm not a stalker), I'd found Jessie was forty, only five years older than Elle and me. She appeared much younger, especially when she and her fiancé exchanged quips on TV like little kids playing in a sandbox. They seemed a perfect match. Not that I knew what went on behind closed doors. Truly, I'd been duped more than once by outward appearances—a few of those times by cold-blooded killers.

Emilio turned to me and said, "Are you thinking what I'm thinking?"

"I'm sure I am, Emilio," I said. "With the light filtering through the window and the tulip in her hand—"

"It would be a great shot for the book," Emilio finished, excitement flushing his cheeks. "Let me set up my camera before we lose the moment." He went to his rolling bag near the door to the hallway, reached down and started to unzip it.

"Hurry!" I said to Emilio.

"Meg, did I say I missed you and your impatient demands? My bad," he said, laughing. Then he pulled out an aluminum tripod.

"Hey," I said, "you're the one who taught me about the importance of catching the perfect light in photography."

Jessie looked on in amusement.

Suddenly, there was raucous barking coming from the hallway. Two seconds later, Lauren charged through the open doorway. Following close behind were Jessie's dogs, Boo and Ridley.

Lauren pushed past Emilio, almost knocked him to the floor, then ran to Jessie's side.

"What's going on, Lauren?" Jessie asked, visibly shaken.

Lauren stopped short. "Oh, cuz, it's terrible. I can't even tell you." Lauren went to the small love seat next to where Jessie stood and sat down. Patting the off-white cushion, she said, "Come sit."

Jessie took baby steps and sat next to her. "Lauren, you're scaring me. Why are you crying? You never cry."

I thought I saw Lauren give her cousin a look, but it was soon erased.

Both cousins shared the same olive complexion and high cheekbones. Their long black hair was almost the same length, only Jessie's was a smidgeon longer. Lauren was a couple inches shorter than her cousin. Her posture slightly hunched. I knew Jessie was a few years older. Except for the color of their eyes and their different fashion styles, they could pass for twins.

Lauren took Jessie's hand, then said in a whisper I could barely make out, "It's Travis, sweetie . . ." A single tear trailed down Lauren's cheek, then pooled onto her quivering bottom lip. "Conrad just called me with some terrible news. He's on his way here." Lauren took a deep inhale, then said, "Travis . . . he's dead."

Emilio dropped his tripod, the dogs growled, and Jessie fainted into the love seat's down cushions.

And there it was. Another job, another dead body . . .

Chapter 5

An hour later, if you'd told me my best friend Elle's husband, Arthur Shoner, lead detective on the East Hampton Town Police Department, would be sitting across from me in the Tulip Room, drinking a cup of Dahlia Lane Farms organic tea, I would have told you it was indeed a small world. But what made it minuscule was the fact my father, Jeff Barrett, retired homicide detective on the Detroit PD, was sitting next to him.

I'd been the one delegated to answer the clang of the bell at the windmill's front door. Not a chore. I was more than happy to escape the tragic scene in the Tulip Room.

As soon as Arthur saw me, he'd put his hand in front of my face in a blocking gesture. "Save it, Meg. Your father already told me you'd be here." Then I'd glanced over Arthur's shoulder to see my father coming up the cobblestones dressed like the lead character in Hemingway's *Old Man and the Sea*.

When my father passed by me, he'd whispered into my right hearing aid, "I was fishing with Doc when they found Travis's body. Arthur said I could tag along."

Doc was my father's best friend and my surrogate uncle. Former Detroit PD coroner Doc had moved to Montauk a few years ago to pursue his love of sportfishing. I also suspected he moved to the Hamptons to spy on me and report back to my father, who at the time lived in my childhood home of Detroit with his wife Sheila.

Fast-forward to the present day. My father and Sheila had recently signed on the dotted line for an amicable divorce. Now Jeff Barrett was bunking at Doc's cabin in Montauk. I'd offered my cottage guest room. My father declined, saying he didn't want to add any speed bumps to my blossoming romance with Patrick. *What a guy.*

Amazingly enough, my father and Patrick had become fast friends—not the case with my father and my former fiancé. Maybe it had something to do with the fact Patrick wasn't a big fat cheating, pompous, narcissistic jerk like Michael.

Patrick and my father also shared a hobby I benefited from. They were both gourmet home chefs and had struck up a friendly rivalry by switching off nights preparing fabulous entrées. Leaving me as *Top Chef's* judge, Tom Colicchio. Not that I'm complaining. I was delighted to weigh in on the winner. However, after one of their gastronomic showdowns, I wasn't as thrilled about weighing myself on the bathroom scale.

Now that my father lived in Montauk, except for the years with my mother, I'd never seen him happier.

After I'd closed the windmill's front door and led Arthur and my father to the Tulip Room, I'd wondered how my father knew who Travis Sterling was. Then I'd remembered my father and Patrick sharing a couple beers while watching a few episodes of *Dahlia Lane Woodworks*—my father a nonalcoholic beer and Patrick his favorite Montauk craft beer.

• • •

"At this point," Arthur said, looking uncomfortable, "it looks like a hit-and-run." Arthur glanced at Jessie, then nervously adjusted his vintage YSL tie. He'd always dressed impeccably. But now that he was married to Elle, owner of two room-sized closets filled with vintage clothing, shoes and jewelry, Arthur must have caved to her demands of adding some old-school designer flair to his wardrobe.

My father, on the other hand, was dressed in waders and a stained long-sleeve khaki shirt with dozens of pockets. In his hand was Doc's fishing hat. Fishing lures, lethal enough to poke out an eye, dangled from the hat's crown.

Arthur continued, "Your brother was found unresponsive in the seagrass next to the parking lot divers use when exploring the *Culloden* wreck site."

Everyone who lived in Montauk, including me, knew all about the HMS *Culloden*, the English ship that arrived in nearby Gardiner's Bay in 1781 to help set up a blockade to keep the French ships protecting the American Patriots at Newport, Rhode Island, from leaving the harbor. The HMS *Culloden* ran aground eighteen feet off the point, in the murky shifting sands of Montauk's Fort Pond Bay. The *Culloden* shipwreck was one of Long Island's most popular dive sites because it had easy access from the shore.

"A hit-and-run!" Lauren said. "I hope you got the monster who killed my cousin."

"I'm sorry," Arthur said. "We're doing everything we can to find out what happened. We'll know more when I meet with my crime scene team as soon as I leave here. But rest assured, we'll get him or her. Plus, there's always the possibility that someone's conscience will make them come forward. I've seen it before."

"Were there any witnesses?" Jessie sobbed.

"Not at this time," Arthur answered.

Lauren shot up from the love seat. "Then how the hell can you catch this monster, if no one saw it?"

Arthur shifted in his chair like he was sitting on shards of glass. "Our department will ask the public for help."

Jessie gulped for air, then said, "If my brother still had on his wet suit, as you said, it must have been right after he talked to me. He told me he was done diving and on his way to the Shoppes at the Hangar to meet someone. I think you've made a mistake. It can't be my brother."

"Oh, Jessica, I am so sorry," Lauren said, sitting back down. She reached into her large handbag and removed a packet of tissues. She took one for herself, dabbed her eyes, then handed the packet to her cousin. "I'm here for you, Jessica. Whatever you need. Just tell me."

Jessie didn't answer, but turned to Arthur and managed to choke out, "Detective, maybe it was someone else—not my baby brother? Who would do this? Just leave him without calling for help?"

"I'm sorry, Ms.—" Arthur said softly, then glanced down at his notepad.

"Sterling," I said.

Arthur shot me one of his trademark dirty looks. One he'd perfected from the first time we'd met over the dead body of Caroline Spenser at the Seacliff estate—our first shared murder investigation. With more to follow.

"He was identified by someone who knew him." He glanced at my father. "And we found his wallet in the glove box," Arthur mumbled, not meeting Jessie's pleading eyes. "And the hatch of his Escalade was open, his oxygen tanks, diving hood and flippers inside. He must have been hit while standing at the back of his car."

"Okay, you've delivered your news. No more details. Now leave us in peace," Lauren snapped.

"Oh, Jessie, I'm so sorry," a male voice said. Glancing toward the hallway, I saw Lauren's husband, Conrad Kincaid, standing under the threshold of the open door. I recognized him from his wedding to Lauren on *Jessica's Table*. I also knew from reading the masthead on the inside cover of *Dahlia Lane Journal* he was Dahlia Lane's financial and marketing VP. Ever since leaving *American Home & Garden,* I had a habit of looking for colleagues I knew in the business.

Conrad stepped inside the room and immediately went to Jessie's side. He knelt next to her and gave her a warm hug, then, in an intimate gesture, wiped a tear from the corner of her right eye. "I'm so sorry, Jessie. What can I do?"

"Bring my brother back," Jessie said softly, causing me to read her lips. "I want to see him. I refuse to believe—This can't be true," she sobbed, looking first at Conrad, then to Arthur.

"It's okay, honey," Conrad said, stroking the top of her hand as if it was covered with fur. "We'll get to the bottom of this." Conrad was tall and lean, with short, neatly trimmed hair that had more pepper than salt. He had a tan, not a fake orange tan, apparently having spent more time on the tennis court than in Dahlia Lane's boardroom. He seemed a lot older than his wife, Lauren. A couple decades older. So maybe it was a pickleball court he played on. Either way, he was attractive for his age. The word *debonair* came to mind.

Possibly jealous of her husband's attention, Lauren grabbed Jessie's wrist and said, "You can see Travis. I'll take you. No matter what you say, Detective."

Again, Arthur glanced at my father. "You can identify him today. But the body won't be released until the autopsy results are in. We want to get everything right. Hopefully someone will turn themselves in and we'll know more."

"Who found him? Did someone see the accident?" Conrad asked.

"I'd rather not share information until we know more," Arthur answered.

Lauren placed a hand on both sides of Jessie's head, forcing her to make eye contact. "Jessica, Conrad and I will handle everything." She looked over at her husband. "I think right now, you should take one of my pills. It will calm you."

Jessie didn't say yes or no to the offer. She just collapsed back into the love seat's cushions and silently wept.

Conrad moved from Jessie's side and stood at the back of the love seat. "That's a good idea, Lauren. Why don't you go fetch Jessie a few of those pills?" Then he gingerly put his hand on Lauren's shoulder.

"I'm not a dog, Conrad," Lauren snapped. "I don't fetch anything on your command."

It appeared Lauren's husband was the dog, and it wouldn't have surprised me to learn he'd spent an inordinate amount of time in the doghouse.

I wasn't an FBI profiler, but due to my hearing loss I was able to pick up on visual details others might miss. Lauren's flinching when Conrad put his hand on her shoulder had been one of those clues. It was possible that by Lauren marrying Dahlia Lane's business and marketing VP, who had a close relationship with Jessie, their union had paved the way for Lauren's return from exile.

Lauren turned to her cousin and said, "*Jessica*, you need to rest. Go to the farmhouse and I'll bring you something to help you take the edge off." When Lauren said her cousin's name, she sounded like a mother or schoolteacher talking down to a child.

Jessie shook her head. "I don't take pills. You and Conrad know that."

Lauren took a deep breath, then narrowed her eyes in Arthur's direction. "How long do you think it'll take for the autopsy?"

"Autopsy results take a while," Arthur said. "However, it's pretty clear how he died."

"That's routine for the autopsy results to take some time," my father piped in. "Don't be alarmed." His smooth voice and gentle smile seemed to calm Jessie.

Unfortunately, his words seemed to have the opposite effect on Lauren. She shot up from the love seat and gave my father the once-over. Just like she'd done with me at our first meeting. "Who the hell are you, anyway?"

"Jeff Barrett," he said, extending his hand. Lauren didn't take it.

Emilio saved the day by stepping into the room with an armload of water bottles. He immediately went to Jessie, unscrewed the top from one of the bottles, then handed it to her.

"Emilio, I'll have one too, if you don't mind," Lauren said, shaking her head. "Aren't you just Jessica's perfect little gopher. What's wrong with Philomena? She should be serving us. This is outside your pay grade."

"You mean Wilhelmina?" Emilio said with a clenched jaw.

"Lauren, she's been Dahlia Lane Farms' part-time housekeeper for the two years I've been working here, and you don't even know her name. She only works Friday to Sunday. She takes care of her mother during the week."

"Excus-s-e me. I don't need to be chastised by the hired help."

"We're all out of sorts. Let's try to be kind to one another," Conrad said.

Emilio glanced around the room. Ignoring Lauren's outstretched hand, he said, "Anyone else want a water?" When he noticed my father, he said, "Jeff, so sorry we had to meet under these circumstances. Meg just told me you've retired from the Detroit Police Department and moved here."

"This dirty fisherman's your husband?" Lauren asked, turning to me.

"No. My father."

I was glad Jessie didn't question why my father was here with Arthur.

Conrad went back to Jessie's side and whispered something into her ear.

I didn't have to read his lips because of Jessie's response. "I'll do no such thing! Shoppes at the Hangar was Travis's project just as much as it was mine. Travis poured his heart and soul into every aspect of its planning. Conrad, you of all people know what it meant to him. Unlike some people in this room." Her gaze fell on Lauren.

So, there it was. It was the first time I saw Jessie wasn't as enamored with Lauren as I'd thought. Jessie continued, "Travis is the one who got the local artisans on board to fill the shops. I won't postpone it. He wouldn't want that."

I was stunned. With such tragic news, I was sure the mega extravaganza planned for the grand opening of Shoppes at the Hangar on the Fourth of July would go to the back burner. Along with the windmill coffee table book, rendering my services unnecessary.

"Cuz, Con might be right," Lauren said, sitting back down next to Jessie and pulling her into an embrace.

Jessie wiggled out of Lauren's arms and stood. "I won't change my mind." She called to the dogs, "Boo. Ridley. Come. I need to call Chris. Oh, Trav—my baby br-r-other. He and Chris are—were—best friends. How can I possibly tell him?"

Earlier, Jessie had told me her fiancé costar was in Ecuador working on a building project for Habitat for Humanity. Chris Barnes's upbeat personality and smiling eyes would have been a big plus right now.

Jessie walked slowly toward the door. The dogs emerged from where they were hiding under the coffee table. Or, should I say, the small French bulldog was hiding. Because of his weight and girth, the Olde English bulldog could only fit his head and front legs under the table, leaving his large rear end sticking out for all the world to see.

The dogs silently followed behind Jessie, not a tail wagged. It was as if they knew something tragic had happened to someone they loved.

Emilio stopped Jessie at the door. Then he leaned in to whisper something into her ear. Jessie reacted by putting her arms around Emilio's neck as if he was a lifesaver ring, rescuing her from rough seas. I read her trembling lips as she mouthed, "Thank you." She kissed him on the cheek, then she and the dogs exited the room.

At the thought of rough seas, my mind went back to poor Travis Sterling. He was too young to have died so tragically.

"Should I go after her?" Emilio asked, looking panicked.

Jessie's kiss made it obvious that in the two years Emilio had worked for Dahlia Lane, they'd forged a close relationship.

"No," Conrad said. "I'll see to her."

"*We* will see to her," Lauren corrected her husband.

I felt tears spill down my cheeks. It was all so gut-wrenching.

Lauren shot me a nasty look. Apparently, she didn't think my waterworks display was genuine. But I didn't give a damn what Jessie's cousin thought. I'd noticed her tears had stopped as soon as they'd started.

Maybe I was being too judgy? After all, I was known to cry at weddings and laugh at funerals. If my assignment at the windmill continued, I made a pact with myself to steer clear of Lauren. Until Jessie's fiancé, Chris, came home, I would hone my spider-sense when it came to her and find out from Emilio everything I could about any weird family dynamics.

I knew what Elle would say about my meddling. Stay out of it. There doesn't have to be a mystery behind every closed door.

I begged to differ.

Chapter 6

Silence fell on the room. The only sound was the chiming of the Dutch moon-phase clock on the mantel.

"We'd better follow," Conrad finally said. "She mustn't be left alone."

I was sure he'd said mustn't, not shouldn't. Which was strange. Not that anything that happened in the last hour wasn't strange.

"Yes, we better," Lauren answered. "Talk some sense into her about the hangar grand opening before she gets goofy Chris involved."

I added my unsolicited two cents. "I'm sure speaking with her fiancé will help her cope with her brother's loss."

Lauren looked down her nose at me. "And how would you know what's good for my cousin? What are you doing here again?"

I'd obviously overstepped my tenuous boundaries. "I'm here as the photo stylist for the Windmill Cottage book."

"I should be the one styling the book. I'm family. And Jessica will need family right now. Not outsiders. Including Mr. Photographer over there. His and your services are no longer needed. Everything must be put on hold. Including the book and the Fourth of July at the stupid airplane hangar."

"But Jessie just said—" I sputtered.

From behind Lauren's back, I saw my father give me the zip-it sign.

"Enough, Lauren. Let's focus," Conrad said, glancing first at me, then directing his gaze at my father and Arthur. "As you can see, now's not a good time. We'll take care of things. Thanks for coming." He reached into his pants pocket and took out a business card and handed it to Arthur. "Here's my contact info. Please don't bother Ms. Sterling. I'll pass on any news about Travis to her. And let me know when I can make funeral arrangements."

"Yes, do that, Detective," Lauren snarled, her bottom teeth biting her upper lip, piranha style. "Leave us in peace."

At the same moment Conrad grabbed his wife's wrist and pulled her toward the door, my father raised an eyebrow in my direction. I raised mine back. Though I didn't know why.

After they'd gone, I said, "That was intense."

It was unimaginable I'd mistaken Lauren for Jessie. It had only taken a short time to realize Lauren and Jessie were nothing alike. Which made me wonder about Conrad. He seemed genuinely concerned for Jessie. Something Lauren hadn't seemed thrilled about.

I searched my father's face but couldn't read him. Which was unusual because I thought I knew him like a proverbial book. "Excuse me," he said, "I need to visit the little boys' room."

Emilio pointed to the hallway. "Second door on the right."

After my father left the room, I introduced Emilio to Arthur.

"How awful," Emilio said, shaking his head. "One minute everything's all sunshine and laughter, then . . ."

Suddenly, the room darkened. Sooty thunderheads had rolled in from the direction of the ocean.

I glanced out the window behind the table. Was it possible that just a little while ago, Jessie had been happily arranging tulips?

My first thought was *good*, we needed the rain. But after a zigzag of lightning, followed by a boom of thunder that rattled the window frame, my second thought went to a quote by Poe. One I'd left in the sand in front of my former rental cottage when I'd first moved to Montauk. I'd been in a melancholy state of mind after my breakup with my jerk of a fiancé and was questioning my decision to leave the magazine . . .

Out—out are the lights—out all!
And, over each quivering form,
The curtain, a funeral pall,
Comes down with the rush of a storm.

"I hope your father doesn't take long," Arthur said. "I need to go talk to my team. If it rains, the crime—I mean the scene will be compromised."

"Hope you'll keep Dad and me in the loop," I said. "There's no chance Travis was purposely hit, is there? That would be vehicular homicide, or would it be premeditated manslaughter?"

"Cool it with the television jargon, Meg. I'm—" Arthur glanced sideways at Emilio.

"Oh, Emilio's cool," I said. "We go way back. Don't worry about sharing any intel in front of him. Elle will also vouch for Emilio."

Emilio appeared confused.

"You don't know, do you? Detective Arthur Shoner of the East Hampton Town Police is Elle's hubby."

"Congrats on your marriage," Emilio said. "You're one lucky guy. They don't get much better than Elle."

Arthur's face pinked. "You've got that right." Arthur stood and Emilio went to him and gave him a vigorous handshake.

Looking back at me, Emilio said, "What about you, Meg? Are you married? Hope not. I'd be really upset if you didn't invite me to the wedding."

It was my turn to feel heat on my cheeks. The Barrett blotches had traveled up to my face in record time, a family curse that reared its ugly head during times of embarrassment, stress, joy and terror.

Before I could answer, my father stepped back into the room.

"She's not married yet, Emilio. But if I'm not mistaken, it might be sooner than later. So get ready, daughter."

"Dad! Stop. We're taking things slow."

"Wish I'd taken it slow with Sheila," he said wistfully.

"You were meant to be here with your family and friends," I said, standing up and walking over to him. "No regrets. We learn from our past and need to stay in the present because that's all we have."

"When did you become so wise?" he said with a grin.

"Yeah, when?" Emilio teased.

"Uhm, I think it was you, Dad, who coined those words after my breakup with Cole."

"Cole?" Emilio asked.

"A story for another time," I answered.

"Okay. But you're not getting away that easily. Now that I'm living in Amagansett, I'll be able to hear all about it. We can commiserate about our past relationships over a good glass of red and some Motown. And you can tell me about your current relationship. I can tell Jeff likes him. So he must be a good guy."

"Patrick Seaton," my father offered.

Emilio's eyes lit up. "Patrick Seaton the author? The reclusive writer of all those thrillers?"

"The one and only," Jeff answered, as if proud his daughter hooked such a catch.

"Wow. I'm happy for you. You deserve someone other than that obnoxious Michael."

Changing the subject, I said, "Hard to believe we never ran into each other in the Hamptons. Especially if you've been working for Dahlia Lane for two years."

"Oh, I've only recently moved here. Before that I was staying at a B&B in Northport. I recently got a steal of a deal on a small cottage/ shack in Amagansett."

"Welcome to the neighborhood," my father said.

"Not to change the subject, father dear. But what were you doing snooping around the windmill?"

"What are you talking about, daughter dear? I wasn't doing anything of the kind." He took a furtive glance in Arthur's direction.

Arthur didn't answer my father's peaked eyebrow. He was busy reading something on his phone with a clenched jaw. Whatever he was reading, it wasn't good.

My father looked from Arthur to me. "I really did need to use the restroom. These waders make things hard when it comes to that."

Arthur shot up from his chair. "I must leave."

"Why? It's not Elle, is it?" I asked, my heart pounding.

"She's fine. It's something else."

"I'd bet it has to do with Travis Sterling." I walked up to Arthur until we were nose to nose.

Arthur ignored me and headed to the door. "Jeff, I have to leave you with Meg to get a ride home. I'm heading to the station. I'm sure Nancy Drew will be more than accommodating to give Carson Drew a lift."

I smiled. "No problem. As long as you keep us in the loop."

"Oh, no, Ms. Barrett. There's no us." Arthur pocketed his phone.

"I agree," my father said, pretending to look stern. "Since moving to Montauk, Arthur and Doc have filled me in on all the things you've omitted to share with me since you moved to the Hamptons."

"What kind of things?" Emilio asked with a peaked brow.

"Oh, nothing, Emilio," I said. "I can't help it if inquisitive genes run in my blood. I'm just a chip off the old block."

"Well, I might be the old block, but now that I'm here, no need to get yourself in dangerous situations."

"Yes, Father," I said coyly, looking down at my sandals.

When I glanced up, I saw Arthur was already at the open

doorway leading out to the hallway. He took one glance back at my father, then disappeared.

A few seconds later we heard the windmill's front door slam.

Boy, was he in a hurry.

I wondered why.

Chapter 7

The rain never materialized. The sun was gallantly attempting to make its way through dark clouds as my father and I headed toward my woody Wagoneer, parked on the circular drive in front of the windmill. I thought back to what seemed a lifetime ago when I'd cheerily punched in the code to open the gates for my first official day at Dahlia Lane. "Poor Jessie," I said to my father. "I'm glad Emilio went to check on her. I don't trust Lauren." Then I told him about how frightened Lauren seemed yesterday when she'd answered the Windmill Cottage door.

Instead of commenting, he stopped short. His phone must have buzzed because he pulled it out from a pocket beneath his waders, then looked down. After reading, his eyes met mine and he said, "Arthur."

I waited until he stowed his phone back in his pocket. "Well? Did they catch the person who ran Travis over?"

"I promised Arthur anything he shares with me will be in strictest confidence."

"You need to talk to him. Say I should be included in the investigation. I'm the one working at Dahlia Lane. Think about what info I could get on the inside."

"A promise is a promise. But I'll have a talk with him. Why do you think someone here has something to do with his death? It happened miles away. More than likely, it was an accident and someone panicked. Maybe they'll do the right thing and turn themselves in."

"It's just a feeling, Dad."

"Oh, one of your feelings, huh," he said, raising an eyebrow.

"Trust your gut, you always say. Here's the key to the woody. I forgot something."

He caught it in midair and grinned. "You really expect me to buy that one?"

"Did you really expect me to buy the *little boys' room* routine?" I answered.

"You should, it was the truth."

"Okay, if you tell me there is no way Travis was deliberately hit, I won't go back inside to get the reading glasses I left behind. Tell me, father of mine, what should I do?"

"Reading glasses? You have twenty-twenty vision," he said. "But yes, maybe you should go retrieve those glasses. Although it's still early in the investigation."

I was right. Arthur must have shared intel with him about Travis's death.

Jessie's words came back to me from yesterday. She was worried about her brother, saying he wasn't himself. And what was the deal, when Travis almost caused me to drive off the road into the pine trees? He was angry. Now he's dead. Then there was Lauren's nervous behavior when I'd shown up at the front door of Windmill Cottage, wanting to know if I'd been followed.

I hadn't been lying when I said I'd left my glasses in the Tulip Room. After I saw Arthur's reaction to the message on his phone, I'd planted the glasses on purpose. And it's possible I hadn't completely closed one of the Dutch doors as I'd followed my father outside.

"Okay. You keep watch," I said. "If I don't come out in a few minutes, send in a swat team."

"Funny."

"Oh, and maybe while you're waiting, you might want to jot down the license plates of that Mercedes, Kia and Lexus SUV behind my woody. Couldn't hurt. Just in case."

"Case of what?" he asked, smiling.

I didn't answer, just turned toward the windmill.

I climbed the three brick steps, gently pushed open one of the Dutch doors, then slipped inside.

Bam! My forehead hit something solid.

A sequoia tree trunk?

No, a man's chest.

As I gazed up—I mean way-y-y up, because the guy in front of me was at least six foot six and built like the actor who played Aquaman. It took everything I had not to keep my jaw from dropping to the floor.

"What do you want, trespassing lady?" he said menacingly. "Do you always walk inside strangers' homes or windmills unannounced?" His voice was so deep, I expected him to add a fee-fi-foe-fum to the beginning of all his sentences. Frowning, he narrowed his moss green eyes and looked down at me. Under his black tank top, muscles upon muscles glistened like he'd bathed in Vaseline. With his thick tight-end neck and huge head and shoulders, I was sure an NFL football team would welcome him with open arms. The only thing that didn't go with his height and weightlifter physique were his tiny, pink bowed lips. Even his G.I. Joe blond buzz cut fit his physique—but not those lips.

I extended a shaky hand. "Meg Barrett. I'm Ms. Sterling's photo stylist. I was just here a few minutes ago and left something in the Tulip Room."

He looked suspiciously at me—*as well he should.* "I'll have to verify your story with my uncle."

"Who's your uncle?" I asked.

For a second, I didn't think he was going to answer. "Mr. Kincaid. Let's see some ID."

I had no clue what kind of ID he expected me to produce to prove I was here to work on the Windmill Cottage book. I reached into my handbag and withdrew one of my Cottages by the Sea business cards and handed it to him. He peered at it, then stowed it in the pocket of his shorts.

"So, Conrad's your uncle," I said, like Jessie's financial VP and I were old friends and I hadn't just met him for the first time. "I didn't catch your name?"

"'Cause I didn't throw it," he said, then laughed at his own joke. At least he could laugh.

"Good one!" I said for brownie points.

"You stay here," he grunted. "I'll get whatever you left. Now's not a good time."

"So you've heard."

"You mean about Travis? Yes." He extended his arm in the direction of my head. I thought he was going to punch me with a hand capable of cradling a basketball as if it was an egg. Instead, he pushed at the Dutch door until it clicked shut, then turned the lock.

"What did you leave?" he asked impatiently.

"My reading glasses. I was sitting on the chair closest to the fireplace." *And had hidden them between the arm and the seat cushion.*

"Stay here," he repeated.

"Wait," I said. "Won't it be easier if I get them myself?"

"No—"

34

"Bryce!" A diminutive young girl, holding a blue folder in her arms, charged toward us from the end of the hallway. "There you are. Mrs. Kincaid has been looking for you." She stopped in front of us, then bent at the waist to catch her breath. When she stood, I saw her large amber eyes in her creamy mocha face were filled with pure unadulterated fear.

Looking up at skyscraper Bryce, she said in a quivering voice, "Mrs. Kincaid said you need to get over to the test kitchen right away and unlock the door. I must start pulling ingredients. I guess she's taking over for Ms. Jessica because of—you know, what happened to her poor brother."

Taking a few small steps closer, her foot caught the edge of the runner and she went stumbling forward. I caught her, but not before the folder she was holding went flying, its contents spilling onto Bryce's clown-sized sneakers.

"Oh, I'm such a ditz," she squeaked. "I'm so nervous. The last time I worked with *her* it was such a disaster. She'll probably fire me."

"Kayla, how can you get fired?" Bryce asked in a soft tone. "You're an intern. You don't get paid."

"Still, if I lose this internship, I'll simply die. This has been my utmost dream to work at Dahlia Lane with Ms. Jessica. We get along so well. Not the case with . . ."

She didn't need to finish her sentence. I knew who she was talking about. Mrs. Kincaid, aka Lauren.

Because no one else seemed willing, I bent down, corralled the papers Kayla had dropped, then returned them to the folder. I was happy I did, because each page in the folder was a printed recipe with a heading that read *Jessica's Table*. They must be recipes she would be featuring on her show.

What I wouldn't do to steal a few, then pass them on to my father and Patrick. Especially the recipe on top for pan-fried striped bass with lemon garlic herb sauce. Not that I would attempt to make the dish myself. I was banned from the kitchen until it was time for cleanup. A rule both my father and Patrick adhered to after one of my many mishaps. However, I *was allowed* to provide herbs from my garden. Besides being called a "murder magnet," my buddy Elle also christened me an "herb whisperer."

"Kayla, chin up. You'll be fine," Bryce said, grabbing the folder from my hands, then handing it to Kayla.

Kayla looked over at me with tear-filled eyes and mouthed, "Thank you."

"Lauren won't bite," Bryce said, not appearing too sure.

If I had to guess, Bryce looked to be in his mid to late twenties. Kayla looked too young to order a beer.

Bryce grinned down at her. "That's unless you make another one of your catastrophic mistakes. Like setting out cayenne pepper instead of cinnamon. Better you deal with *Auntie* Lauren than me," he said, patting Kayla on the head like she was a toddler.

Size-wise she looked like one. I was five foot seven. Kayla appeared to be six or seven inches shorter.

"Thanks for reminding me." Kayla sniffled.

"Just teasing," he said, grinning.

"Now's not the time for teasing, Bry," Kayla moaned. "There's only one difference to what happened with the cayenne. I was assisting Ms. Jessica. She never gets angry. 'Lesson learned,' was all she'd said to me." Kayla glanced nervously toward the end of the hallway. "Ple-e-e-se, Bry, let's go."

If I'd thought Kayla was afraid of Bryce, then I'd been wrong. It seemed Lauren was the cause of Kayla's trembling lips. In fact, there might have been a little flirtation going on between the pair.

Bryce glanced at me, then Kayla. "I'll go unlock the kitchen studio and put on the AC. You can escort—"

"Meg," I said.

"To the Tulip Room. Don't let her take anything except those glasses."

"I need to go, now," Kayla whined, sticking out her bottom lip. "We don't have much time. Mrs. Kincaid will be here soon. Along with the camera crew. Remember what happened when you—"

I saw a flash of panic cross Bryce's green eyes. "Okay. Okay. Let's go."

They started toward the same door Lauren had exited through after yesterday morning's not so charming meet-and-greet.

Now it was my turn to whine. "Wait! What about me? I need those glasses."

Before stepping through the door Kayla was holding open, Bryce ordered, "Run into the Tulip Room, then scoot via the front door, lickety-split. And don't think I won't check the outdoor camera to see how long you take. Any shenanigans, I'll report them to Uncle Conrad."

I gave him a military salute. "Promise. At least I hope that's where my glasses have gone to. With all — "

Bryce narrowed his eyes and gritted his teeth, stopping me in mid-sentence.

"Okay," I said. "Promise. I'll be fast."

I waited until they were out of sight, then hurried down the short hallway. My covert mission in the Tulip Room was to rifle Bryce's Auntie Lauren's handbag.

After I stepped inside the room, I waited a few seconds to make sure Bryce hadn't changed his mind and decided to check on me. I went to the love seat, reached down and grabbed the handbag from the floor. The same handbag I'd noticed earlier Lauren had forgotten when she and her hubby left in search of Jessie.

Now that I thought about it, how did Lauren and Conrad hear about Travis's death before Jessie? Lauren had told Jessie, after Conrad had told her.

Realizing there was no time for ruminating, I searched the handbag's contents. It was packed with everything from a half-used roll of toilet paper to a baggie of assorted screws and a Philips head screwdriver. Not that I could fault her on the screwdriver. My own handbag contained a Swiss army knife with a screwdriver attachment. There was one prescription bottle without a label. Her Dahlia logo key ring had a Mercedes remote key on it, along with a small brass key. Lauren's tiny Fendi wallet only had her driver's license and two dollars in cash. No bank cards. I soon found out why. Inside a large cosmetic case that didn't hold cosmetics, I found–I kid you not—at least twenty credit cards. Not debit cards. Credit cards. Most of which had Lauren's husband's name on them or her cousin Jessie's.

Was she opening accounts in Jessie's name? One more reason to dislike her. Though it was none of my beeswax, as my mother would say. Still, I could tell something wasn't on the up-and-up with Lauren Kincaid.

As I placed the handbag down on the floor, I noticed a white piece of paper sticking out of the front pocket. I glanced behind me to make sure the coast was clear. I wasn't being paranoid. I just knew that even though I was wearing my hearing aids, there were still some sounds I had a hard time picking up, like footsteps from the incredible hulk. I grabbed a tissue from the table then used it to take out the paper. No need to leave my prints on it, if it had to do with Travis's death.

I held it to my nose. It was a handwritten note on a large white Post-it. The message written in red marker was simple — *L, your time is coming. Better keep looking over your shoulder. I'm watching you.* There wasn't a signature. The *L* was obviously for Lauren. I thought about Lauren's behavior yesterday. Was someone stalking her? Was it related to Travis's death? Maybe Travis was getting his own notes addressed with a *T*. Jessie with a *J*? More importantly, were they related to Travis's hit-and-run?

I took out my phone and shot a picture of the note and a couple more of both sides of a pill that was in the pharmacy bottle with its label ripped off.

As I headed toward the door, my mind was filled with questions.

One thing seemed clear: I needed to find out everything I could about everyone at Dahlia Lane Enterprises.

Chapter 8

Five minutes later, remembering Bryce was keeping track of my movements, I hurried from the Tulip Room. As I stepped toward the front door, I noticed a piece of paper on the floor I'd missed when Kayla dropped her stack of recipes. I snatched it up and looked down.

Wow! This one was a real keeper—crab cakes on top of fried green tomatoes. Someone had written a note in the margin—*Do Not use canned crab!* I didn't know if it was Jessie's handwriting or her cousin's.

I'd watched every episode of *Jessica's Table*. Following Lauren's Lavender Fields failure, she hadn't been on a single episode, except for her wedding to Conrad. Before she'd left Dahlia Lane, Lauren would occasionally be on camera assisting her cousin.

It seemed logical, after the news about her brother's death, Jessie wasn't ready to tape the show. But the show must go on, and all that. It would be interesting to see how Lauren planned on taking over in Jessie's stead.

I glanced at the paper in my hand. The recipe looked important. Really important. *Didn't it?* It would be prudent of me to deliver it to Kayla in a timely manner. If only to save her from Lauren's fury.

I hurried toward the double Dutch doors, turned the bolt Bryce had used to lock them, opened the right one, then stepped onto the porch, making sure the door locked behind me. Then I flew down the front steps. That's when I tripped on an uneven brick on the walkway, got up and dusted myself off.

"Are you okay?" my father called out. He was sitting on the hood of my woody. "Need a medic? I'm trained in first aid." He'd taken off his waders and had on a pair of lightweight pants with a zillion pockets.

When I reached him, I grabbed his wrist and pulled. "I'm fine. Come. We have a fun mission ahead of us."

"Mission, what mission?"

"One you'll love. I promise." I showed him the recipe. Earlier, when Jessie and I had been in the glass atrium collecting flowers, Jessie had pointed out a cottage behind the farmhouse used as Dahlia Lane's television studio and offices. The same building where she filmed her cooking show. This would be the perfect time to see where the show's magic happened and a chance to drool over the studio kitchen's interior.

"Crab cakes on top of fried green tomatoes," he read. "Film date July 1. *Jessica's Table*, S5, episode 62."

"I'll explain on the way to the filming studio," I said. "But didn't you notice one of your favorite ingredients in the tomato and crab cake breading?"

"Yes. Saffron. I'm in." He jumped off the hood. "But first—" He took my hand and searched my face. "On the way, you'll explain what you were doing inside. And more importantly, what you found."

"Sure, but not now. And, I want to know what Arthur texted you. We can share intel." I'd tell him on the way back to Montauk about the photos I'd taken. One of which I was sure he'd find extremely interesting—the threatening note.

"By the way," he asked, "who's Kayla?"

"Jessie's intern," I said. "Let's go."

We followed a path to the right side of the windmill, passed the white farmhouse and continued until we came to a large white cedar shake cottage.

My Dahlia Lane fangirl pulse quickened.

When we reached the door, I opened it, and we silently slipped inside. We took a hallway to the left and followed the sound of clanging pots and loud voices. Luckily none of the voices sounded like Lauren's.

"Hey," I announced, pushing open the studio kitchen's swinging doors like a gunfighter entering a noisy saloon.

A startled Kayla glanced over at me with surprise, her dark eyes large in her small delicate face. The ceramic bowl she was holding slipped from her fingers and crashed onto the floor.

Oops. I waved the recipe in the air. "Sorry, didn't mean to scare you. You forgot something. Looks like today's appetizer recipe. Crab cakes on top of fried green tomatoes."

In a less dramatic fashion, my father slunk in behind me. His jaw dropped as he scanned the studio kitchen that any chef or non-chef like me would envy.

Two cameras on dollies were stationed in front of a long rectangular wood island with a concrete top. On top of the counter was a line of clear vintage Pyrex custard cups filled with ingredients I assumed were in recipe order.

Behind the island were glass-fronted whitewashed cabinets filled with 1930s pale green translucent jadeite dishes. I knew they were just for display, but they sparked an idea for one of the cottages I was working on at the former Sea Breeze Motor Lodge.

Bryce charged out of the pantry. "What was that crash!" He scanned the studio floor until his eyes stopped on the broken glass.

"Just clumsy me," Kayla said.

Bryce scowled at me. "What are you doing here? I told you to get your glasses and leave." Then he raised an eyebrow and addressed fisherman Jeff Barrett. "And who the hell are you?"

"Bry," Kayla said, her voice quivering. "Help me find these ingredients. Or better yet, clean up the broken dish. I'll try to find everything. I'm doomed. I'll never make it before Lauren and the crew show up."

"Will do," he said with obvious relief. "You're better at finding things in that monstrosity of a pantry than I am. I didn't have a clue about half of the ingredients in that dessert recipe we just set up. Dandelion petals, for God's sake. As soon as I escort these two out, I'll clean up the broken glass." Bryce turned to me. "Again, why are you still here?"

I reached up and waved the recipe in front of his face. "I thought you might need this recipe. It's dated today."

Kayla scurried over and grabbed the recipe from my hand. She said, "Bryce! Don't be so rude. She's done me a big favor." Looking down, she said, "Wondered what the crab in the walk-in was for. Though, I have no clue where to find the saffron." She looked over at us. "With the crab?"

"No," my father said, "it would be with your other spices in a cool dark place. I'm Jeff, by the way. Meg's father. May I help you find it?"

Kayla looked at me for reassurance.

"You can trust him." *If you trust me at this early stage,* I thought. "My father is the best home chef there ever was. I don't think there's an ingredient he hasn't heard of or used."

"Wow! I might just pull this off," Kayla said, grinning. With recipe in hand, she grabbed my father's elbow and steered him into the pantry.

I took a seat at the counter and watched Bryce broom up the glass from the broken bowl. A minute later, my father emerged holding a round silver tin in his right hand. Kayla followed, her arms laden with breading ingredients for the crab cakes and fried green tomatoes.

"I never would have found the saffron," Kayla said. "Thanks, Jeff."

"No problem. It's important to store it away from the light," my father said. "Plus, it tends to be quite expensive. You wouldn't want any of the camera crew to steal it, especially this brand of golden saffron. "You know —"

Here he goes, I thought, *giving one of his culinary lessons.* Not that I minded. I just hoped we'd be out of here before Jessie's cousin showed up.

"Saffron," he continued, "is such a delicacy that you only need" — he twisted off the top of the tin — "three or four strands for an entire dish. If you were adding it to risotto or the like, you would first soak the strands in hot water — not boiling water — so it blooms in all its magnificence. Then, after twenty minutes, you add the liquid and the threads to your dish. Golden saffron contains crocin from the crocus flower's female stigma and must be handpicked. The reason it's so expensive. Saffron's also known to have magical neuroprotective powers to help anxiety, not to mention it's an antioxidant and anti-inflammatory."

At the word *anxiety,* my mind went back to the bottle of pills I'd spied in Lauren's handbag. I'd taken a photo of the front and back of a white oval numbered pill. It would be easy to look it up later. It was a huge stretch the pills had anything to do with Travis's hit-and-run. However, ripping off the label was strange. Then there was that creepy note — maybe that was the reason for Jessie's cousin needing the pills.

"Remember, Dad," I said, "that time when I was about four. I opened one of your saffron tins and the entire contents fell to the floor. Starsky lapped it up in seconds flat. Back then, you said he'd just enjoyed a hundred-dollar delicacy."

"Now, a pound of saffron would set you back about five thousand dollars," he said.

"Kind of like white truffles," I said.

"True," he said. "Those would set you back at least a hundred and fifty an once."

"Oh, no," Kayla said, laughing. "You two seem to have a great relationship. Just like my dad and me. Only he's not a cook. He's—" Kayla's chin quivered, and she looked down at the counter. When she raised her head, I saw her eyes were watery. She blinked away tears, then said with a smile, "I bet you guys have father-daughter cooking competitions."

I grinned at my father. He grinned back and said, "Meg is culinary-challenged, but she makes a great assistant—just like you, Kayla."

Kayla grinned. "Thanks, Jeff."

Bryce was standing sentry at the kitchen's swinging doors, his eyes laser focused on Kayla. "Not to break up this admiration society," he said, "but Kayla, I think you should be doing more preparing and less talking. And these two need to vamoose asap."

"Bryce!" Kayla snapped. "Stop! No one's leaving. We still need Jeff's help."

"Well, I need to go," he said. "Sure you want to be alone with these two? We've only known them for a red-hot second?" Bryce looked over at my father, but he was too busy inhaling saffron to notice. "I'm only thinking of you, Kayla."

"I'm fine. No need to worry," she said. "Plus, if Ms. Sterling is working with Meg, that's all I need to know about her."

"If you're sure?"

"I'm sure. Now you're the one holding us up, Bryce," she said with a wink.

"Okay. Okay." Bryce raised his muscled arms in surrender. "I'm going to walk the perimeter to make sure that lunatic stalker hasn't left one of his notes again. Keep your phone handy. I'll also tell you if I see Lauren coming this way."

"Oh my gosh," I blurted out, faking surprise. "There's a crazed stalker?"

Bryce shrugged his shoulders.

"Has anyone been hurt?"

"Nope. I have it under control. Just some crackpot."

"You never caught them on camera?" I asked.

"No. But we just upgraded the system. We'll get him. We think he's been hiding out in Travis's workshop. A couple days ago, Travis found a red marker in the same color as the ink the dude used on his latest note."

"His latest? There's been more than one?" I said, thinking of the one in Lauren's handbag. It had also been written in red marker. "Did you tell the police? My dad's a retired cop," I said, nodding over at my father, who looked the furthest thing from a tough Detroit homicide detective with his tongue sticking out as he concentrated on pulling rust-colored strands of saffron from the tin.

"Just smell the heavenly floral, earthy aroma," he moaned, waving the strands under Kayla's nose.

Kayla leaned in closer, coming away with a dot of orange at the tip of her small nose.

"I don't need no old cop," Bryce said, sticking out six-pack abs that looked more like twelve-pack abs. "I've got things handled. I don't think the police would be too interested in a red marker. Plus, have you looked at these guns?" he said, flexing his biceps. "The creep won't know what hit him." To prove his point he reached into his back pocket and removed a gun. Not a gun gun—a Taser gun.

"Taser's aren't legal in New York," I said.

Bryce pocketed the Taser. "Only a class-A misdemeanor. Not a big deal."

"I would think you'd have a better chance of punching the guy. Unless he's big like you?"

"No one's as big as me."

I wasn't about to argue that one.

"And I'm sure the police would like to see those notes. Right, Dad?"

Not surprised he'd been covertly listening, my father said, "You told us you don't have the person on camera. Then how do you know it's a guy?"

"Don't worry, his or *her* days are numbered. And I'm not worried about someone arresting me for owning a Taser. Uncle Conrad knows people in high places at the courthouse. They'd drop the case against me in a heartbeat."

"How many notes have there been?" I asked Bryce. "When was the first note found? Have they only been found here, at Dahlia Lane?"

"About a month ago. As I've said, Uncle Conrad is on top of it. He won't let anything happen to his wife. How does it concern you, anyway?"

"If I'm going to be working here," I said, "I want to make sure I'm not in danger."

"Forget I said anything," Bryce warned.

I was waiting for him to say *Or else,* but his phone must have vibrated.

He reached into his pocket, pulled out his phone and looked down. "Oh boy. Looks like the news broke about Travis's death." He turned to Kayla. "I need to fortify the front gates before the press and Dahlia Lane fans try to get inside."

Kayla looked at him, smiling. "Okay. Thanks for your help. I couldn't have done it without you."

With a flushed face, Bryce gave her a silly grin, then exited through the swinging doors.

Kayla glanced at my father, who was in the middle of crushing crackers for the crab cakes. "Thanks to you, too, Jeff. Meg, you're one lucky girl." There it was again, Kayla looked ready to cry. "I'm sure happy you both showed up. Don't mind Bryce. His bark is worse than his bite. He's really a big softy."

"Maybe with you," I said with a laugh. The guy still scared me. "Kayla, what do you know about these notes?"

"Mr. Kincaid told me about them. Said I needed to let him know if I see anything strange. That's all he said—" She looked nervously toward the swinging doors.

"Meg, why don't you check out the pantry," my father said, giving me *the look.* "I know how you love a good pantry."

"Sure." I knew what he was trying to convey. He could get more information about the notes than I ever could.

And, *oh,* what a pantry it was. My entire kitchen would have fit inside. Even though I wasn't a cook, I could still appreciate a well-stocked kitchen. This was just the *studio* kitchen, making me fantasize if we ever went back to shooting the Windmill Cottage book, Jessie might invite me over for a homemade meal in Dahlia Lane's farm-house kitchen.

Last week, on an episode of *Jessica's Table,* Jessie made a ploughman's lunch for her fiancé sidekick Chris. I was confident even a non-chef like myself could pull that one off.

I visualized Patrick and me on a romantic picnic at the Montauk Point Lighthouse. I would use my vintage picnic basket and serve him what Jessie had made for Chris—crusty, thick-sliced sourdough bread—only mine would come from Montauk's new Blissful Bites Bakery. A slab of cheddar from Mecox Bay Dairy in Watermill. A bottle of wine from Patrick's and my last trip to Channing Daughters Vineyard in Bridgehampton. Hard-boiled eggs (yes, I can boil an egg). The prosciutto and marinated olives I could snag from my favorite restaurant's, Pondfare's, newly opened gourmet shop. And last, but not least, a jar of Dahlia Lane Farms chutney.

When I stepped out of the pantry, I saw Kayla and my father were laughing over something.

"What's so funny?"

"I was just telling Kayla about the time you helped me make coq au vin."

"Not fair," I said. "I think I was nine at the time."

My father grinned. "Well, let me just say, Kayla, a fire extinguisher was used."

"Ha-ha," I said. "We better skedaddle, Daddy-o. Lauren might be here any minute."

Kayla's smile turned upside down. "Yes. You better. Thanks for everything."

I wished we didn't have to leave, but after rifling Lauren's handbag, I didn't want Lauren to show up and see I was still on the grounds. Kayla might be a wealth of information if it turned out there was foul play in Travis's death.

If my father hadn't gotten anything out of her about the threatening notes, we could always invite her to Mickey's Chowder Shack for Mickey's famous shrimp fritters and a glass of wine or beer— if she was old enough to drink. Because of his blood ties to Conrad, we'd leave Bryce out of it.

"Okay, we're all done," my father said.

I went to Kayla and handed her my business card. "You take care of yourself. Call us if you need any help, culinary or otherwise. I'm working with Jessie on the Windmill Cottage book. Hopefully, I'll see you when things settle down."

"Oh, I hope so, Meg. My internship covers the meal prep and gardening segments. I'm sure we'll meet again." She stowed my card in the pocket of her *Jessica's Table* embroidered apron. "And Jeff, it's been a pleasure," she said, extending her hand. "Can I reach you from Meg's number?" She grinned. "Just in case I find myself in a culinary pickle again."

He took her hand in his and winked. "Please do. We'll leave Meg in charge of interior design. You and I will stick to the kitchen."

"Nice meeting you both," she called after us. I glanced back at her before going through the swinging doors. She seemed a different person from the one inside the windmill. She exuded confidence. My father had cast his spell.

I just hoped Lauren wouldn't squash it . . .

Chapter 9

As we walked toward my car, I said, "Oh, look, there's Jessie's Olde English bulldog, Boo, or maybe it's Ridley. And I bet that woman is Wilhelmina, the housekeeper Emilio mentioned. Let's go talk to her."

"For what possible reason? I'd really like to get out of these clothes. It's been a really long morning," my father said.

"I have an excellent reason to talk to her, or at least introduce myself. I'll tell you why when we get in the car."

We turned toward the grassy area next to the gazebo, but we didn't need to go any farther, because the Olde English bulldog came bounding in our direction. Even though he had to weigh eighty pounds, he reached us in seconds. Which was not the case for the short, squat woman trailing behind him, her face hidden under a floppy straw hat.

The dog stopped in front of my father, then dropped a stick from his drooling mouth onto my father's flip-flopped feet.

"Boo, you naughty boy," the woman said, panting harder than the bulldog. "I apologize for his manners. I'm Mrs. White, Wilhelmina. I work for the family. Usually only on weekends, but I got a call about the tragedy. So here I am. Are you here for condolences? Isn't it so awful? I was at the market for Mother when I got the call from Mr. Kincaid. Travis was such a wonderful, loving person. And poor Jessie. She and Travis were so close."

Under her floppy straw hat, short russet curls sprung out in all directions. With her full red cheeks, bright emerald eyes and short curvaceous body, she reminded me of Mrs. Patmore from *Downton Abbey*.

"We're new acquaintances of Jessie—Ms. Sterling," I said. "We were with her when she received the terrible news."

"I'm sorry," she said. "How I prattle on. And on. As my husband says. My poor, darling Jessica was fast asleep when I arrived. She had little Ridley in her arms. This rascal," she said, patting Boo on his giant head. "The old boy needed a walk. Lots of nervous energy. Dogs are very perceptive when it comes to tragedy."

"They certainly are," my father said, picking up Boo's stick. He threw it a short distance and Boo took off, sending clumps of sod behind him.

"See what I mean," Wilhelmina said. "Tons of energy. I better get back. I want to make Jessie a meal before I take the train back to Amityville. I'll be back on Friday. Mr. Kincaid said Jessie still plans to open the hangar. It's all so sad," she said, wiping away tears. Boo scampered to her side. He dropped his stick and looked up at Wilhelmina with a soulful gaze. "I know, sweet thing," she said. "We will both miss Travis. Come, let's see if Mommy is awake."

She and Boo walked toward the farmhouse. A few yards away, she turned and gave us a wave.

"Looks like Jessie is in good hands," my father said as we moved toward the front of Windmill Cottage.

"True. But what happens when she leaves? Jessie will be left alone."

"Her cousin will be there for her."

"I suppose," I said grudgingly. "I'll fill you in when we get in the car."

On the way back to Montauk, I showed my father the photo of the note from Lauren's handbag. I handed him my phone and said, "You can send it to your phone. But I wouldn't show Arthur, unless you want to put up bail money when they arrest me for foraging in her handbag. Of course, you can tell him about the notes in general because Kayla and Bryce discussed it with us."

"Slow down, Meg. Of course I wouldn't throw my own daughter under the bus," he said as I turned onto the long rutted dirt lane leading to Doc's cabin. Tall pines stood sentinel on either side of us. We came to a stop in front of a two-story log cabin that butted up to the banks of Fort Pond. It was the perfect idyllic hideaway for two retired police and fishing buddies.

My father put his hand on the door handle. Before getting out, he gave me a kiss on the cheek and said, "You're right, Arthur is a by-the-book kind of cop."

"Just like you were," I added.

"I'll let him know about the notes and what Kayla told me when you were perusing the studio kitchen pantry."

"Dad-d-d! Say what? What did Kayla tell you?"

"I didn't get any info on the threatening notes. But—"

"Yes?"

"Kayla overheard Travis talking to Conrad. Travis told Conrad that he wouldn't be surprised if Lauren was writing the notes to herself. Kayla also said Bryce told her that Lauren was the only one receiving them. Kayla had no need to worry about her own safety."

"Well, that's a relief."

"A relief for everyone but Lauren," he said. "I don't know what you have against her. She can be caustic and uppity, but remember she's being threatened by someone. Remember what Sherlock said—"

"'The game is afoot'?"

"No. 'Presume nothing.'"

"But you just said Travis told Conrad he thought Lauren was sending the notes to herself."

He opened the door, got out, then stuck his head back in.

"Presume nothing, daughter."

"Hey, don't go. I shared the note with you. Now you need to tell me why Arthur rushed off and why you don't believe Travis's hit-and-run was an accident."

"Later. I need to get out of these stinky clothes. And discuss with Arthur what I can and cannot share with you."

"Understood," I said.

I watched him trudge slowly up the stone walkway, carrying his waders and Doc's fishing hat. I couldn't imagine the long day he'd had, and it was only noon.

I also couldn't imagine the horror of seeing Travis Sterling's dead body.

My father had always been my rock. But who would be his, now that he'd divorced Sheila?

One thing was for sure. I was so darn blessed to have such wonderful men in my life. Doc included. And Patrick, of course.

At least Jessie had her fiancé to lean on. A small silver lining in a very tarnished day.

Chapter 10

"So, you're telling me you went through this woman's handbag just because you don't like her?" Patrick said. "You suspect this Lauren of killing or having something to do with her cousin's death and you don't even know if the hit-and-run was deliberate?"

When Patrick put it that way, it did paint me as loon. I said, "You sound like my father."

"That's a compliment."

"How about the threatening note I found. My instincts were spot-on. She's done something to someone."

It was my favorite time of day, an hour before sunset. We were on my oceanfront deck, sitting on the bench Patrick made for me in his workshop, sharing a glass of local organic sulfate-free wine and nibbling on a cold seafood platter that was missing two shrimp because of my naughty Maine coon Jo.

I didn't need to look behind me to know Jo had her fat nose pressed against the glass of my French doors, her one eye boring a hole into my back. The reason being, I'd swiped a couple of shrimps from between her mighty jaws, then hid them away in the fridge, telling her if she ever hopped on the counter again, she'd be eating dry kibble for the rest of her days. Jo didn't like being scolded. She'd taken a few swipes at my ankle, then sulked off to my reading chair by the fireplace.

As a reward for good behavior, I'd give her the shrimp later. Who was I kidding? Jo didn't know the meaning of "good behavior." I was sure the shrimp would soon find their way into the compost heap. Except for my bleeding ankles, I did admire Jo's moxie. Life was never dull with Her Fatness.

In perfect contrast, Patrick's greyhound Charlie was peacefully lying at our feet, taking a siesta after our romp down the beach, the ideal example of a well-mannered pet.

"I do have a strong feeling Travis Sterling's death wasn't an accident," I said, glancing out at the gently rolling waves.

"And why would you think that?" Patrick asked.

"It happened in broad daylight. Also, there was something about the way my father and Arthur were looking at each other. The way Arthur fled the Tulip Room."

"Fled? Tulip Room?" Patrick said.

I explained how Jessie had named each room in Windmill Cottage. "Until he talks to Arthur," I said to Patrick, "my father won't tell me much. In the meantime, if someone ran Travis over on purpose, Lauren Kincaid is my lead suspect."

"Didn't you just tell me the note was addressed to Lauren, not Jessica."

"What if Travis was threatening Lauren? She found out and ran him over."

"There's always the chance the notes and the hit-and-run aren't related," he said.

"Then there's Lauren's husband, Conrad. He's Dahlia Lane's financial guy, who happens to be a VP and on Dahlia Lane's board of directors. And we can't leave out big boy Bryce, who I told you is Conrad's nephew and Dahlia Lane's muscle security guard. I almost forgot about Peat Moss Pete." I went on to explain to Patrick about the romantic scene I'd witnessed between Lauren and Pete. "I suppose I should add Jessie's intern, Kayla—"

Patrick smiled. He had the best smile. "You do, do you?"

"But Lauren's still in the top slot."

"What about your friend from the magazine? The photographer?"

"Absolutely not. When I lived in Manhattan and worked at *American Home & Garden*, Emilio was like family to Elle and me. I can't wait until you meet him."

Patrick grinned. "Hmm. If there's anything you've learned from you checkered past, when it comes to murder you can't count on anyone being in the clear. Even your style influencer, Jessica Sterling."

"Okay. I get your point. Except for Jessie and Lauren, this was my first day meeting everyone. I guess if we put Emilio on the list, we need to put Chris Barnes, Jessie's fiancé, on it too. I know you're a fan of his. So am I. I love his sense of humor on *Dahlia Lane Home Makeover*."

"There's no way Chris Barnes should be on the list," Patrick said, sitting up straighter and looking me in the eye. "Didn't you say he was in Ecuador or somewhere?"

"Are you forgetting about all the hit men you put in your action-packed thrillers?" I said. "He could have hired someone."

"No way," he repeated.

"Well, if Jessie has to be on the list," I said, "so should your guy-crush, Chris."

"It's hard to fathom that Travis Sterling is dead," Patrick said, adding a sigh. "No one did woodworking like him. Well, maybe my father."

"So that's where you learned it from. Too bad my father couldn't pass on his culinary skills. Lord knows, he tried."

"He did pass on his sleuthing skills," Patrick said with a smile, shooing away a seagull who'd landed nearby and was eyeing the last crab claw. "I think you're getting way ahead of yourself. I think, before getting involved, you should take a deep breath."

"Too late for that. Just knowing Jessica for such a short time, I can't help being concerned."

"Well, I'm happy Jeff's here to keep you in line while I get this first draft of mine finished."

"I resent that! No one must keep me in line. I'm a big girl. I don't need my daddy, or you, worrying about me. Look at my track record. I've come out okay after more than a few sticky situations."

"Okay," he said, turning to me with a grin. "Let's do a recap. After murder number one, you ended up in the hospital. Murder number two, same scenario. Murder number three, darn, what was that one — they're all running into each other!"

"He-he. Don't forget what happened at the lighthouse. We *both* came out of it unharmed."

"Yeah, we were lucky."

A gust of wind blew back his sandy blond hair. I saw, even though he was smiling, his blue-green eyes were clouded with concern. I didn't want him to worry about me. He was right, there'd been quite a few close calls. I'd *try* to keep close to my father and let him and Arthur handle things.

I admired Patrick's profile as he looked toward the calm ocean. He'd gone through such a metamorphosis from when I'd first spied him walking the beach in front of my old rental cottage, all melancholy and despondent. Back then he'd had good reason to be sad. His wife and little girl had been killed in a car accident. Patrick had recently shared that he blamed himself for the accident, thinking if he'd been with them, he could have avoided the drunk driver in the other car.

Like me, Patrick had moved to Montauk in order to heal. Though there was no comparing a cheating fiancé to his losses. The good news was, he'd seemed less introspective and more lighthearted in the past couple months.

"You promised you'd be good while I'm hibernating with my laptop," he said.

I took a sip of cabernet, savored it, then swallowed. "You're right."

"Say what?" Patrick said in mock astonishment. "You're saying I'm right?"

"Well, we've only been able to snatch a few moments together since you started writing your book. I don't want to waste time talking about murder."

"Possible murder," he added.

"I'm sure you have enough murder in your new thriller. The same one you won't let me read that keeps you burning the midnight oil in your attic writing cave."

"I thought that was you last night," he said. "You shouldn't be wandering the beach alone. Even if it is Montauk." He looked to the west. "You're more secluded here than I am."

"Please," I said. "I'm never alone on the beach in the summer months. Too many vacationers. Even at midnight."

He gave me a fatherly look. "Well, I did appreciate the quote by Khalil Gibran you left in the sand. Though it was perhaps a bit dramatic. I'm only a mile down the beach."

I recited, "*And ever has it been known that love knows not its own depth until the hour of separation.* I haven't seen you in four days. I was going through withdrawal." I reached over and gave him a kiss on his rough cheek. Apparently, not shaving was a writer thing. Along with not trimming or combing his wind-tossed hair. I liked the look. Basically, I liked all his looks. But this one the most. "Well, the quote in the sand worked," I said. "'Cause here you are."

He laughed. "I should be finished with the manuscript by the end of July. We can still take that trip we planned to London. You'll finally be able to scratch the Jack the Ripper pub crawl off your bucket list."

"And a visit to 221 Baker Street," I said.

"You do know Sherlock Holmes is a fictional character, right?"

"Then onto Cornwall," I said, ignoring him. "For another must-do on my bucket list. Visit the home of Daphne du Maurier, Victoria Holt, aka Eleanor Hibbert, the Bronte sisters. Even Agatha Christie set a few of her mysteries there." Thinking of gothic mysteries set on the moors of Cornwall, I glanced toward the lighthouse. Occasionally, the stretch of property above the shoreline was labeled the Montauk Moors. One of the reasons I'd swooned when I'd first found the property for my cottage.

"And don't forget," I said with a sideways glance, "you promised we'd rent a castle for a night. So I can play out all my governess and lord of the manor fantasies."

"Funny, that's your fantasy. You don't seem the submissive type."

"Reading gothic romances as a teen in my mother's antiques shop left its mark, Lord Seaton." I bowed my head obediently.

Patrick tilted up my chin, and when I raised my head, he said, "Open wide."

When I did, he stuffed a shrimp into my mouth. "Lady Barrett, I must get back to the quill and parchment if I'm going to meet my deadline."

"Oh, kind sir, please call me Megan, I'm just a lowly governess." I fluttered my eyelashes at the same time a bug flew into my right eye. "Stupid no-see-ums!"

Patrick laughed. "Bet they have no-see-ums on the moors of Cornwall. Not so romantic."

"Don't burst my bubble," I said, "or I'll change the scenario and make you the muckraker stable boy."

"Then I would be the submissive one. That could work too," he said with a wink. "Back to the subject of Travis Sterling," he said, his eyes growing serious. "I don't want to worry about you. Seeing I won't be there to help you survive another *sticky* situation like the lighthouse." He put quotation marks in the air for the word *sticky*. "I need you to follow your father's and Arthur's directives."

His smile returned. I released my hand from his, then lightly punched him on his tanned bicep. "Stop. This is different. I have no connection to anyone at Dahlia Lane. You don't have to worry about me." Then, like an idiot, I said, "If I do go back to, I'll try to get more information on what the other notes say and how many there are. And make sure they were all addressed to Lauren, like I've been told."

"Hopefully the driver of the hit-and-one will be arrested or turn themselves in before you go back."

"Oh, I hope so. Seeing that Ashley got me the assignment at Dahlia Lane, maybe you could chat her up. See if she knows anything about why Lauren Kincaid would get threatening notes. After all, she's your and Jessie's publicist. I'm sure she has her ear to the ground."

"I will. On one condition," Patrick said, trying to sound serious, even though his grin said otherwise. "We get back to something very important. Us. You don't even know for sure Travis Sterling was deliberately killed. I want to savor my short window of Meg-time. Remember, I came out of my gloomy attic room just for you. I have my own plotting problems. Making sure the trail of breadcrumbs I leave won't give away who the bad guy is mid-book."

"I thought your thrillers always told you who the bad guy was up front," I said.

"True. But there's always a secret mastermind."

"I do get to read it before you turn it in to your publisher, right? You promised."

"We'll see how well you behave."

"Stop teasing me."

"Okay. Okay. There's something more pressing I need to do right now." He leaned in and we kissed.

His lips tasted of wine and salt from the ocean air.

I reveled in the feeling.

Poof! All thoughts of death vanished like the setting sun.

Chapter 11

"Are you stalking me?" Arthur asked.

After Patrick and Charlie left for home, via the beach, I'd been waiting for Arthur's Lexus to pull into the driveway next door. So in a way, he was right, I was stalking him. Which in turn reminded me about the poison pen stalker at Dahlia Lane Farms.

"No. Yes. Whatever," I said. "It's been three hours and I haven't heard anything from you or my father. So? Did they arrest the driver of the car?"

Arthur glanced over at Little Grey. His wife, my best friend, could be seen under the overhead light at the kitchen sink. She was the perfect picture of domesticity, watering violets on the windowsill.

While Elle and Arthur were renovating their new home—scratch that, estate—they were staying next door to me at Claire Post's cottage, Little Grey. Poet laureate Claire was in California helping her daughter with her newly minted granddaughter, Sophie. Claire was letting Elle and Arthur stay rent-free until they were finished with their renovations.

Claire's cottage had been nicknamed Little Grey because it was built by the same architect as the infamous Grey Gardens in East Hampton. The same mansion once owned by Jackie Kennedy Onassis's eccentric aunt and cousin, Big and Little Edie Beale.

"It's been a long day, Meg," Arthur said. "You know I can't share anything with you. If, after I talk to your father, he wants to fill you in, he can. I'll leave that decision up to him. This is a high-profile case. I must do it by the book."

"You're sounding like Travis's hit-and-run might not have been an accident. Why did you run out of the windmill so fast?"

"I'm too weary to be interrogated. Yes, his death is suspicious. That's all I'm saying. Please don't mention to Elle that foul play might be involved."

"You mean murder," I said.

"I don't want her to be part of your amateur detecting. Her plate is full to overflowing trying to get this monstrosity of a house we bought ready before Claire comes back and we need to move out."

"Just one thing. Something's bothering me," I whispered, glancing over at Little Grey's front porch, making sure Elle hadn't decided to come out to see what was taking her husband so long. "How did Lauren Kincaid hear about Travis's death before Jessie?"

"Why would that matter?" Arthur said. "If you must know, Conrad Kincaid's business card was in Mr. Sterling's wallet, which we found in the SUV's glove compartment. Your father noticed the Dahlia Lane Enterprises logo, so we called him. Anything else before I go inside?" Arthur asked, loosening his tie. Between the bags under his eyes and his five-o'clock shadow, which seemed more like an eleven-o'clock shadow, he'd had a long-g-g day. He didn't need me adding to his stress.

As Patrick suggested, I would try to keep my nose clean. Then I thought of the photos I'd taken of the items in Lauren's handbag. "Well, you go see your wifey. Give her a kiss from me and tell her I'll be out at the motor lodge tomorrow morning working on the cottages. I'm sure she'll wonder why I'm not going back to work at Dahlia Lane Farms. Don't worry, I'll be quiet as a mouse." I mimicked zipping my lips, then throwing away the key. "Though she's not a delicate flower. And I have to say, she's pointed out a few things in our past cases you and I've missed."

Our past cases. The same ones where you put her in danger," he said. "Let's compromise. I'll tell her about Travis Sterling because it's already in the press. Nothing more. You know how she's been lately, up and down on the emotional scale. Let's keep things having to do with this Dahlia Lane business between the two of us."

"You mean because Elle's *horror*mones, as she's coined them, are out of whack because of the fertility injections?"

"Exactly."

"You're right," I said, laughing. "Yesterday, I read her a poem from the poet chosen for our next Dead Poets Society Book Club meeting. She started sobbing."

"What poem? Something from Edgar Allan Poe, I bet. Meg, you should know better."

"No. Longfellow. 'Nature paints not in oils—but frescoes the great dome of heaven. With sunsets and the lovely forms of clouds. And flying vapors.' Pretty benign quote," I said. "Nothing to cry about. Even though it's beautiful."

"I rest my case," he said. "Leave Elle out of anything having to do with death or poetry." Realizing what he'd said, he grinned then turned and headed up the crushed-shell driveway.

• • •

An hour later, I stood on my deck looking out at a calm ocean bathed in moonlight. Was the hit-and-run an accident? Or intentional? And why was Arthur saying it was suspicious? I could either let it go or put a call into my father to see if he'd learned anything new.

A cloud shrouded the smiling moon. Jessie's tear-stained face, after the news of her brother's death, flashed in front of me. Hopefully, she'd gotten ahold of her fiancé and he had given her some comfort.

When I went back inside the cottage, I ignored the blinking light on my answering machine. I knew it was from Elle. Arthur must have told her about Travis. With so many things relating to his death swirling around in my mind, I decided to call her back in the morning. I needed a time-out. And I knew the perfect place to take that time-out. My sanctuary. My reading and chillaxin' room. The perfect cocooned space to unwind after what happened with Travis Sterling.

I pressed the paneling by the fireplace and *voilà!* the door opened.

I carried my dinner inside. I'd had to reheat it five times because I'd gotten so immersed in all the social media posts about Travis Sterling's death. I shouldn't have been surprised at how fast the bloggers and online papers like *Dave's Hamptons* had gotten ahold of the story. After all, we were nearing the height of the summer season. Paparazzi lurked in every gold-paved alley. For every ten people walking the Hamptons streets, I'd guess five were big-time celebs.

The police hadn't released many details about the hit-and-run, most likely waiting for the person to turn themselves in. They had disclosed that it happened in the cozy hamlet of Montauk. My Montauk.

Placing my dinner and phone on the candlestand next to my window seat, I sat, more like collapsed, onto the window seat's thick cushion, my back sinking into a huge down-filled pillow. Looking toward the east, I soaked in the view of the Montauk Point Lighthouse. Its beacon, bright under the moonlight, soothed my jangled nerves. Its solitary light was welcoming and constant.

I'd designed my hidden space with floor-to-ceiling custom-made bookshelves built from recycled wood. The shelves were filled with my collection of antique nineteenth-century cloth-bound books embossed with gold spines and decorative covers.

I'd gotten the idea for the room after I'd found a dead body—actually, a pile of bones—in a hidden room at one of the bungalows I'd been working on at the Sandringham Estate. Another story I'd rather place on the back burner.

I reached for my dinner at the same time Jo pounced on my lap. She did a couple turns while kneading my thighs, then snuggled down affectionately. She was up to something.

Then it hit me, she wanted my makeshift dinner. Earlier, I'd made a box of Stove Top stuffing, added canned wild-caught tuna, cream of mushroom soup, white cheddar cheese, fresh herbs from my garden and large dollops of sour cream. Where I went wrong was giving Her Chubbiness the water from the canned tuna. After lapping it up, she'd followed me around the cottage like we were bosom buddies.

As if!

"Sorry, sweetie," I said, looking down at her. "You know what the vet said. No table food. Not even Uncle Patrick's home-cooked meals. So be a good girl." I scratched under her chin (first time ever without her nipping at me!), then felt more than heard her rattling purr.

Theatrics at their best. Still, I took advantage of the moment and kissed her on the head. It was my own darn fault for giving her the tuna water. Lesson learned.

At Jo's last checkup, she'd scratched the poor vet's hand so severely he'd received a souvenir for life—Jo's personal branding signature in the shape of a red X.

Either as revenge for his oozing wound or because he was truly worried about her health and recent weight gain, he put Jo on a strict diet of expensive veggie-infused cat food.

I was leaning toward the revenge theory.

When Jo saw I wasn't in a sharing mood, she tried a different tactic. With talons extracted, she jumped onto my shoulder.

"Ouch!"

She swiped her right paw in the direction of the bowl on the candlestand. I pulled her away and deposited her on the window seat's cushion.

Trying one more time to sway my decision, Jo nuzzled her face against my chin. a pouf of fur floated, then attached itself to my lips like Velcro. "Sorry, buddy," I sputtered. "We both have to be strong. It's for your own good."

Jo hissed. I guessed that's where they got the expression *hissy fit*. Before I could chastise her, she leapt off the window seat, the nails from her back paws digging into my bare knees as she went in search of something to destroy.

Had to love her chutzpah.

After I finished my quasi-supper, I placed my empty bowl on top of the candlestand, grabbed my phone and called my father.

The call went through to my hearing aids. "Jeff Barrett's phone," someone answered.

"You're not Jeff Barrett, you're Doc. What's up, Doc?" It never got old.

"Meg, you're a riot," Doc said.

"Well, while I have you on the line, what can you tell me about Travis Sterling? After all, you were Dad's top Detroit PD coroner."

"Oh, no, you don't," Doc said. "Here's your father. Now that he's living in Montauk, I refer all questions to him. I'm not going to worry about you getting into trouble anymore."

"I'm not a little kid, Doc."

"If the shoe fits, missy. Need I go through the list of your past troubles since moving to the Hamptons?"

"Glass half full, Doc. Look at the dénouement."

"The what?"

"The great reveal at the end of all those *past troubles*. Justice was served."

"Don't pull that Hercule Poirot stuff on me." Then I heard him call out, "Jeff, it's your wayward daughter."

My father's smooth, calm voice came on the line. Boy, was I happy to have him living nearby. He said, "I just hung up with Arthur. He told me you've been sniffing around for answers about Travis."

"Did you tell him about the threatening notes?"

"Yes."

"Well?"

"He wasn't that excited. He seems sure the hit-and-run driver will turn themselves in."

"What's your opinion? You were at the scene."

"Give me time to process everything, then I'll use Doc as a sounding board. As for tonight, daughter, let this one go. Let's trust that Arthur and his team—"

"You don't need to talk it over with Doc. You have me now," I said like a petulant child.

"How about this. Meet Doc and me at Paddy's tomorrow morning. We're supposed to have thunderstorms and marine warnings are out. So we won't be fishing."

"Fabulous!" I cheered. "The three musketeers. Or should I say detectiveteers. I've always dreamed of you, me and Doc solving a case."

"You have? Good thing your mom's not here. When you were younger, she's the one who forbade me to share any details in my murder cases with you, even if I made them PG-13."

"Well—about that."

"Megan Elizabeth!"

"I never looked at your files. I swear. But I might have been eavesdropping when you discussed a case with Mom."

His voice softened. "She was always there for me when I'd go off to a dark place in my head about a senseless murder. It's up to law enforcement to make sense of the inner workings of a killer. Hell, they're all senseless."

"So, you're thinking he was deliberately hit?"

"You're getting way ahead of yourself. We don't know a lot right now. Like Arthur, I'm still hoping whoever hit him will turn themselves in. On second thought, maybe meeting with us in the morning isn't a good idea."

"Pshaw! Order me a ham and cheese crepe. I promised Patrick I'd walk Charlie at daybreak."

"Patrick's invited," he said.

"He's trying to finish his newest thriller manuscript. So I won't even ask. I don't want to tempt him. We have that trip to London in August. And don't start discussing things until I'm there. I've only known Jessie for two days, but I'm really worried by the few things she's said. Then there's the threatening note creep."

"We still don't know if any of that is related to the hit-and-run. Try to get a good night's sleep. It will all keep till the morning. Love you."

"Love you back. Hey, Dad—" He'd already hung up. I'd wanted to ask him one more thing. I wanted to know if he and Doc talked to the person who called 911. I guessed I would find out in the morning.

Now, my only problem was getting that good night's sleep.

Luckily, I had the perfect cure for insomnia.

I threw on my flip-flops, went out the French doors and onto my deck, then flew down the thirty-five steps to the beach.

Surely, Patrick could take a two-minute break to kiss me good night. Then I'd sleep like a baby.

Only, when I reached his cottage and climbed the steps to his deck, I stopped in my tracks. Beyond the sliding glass doors, highlighted by a soft backlight, was the silhouette of a tall woman.

What the heck!

Coward that I was, I turned, crept back down his wooden steps, got a splinter from the railing, stifled a scream, then slowly slunk home, ruminating about my strange day—and night.

When I reached my beach, I turned on my phone's flashlight, found a stick of driftwood, then left a couple lines in the sand by Longfellow:

> *Trust no Future, however pleasant!*
> *Let the dead Past bury its dead!*
> *Act, act in the living Present!*
> *Heart within, and God overhead!*

Chapter 12

Thursday morning, before leaving to pick up Charlie for her walk, I searched the cupboards for a couple toothpicks to keep my eyes open. As I'd feared, between Travis's death and the woman in Patrick's cottage, I'd gotten about ten minutes of sleep.

I'd woken to a mouthful of cat fur. Jo had been hogging my pillow, her chubby face just inches from my nose. I should've been used to it by now. Her stinky tuna breath was better than an alarm clock.

I pressed the button on the coffee maker and bent to grab a can of Jo's food from the cupboard. I always filled the water reservoir the night before and had already put in a new pod of Sumatra. I wasn't wearing my hearing aids and didn't realize until Jo jumped onto the counter that I'd failed to put my favorite mug with a caricature of Edgar Allan Poe and the words *I became insane with horrible intervals of sanity* under the spout of the Nespresso machine. Coffee was waterfalling onto the counter, ready to pool onto my kitchen floor.

I took the mug from the dish drainer and shoved it under the coffee machine spout, then grabbed an entire roll of paper towels and used it to dam up the water. After a few, choice swear words, I glanced up at the ceiling and said, "Please don't let this be a precursor to the rest of my day."

Jo gave me her one-eyed, you're-crazy-as-a-bat stare, then sulked off.

She was right. Spilled coffee wasn't a big deal. Not compared to Jessie Sterling's brother's death.

I looked out my west-facing bay window and noticed a churning ocean and stormy sky. I wasn't unhappy about the weather. If the sky let loose its deluge, I'd rejoice. My poor garden needed it.

Feeling snarky and irritated, I was tempted to call Patrick to see if he still wanted me to walk Charlie—or perhaps the woman from last night could do it. I decided not to call.

For one reason.

I needed to find out who the woman was.

I grabbed my rain slicker from the bamboo coatrack, opened the French door and stepped onto my deck. Looking back over my shoulder, I said to Jo, "I'm sure there's a logical explanation for whoever that woman was in Patrick's cottage. But it was ten at night—his prime writing hours, for gosh sakes."

I swear Jo grinned back at me, then meowed something I knew would translate into *You silly adorable fool.* I slammed the door on her smug face.

Stepping toward the deck's railing, I saw a tremulant white-capped Atlantic. Lightning streaked the sky. A boom of thunder followed, vibrating my entire body.

Then it started to pour.

There was no way I should walk the beach in a thunderstorm. And there was no way Patrick's dog, Charlie, should either. One thing I was thrilled about—I knew my garden was rejoicing.

I turned and went back inside, took my phone off the charger, then looked down at the screen. Patrick had texted me at dawn. *Thanks for the offer to walk Charlie. I couldn't sleep, so I took her out before the storm. TTYL. LY.*

"*He* couldn't sleep!" I shouted in Jo's direction. Her eye remained shut, but she twitched her right ear in annoyance. "He couldn't sleep!" I said again. Then I took a step back in my thinking. How crazy was it that instead of confronting him, I was choosing avoidance? Confronting wasn't the right word. I could simply ask. This was Patrick. Kind, loving Patrick. I'd been burned in the past. It didn't necessarily mean the past would repeat itself.

Did it?

It would be as simple as driving over to Patrick's cottage before going to Paddy's and asking him who the woman was.

I took a deep breath.

It always felt better when I had a plan.

Even in the torrential rain, his cottage was only a two-minute drive from mine.

A couple hours later, when I pulled into his driveway, the storm was in full swing. I parked, grabbed my umbrella, and stepped into the deluge. I fought my way toward Patrick's back door. Horizontal gusts of rain carried gritty sand that stung my cheeks. By the time I reached the door, my umbrella was inside out.

I pounded like a madwoman at the glass. I had a key, but after seeing a stranger in his cottage last night, I was too shell-shocked to use it. At that thought, a gust of wind picked up my umbrella and it went flying Mary Poppins–style toward the ocean. Maybe this was a bad idea.

I pounded again, then waited.

I was about to give up when the door flew open.

Patrick reached out a long arm and pulled me inside. "Meg, what's wrong? Everything okay? Are you okay? Didn't you receive my text about Charlie?"

I glanced up at him as water rivered down my raincoat, then dripped onto the mudroom's brick floor.

It was then that I saw her.

Over Patrick's shoulder was a tall, elegantly dressed woman with short perfectly coiffed silver hair. Even though it was only eight in the morning, she was dressed for the day and had on a full face of makeup. She had the same blue-green eyes as Patrick. Only the expression in her eyes wasn't one I'd seen on Patrick. I guessed shock and irritation would sum it up. *Yikes.* This must be Patrick's mother. That's what I got for not trusting him.

As she looked me over, her gaze met mine. My hands flew to my face as I tried to unglue the muttonchop sections of hair pasted to my cheeks. I could only imagine what a sight I was compared to her. "Uh-h, n-o-o," I stuttered, looking first at Patrick, then his mother. "Everything's fine, I was just in a hurry to get out of the rain." I added a faux giggle. "It's a beast out there. I wanted to stop by and say hi before you start your writing day."

"What a nice surprise," Patrick said nervously. "This is, uh, my mother . . ."

"Aurora Montague," she said, without extending her hand. "And who might you be?"

I was immediately aware of two things. One, she had no clue who I was. Which meant Patrick had never told her about me. Just like he hadn't shared anything about his mother to me. Only his long-deceased father. And two, her last name wasn't Seaton. Either she'd remarried or Montague was her maiden name, nom de plume, or stage name.

"Meg Barrett," I said, just as Charlie galloped in from the great room, jumped up and pressed her front paws against my chest. Patrick had to grab me by the shoulders to steady me as Charlie went to town licking my cheeks like I was her personal Dum-Dum lollipop.

I was a dum-dum to worry that Patrick was cheating on me.

"Oh," Aurora said, "you're my son's dog walker. Well, as you can see" — she waved her hand dramatically toward the screen door — "it's not safe to take out adorable Charlotte. Come back when it clears up."

"Her name is Charlie, Mother."

"Charlie is a boy's name," she said disapprovingly. Turning to me, she said, "I suggest you get going before . . ."

I fisted my hand, ready to punch Patrick if he didn't fess up.

That wasn't necessary.

"Meg is not my dog walker. She and I are in a relationship," he said, taking my hand in his, then squeezing it. "Meg, I was planning on calling you to see if you wanted to join my mother and me for dinner tonight at Pondfare."

"Of course," I said. "I'd love to." Looking at Aurora's stern face, I felt like retracting my words.

Aurora grabbed Patrick's arm. "Oh, darling, I thought we were going to Sarabeth's to see her and little Sophia? I'm only in town for a couple days."

Sarabeth was the chef and owner of a thriving restaurant in nearby Watermill. She was also Patrick's deceased wife's identical twin sister. Sarabeth's daughter, Sophia, was Patrick's niece by marriage.

"Well, we could do that," I said in an overly perky tone. "I'd love to see Sarabeth and Sophia. Sarabeth has been so busy after her fabulous review in the *New York Times* Sunday food section, we've barely spent time with her. Right, Patrick?"

Aurora pursed her lips. "Oh, so you've met beautiful Catherine's twin. That means you know all about the tragedy. I'm surprised, dear," she said, turning to Patrick, "you would share something so personal. I'm sure you still need time to grieve. It's seems like only yesterday," she said, her voice trailing off.

"It's been four years, Mother. Hardly a short time," he said, clenching his jaw. "Just like it's been four years since I've seen you."

"I was waiting for an invitation," she answered, adding a sigh. "We didn't quite leave things on good terms, did we, son?"

Patrick gave his mother a look I'd never seen before. Disgust? Exasperation? Certainly not love. "Sarabeth's is out of the question. And you know why, Mother."

The heat of the Barrett blotches worked their way up to my neck, then my cheeks. Talk about awkward. Glancing down at an imaginary watch on my wrist, I stuttered, "Oh, m-m-my, I really need to go. My father and Doc are saving me a spot at Paddy's."

Patrick looked over at me in amusement. He wasn't buying it. Even if it was true. I wasn't lying, but I'm sure I would've made up anything to get out of the embarrassment of the moment.

I placed my hand on the doorknob. "Nice meeting you, Aurora." *Should I have called her Mrs. Montague?* "Just let me know about dinner tonight. I'm free. Wherever you decide to meet."

Why was I so gung-ho on inserting myself into their dinner plans?

That was obvious. Because I wanted to know more about someone Patrick never mentioned. He knew all about my mother, who'd passed away from breast cancer when I was a teen, and he had no problem talking about the close bond he'd had with his father before he passed away. But not a peep about his mother. Had Patrick's father raised him? Not Aurora?

I also asked myself, after Patrick kissed me goodbye as his mother looked on with her lips pursed tightly, hadn't Aurora visited her son in the four years since the accident? And what was up about Sarabeth's restaurant? Something to ponder later.

I waved goodbye and stepped into the storm. Welcoming the pelting rain and escape from Patrick's mother's accessing gaze.

As I fought my way to my woody, I thought, *That went differently than I expected.*

I needed to refocus my energy on bigger mysteries than Patrick's mother showing up out the blue.

I prayed my father would have good news to impart over breakfast.

Once again, I felt blessed he'd moved to Montauk.

Not because he was the best father ever—more because he was also the best homicide detective ever.

Chapter 13

After circling the block a dozen times looking for parking, I was seated at Paddy's Pancake House's red-speckled Formica counter.

My father was to my right, Doc to my left.

Paddy's décor hadn't changed since the first time I came out to Montauk with a group of girls from my dorm at NYU — and I hoped it never would. Old black-and-white photos covered the walls, most of them showing old Montauk from back when it was a fishing village. The female waitstaff were all in their sixties or older, including husky-voiced Rose, whose husband Paddy was the chef and owner. In the winter, most of the clientele were dressed in plaid flannel shirts, jeans and hiking boots. Summer was a different story. You never knew what famous person you might be rubbing elbows with.

"And you won't believe who the woman was!" I said, taking a gulp of coffee. "Patrick's mother! He's never once mentioned her. And I'm sorry to say, I don't think she liked me."

"Meg, lower your voice. Everyone's looking at you," Doc said, holding a finger in front of his trim white beard. "How could she not like you?"

"It was all in her eyes." I glanced around the restaurant. "Plus, no one's looking at me."

"How about that table of forty-something women who look like a well-dressed school of fish out of water?" Doc said.

I swiveled my red pleather bar stool and zeroed in on the table he referred to. Doc was right. Four attractive Botoxed women with large lips were glancing in our direction. I wouldn't be surprised if they were castmates from the myriad Hampton reality TV shows that filmed during the summer.

But they weren't looking at me — more like at my father.

Jeff Barrett always turned heads. I should say, when he wasn't wearing army green waders and Doc's stinky fishing hat. He had that whole Cary Grant/Gregory Peck vibe going. This morning he wore a turquoise T-shirt, a pair of tan cargo shorts, and flip-flops. His short dark hair had the perfect touch of gray at the temples. We shared the same blue eyes, but my fair coloring and blonde hair came from my mother's Swedish side of the family. It wasn't just his looks that made my father attractive. He oozed what my mother had called the three

C's—confidence, calmness and control.

Paddy's wife Rose came over with a carafe of leaded in one hand and unleaded in the other. "Anyone need a refill?"

Doc held out his coffee cup. Rose filled it with decaf, knowing his preference. The perk of being a regular.

"Anyone else?" she asked.

"Thanks, I'm good," I said. "Dad?"

"Wouldn't mind a little octane in my cup." He gave Rose one of his million-dollar smiles. "You make the best coffee. Just like your husband makes the best—uh, everything."

Rose beamed. "Thanks, Jeff."

"Though, I should have ordered the crepes." He aimed his fork at my plate and speared a piece of my ham and cheese crepe.

"Hands off, buddy. Order your own."

Smacking his lips, he said, "I might just do that."

"So, Dad, what do you think of coming out to dinner tonight with Patrick, his mother and me? I could use the moral support. Aurora thought I was Patrick's dog walker. That tells you something. Plus, you're good at smoothing troubled waters. You should've been a diplomat."

"Why not give Patrick's mother the benefit of the doubt?" Doc interjected. "Maybe she'll surprise you."

"You're right, Doc. I only met Aurora Montague for a few minutes. I shouldn't be so judgy."

"Aurora Montague?" Rose said with a frown, then placed a stack of napkins on the counter. She leaned in closer, her eyes wide in disbelief, then shook her head back and forth. The chestnut ringlets on either side on her round rosy cheeks bobbed like springs. "Not *the* Aurora Montague?

"Uh, yes," I said. "Aurora Montague. You know her?"

Putting her hands on her hips, Rose said, "I know *of* her—wish I didn't. Author Patrick Seaton's hoity-toity mother is not welcome here. Not that she would dare set foot. Too pedestrian for her taste. She gave Paddy's our only bad review in the fifty years my husband and I have been in business. According to her, she was some big-time restaurant reviewer for the *Times*—no, wait, *Long Island Newsday*. She's a pariah in Montauk. And we aren't the only ones in the Hamptons who got a crummy review. She's considered persona non grata on the east end of Long Island. For that matter, probably the whole Eastern seaboard."

I was surprised by what Rose said. But not as surprised as I was by what my foodie father said next. "I think at one point she did have a column in the Sunday *New York Times* food and wine section. It was back when you were at NYU, Meg. Remember? We went to that food exposition at the Javits Center in Manhattan. Aurora Montague was on the judges panel for the Top Chefs of New York City competition. Attractive woman. But, Rose, you're right," he said, tipping his head in her direction. "She's the only one who found something wrong with every chef's dish. Wow. She's Patrick's mother. Small world."

Indeed. And here I was worried about being too judgy. Patrick's mother made her living from being judgy. "Good thing I'm allergic to the kitchen. Meaning, she'll never have to critique one of my meals."

"Truly a silver lining," Doc said, giving me a wry grin.

I had a feeling that might be the *only* silver lining in Patrick's mother and my future. So why hadn't mother and son seen each other in four years? Did their estrangement have something to do with the accident that happened with Patrick's wife and daughter? If so, wouldn't that be the time a son needed his mother the most?

Rose must have noticed my worried expression. She sent me a smile and said, "Believe me, I don't blame Patrick for his obnoxious mother. We can't pick who God gives us as parents. And he's apologized a million times. Just do me a favor and I'll give you free coffee for the rest of your days. Don't bring her inside this restaurant. I'm worried about Paddy's heart."

"Rose, order up!" we heard someone bellow from the kitchen.

"I'm coming! Put a cork in it, husband," Rose called back.

Once she disappeared through the swinging doors, and not wanting to dwell on Patrick's mother, I turned to my father and whispered, "So what did Arthur tell you about Jessie's brother's death? Spill, father of mine."

He emptied his coffee mug, then said, "Arthur took some convincing before he agreed I could share a few details with you."

"Only a few?" I said in a louder tone.

Doc rolled his eyes. "Not just Arthur needed convincing. I voted against involving you in the investigation. But now Jeff's moved here, I'll gladly defer to him when it comes to my wayward niece." Doc and

I weren't blood relatives, but we might as well have been. He was also my godfather, and since my move to Montauk, he'd tried to keep me in line. "Snap, Doc. I didn't know I was such a burden."

That got him. He put down his fork and squeezed my hand. "You know I love you. But now your father's here, I'll let him take the reins."

My father swiveled to face me, allowing me to read his lips for any missed words. "As you know, Doc and I were fishing near the old shipwreck site. Suddenly, we heard the wail of sirens and spotted an ambulance and police cars down the shore."

"That was lucky."

Retired coroner Doc elbowed me. "There's nothing lucky about death."

"You're right, Doc. Sorry." Doc wasn't a typical coroner like the ones you see in cop shows, bone saw in one hand, tuna sandwich in the other. He'd cared about his patients, telling me he should have been an obstetrician. He said he wished he could bring them in whole instead of taking them apart.

My father continued, "When we got to the back of what I now know was Travis's Escalade, Arthur waved us over to where he and his team were standing. Travis's body was off to the side, in the grass. He was on his back and still wearing his wet suit."

I tried to picture the scene. "How could you tell he was hit by a car? Was he still alive when Arthur arrived? Did you talk to the person who called it in?"

"One thing at a time, daughter. It was obvious from the tire marks in the dirt parking lot that the vehicle that hit him stopped at the rear of the Escalade. When Arthur's CSI turned him over, it was also obvious by his injuries that he was hit from behind and pinned to the Escalade. The hatch was up. He must have been in the process of taking off his wet suit when he was hit. His hood, flippers and oxygen tank were inside the cargo area."

"Dad, why doesn't Arthur think it was just an accident? Perhaps the driver got scared and simply left the scene in a panic. Also, is there a way to match the tire treads to the car that hit him? Any paint transfer from the other car to Travis's?"

"A few things point to it being deliberate. One, the body was found too far away from where he was hit—a couple hundred yards in the seagrass. The evidence is clear that he was pinned, not thrown in the air. His injuries —"

"I believe you. No need for details," I said.

"As for your other questions," he said. "I'm sure the East Hampton Town Police will look for all the things you mentioned."

"They should search the vehicles at Dahlia Lane Farms to match the tire treads," I said, thinking of Lauren's car, the gold Mercedes I'd seen in the driveway and the Mercedes key fob in her handbag.

Then I told them about Tuesday morning when Travis had come barreling by me in his Escalade, nearly sideswiping my woody. "He looked so angry. How could I not think someone at Dahlia Lane might be involved? Dad, back to Travis's body being so far from the point of impact. Couldn't he have crawled there after getting hit?"

"The imprints in the grass collaborated the theory that someone grabbed him from under his armpits, then dragged him in an attempt to hide his body until they could get away."

"And he was on his back," Doc added. "He looked like he'd been posed. All he needed was a rose between his hands."

"Maybe that points to the fact whoever hit him knew him," I said, turning to Doc. "Could it be they were trying to scare him, and it went terribly wrong?"

"Meg, we could speculate until the sun goes down," Doc said. "We need to let Arthur do his job."

I sighed. "And all this happened in broad daylight? Pretty brazen. Someone has blood on their hands," I said, more as a statement than a question, trying to get the scene out of my mind. "And no one saw any of this?"

"No," my father said, shaking his head. "Another thing we were surprised about—" He looked at Doc for confirmation to continue. Doc just shrugged his shoulders. "His cell phone was missing."

"Really? Wow. Missing? That explains what Arthur told me last night. They called Conrad from a business card they found in Travis's wallet, not from his emergency contact in his phone. Conrad Kincaid is Dahlia Lane Enterprises VP," I said, turning to Doc. "He's married to Jessie's cousin Lauren. Poor guy."

My father gave me *the look*. And here I thought only Elle and Patrick had patented the look. He said, "The phone was nowhere to be found. Doc and I even put on booties and helped the team search for it. I thought Arthur would call and say they'd found it. But as of last night, there was no sign of it."

"I knew it," I said. "You were holding back. Was the missing phone the reason you were okay with me going back inside the windmill to look around?"

"You did what?" Doc mumbled, choking on his French toast. "Jeff, maybe you won't be a good influence on my goddaughter. Shame on you."

"Oh, Doc, a little snooping never hurt anyone."

"Said the fly to the spider." Doc threw his hands in the air. "I surrender. I just hope you know what you're doing, buddy. Arthur is a great detective. Leave it to him and turn your thoughts to the fishing competition on Sunday. That goes for you too, missy." He picked up his napkin, wiped his snow-white beard, then put the napkin on his empty plate. Even Jo couldn't have gotten it cleaner.

"You know I don't fish, Doc," I said. "Too gruesome."

"Ha, said by a woman who's known for taking photos of more than a few murder scenes."

Now it was my father's turn to look at me disapprovingly.

"So it sounds like whatever happened, happened soon after his call to his sister," I said. "Jessie told us at the windmill, when she talked to Travis, he was heading to the airplane hangar to meet with someone. She also told me he'd been upset lately. Not his usual self."

"Airplane hangar?" Doc questioned, raising a thick, furry white eyebrow.

I filled Doc in on Saturday's grand opening at Dahlia Lane Shoppes at the Hangar. Then I said, "Who called 911?"

"A woman who lives nearby. Actually, she didn't find him, her spaniel did."

Doc took a sip of coffee, then looked at me. "How do you do it?"

"Do what?" I asked innocently.

"Invite trouble everywhere you go."

"Just lucky, I guess. Dad, what was Arthur's reaction when you told him about the notes?"

"What notes?" Doc asked.

I explained about the threatening notes Bryce told us about, leaving out the part of me photographing one of the notes after going through Lauren's handbag. If my father hadn't told Doc about that, I certainly wouldn't.

"Maybe Lauren is sending the notes to herself. Wanting her cousin to feel sorry for her," I said, remembering what Kayla had told us.

"It's early days, daughter. Early days."

"Enough, you two," Doc said. "Finish your breakfast. I need to hit the tackle shop. I have an important date with a sea bass tomorrow."

"Good idea," my father said. "Let's change the subject. I bet Patrick's happy his mother's in town."

Not the subject I would have chosen.

Sticking out my bottom lip, I said, "Does that mean you'll be my wingman if we go out to dinner tonight?"

"Hmmm. I don't know," he answered.

"It'll be either Pondfare or Sarabeth's by the Bay." I was banking on Pondfare after seeing Patrick's reaction to his mother's suggestion of going to Sarabeth's. *What was that about?*

A smile spread across my father's face. "I'm in."

"How about you, Doc?" I said. "Bring Georgia." Septuagenarian bookseller Georgia, the owner of the Old Man and the Sea Books in Montauk, was in a relationship with sexagenarian Doc.

"Oh, no," Doc said, shaking his head. "After what Rose just said about Patrick's mother, I think you should keep it a family affair."

"Coward," I said.

Doc laughed, his kind gray eyes lighting up. "And you aren't? Taking your father as wingman?"

He got me there.

"Hey, I just had a great idea. I have to head to the cottages after this. How about this afternoon you two take me to the scene of the hit-and-run? Six eyes are better than four looking for Travis's cell phone."

"We can't. And you can't, daughter. The scene has been methodically searched. Don't make me regret sharing things with you."

"Wouldn't think of it," I said.

"I don't like that look in her eye, Jeff. She's up to no good."

"Am not."

"Are too," my father said.

Chapter 14

"I think the rug should be moved more to the center. What do you think?" I asked Emilio, already changing my mind.

He shot me a questioning glance. "I'm at a loss as to why you wanted my help. You know how to arrange a room. Isn't that why your Cottages by the Sea clients pay you the big bucks?"

"This is different. I want this mini cottage to please both a mother and her children. Elle spent so much money fixer-uppering the exteriors of the cottages. I don't want to let her down."

After leaving Paddy's, I'd called, more like begged, Emilio to help me with one of the cottages at the rehabbed motor lodge. I really did want his discerning eye, but mostly I wanted to know more about Jessie and her crew. Even if a stranger caused Travis's hit-and-run and it wasn't premeditated, which seemed more doubtful as time went on, it couldn't hurt to get Emilio's take on everyone at Dahlia Lane.

Emilio put his hand on his hips and glanced around the open-concept space. "Well, if anyone knows how to transform a small space, it's you. It's noon. How soon will we be done?"

"You've been a trooper. Only a few finishing touches. How about we grab some lunch from Mickey's Chowder Shack? Now that the rain's stopped we can sit on the deck and watch the commercial fishing boats coming into the harbor. Maybe they'll throw some fresh catch onto our table. If you haven't been there, you're in for a real treat. Although I'm still full from my breakfast crepes. Another Montauk place you have to check out—Paddy's Pancake House."

"Paddy's, Mickey's. Sounds like some very un-Hampton-like eateries. My kind of places."

"You okay after everything that happened yesterday?" I asked him. "I thought I had a restless night because of Travis Sterling's death, but those dark circles under your eyes tell me you didn't sleep at all."

He glanced in the mirror over the love seat. "I do look pretty haggard. I can't wrap my head around what happened to Travis. Jessie—"

I waited for him to finish his sentence. Instead, he walked over to a corner cabinet and picked up a vintage McCoy pottery vase. "Are you doing the interiors of the other cottages the same as this one? It would save time." Emilio noticed my silence and turned to me. "What? Why do you have that look on your face?"

"I'm insulted. I thought you knew me. Would I, Meg Barrett, ever curate cookie-cutter décor in these cottages?"

Emilio laughed. "Ex-cuse me for insulting your design aesthetic."

I placed a sea-green glass candleholder on an old chest fronting the love seat. The chest would add storage space and at the same time double as a coffee table/ottoman. Inside the candleholder was an electric candle. I swore, once it was switched on, you couldn't tell its flickering flame wasn't real. Knowing little ones would soon be living here, the faux candle seemed a safe choice, while still adding a cozy vibe. "Plus," I added, "as you can see, the few smalls I've scattered around are one-of-a-kind vintage—irreplaceable."

"Once again, I apologize," he said. "I can't wait to see your humble abode. Maybe I can talk Jessie into doing an article in *Dahlia Lane Journal* about your cottage and your Cottages by the Sea interior design business. I'll be the photographer."

"I don't know about featuring my small cottage in the journal, not that I wouldn't welcome it. Jessie might instead want to do something on the house Elle and her hubby are staying in. It's next door to mine. Until Elle's place is habitable, she's renting from my friend Claire. It was built by a famous architect."

"Speaking of Elle, when the heck am I going to see her?" Emilio asked, taking a seat on the white *washable* slip-covered love seat.

"You might want to put that off for a while. She's going through fertility injections. You never know if you'll get Ms. Jekyll or Ms. Hyde."

"I'll take my chances. I'm sure you're exaggerating."

I laughed. "Oh, no, I'm not. I bet right now Elle's out at her estate, bossing around my construction guys. Before going over there, I usually give Duke Sr. a call to see how her mood is. Wow. An even better idea for *Dahlia Lane Journal*. A before-and-after of Elle and Arthur's estate. Maybe Jessie and Chris will get involved and film it for *Dahlia Lane Home Makeover*."

"Great idea. I'd love to see Elle *and* her new home."

"More like an old abandoned mansion she's sure is haunted."

"Even more reason to go there," he said with a grin. "And I would love for you and Elle and your significant others to come to the opening party of my photo installment tomorrow night at the Green Room Art Gallery in Bridgehampton. I'm a bit nervous. The Hamptons summer people are in a class of their own. This show will have a completely different clientele than those you've attended at my small Brooklyn Heights pop-ups. I was thinking of canceling because of what happened to Travis—"

"I wouldn't. I'm sure Travis wouldn't have wanted you to."

"I guess you have a point. Travis was a big supporter of my photography."

"I remember your shows. You're being modest. They were more than small pop-ups. The fact you're in an art gallery in the Hamptons means you've arrived."

Emilio rubbed the palms of his hands together. "I would hold back judgment until you see my choices for the exhibit. I've gone in a completely different direction from what you've seen."

"Stop! I'm sure it will be amazing. And of course Elle and I will be there. We'll try to get Patrick and Arthur to come. And I'll let Ashley, Patrick's and Jessie's publicist, know about it. She'll invite all the in-crowd."

"In case I fall on my face, I don't want the in-crowd. Just friends."

"Did you invite Jessie?" I asked.

"I did. But I'm sure she won't show up because of what happened. And she'll be too busy. She still plans on opening Dahlia Lane Shoppes at the Hangar on Saturday. I'm sure my little gallery opening is probably the last thing on her mind."

"Well, I'll be there. Come rain or shine or hurricane."

"Thank you."

"What's your opinion about having the grand opening so soon after Travis's death?" I asked, searching his face. "Is she crazy to try to open? Like you said, her cousin Lauren and her husband don't want her to."

"I was super surprised Conrad didn't want her to open. He sure seemed excited about it at the beginning stages. He and Travis worked closely together on ordering all the things Jessie wanted to go in the shops. Conrad's the money man. But Travis had final say on the budget."

"Maybe Conrad's wife, Lauren, swayed him. She's pretty intimidating, don't you think? Or maybe she really does care about her cousin."

Emilio laughed. "I doubt it. Lauren only cares about herself. She doesn't intimidate me. I've stood up to her more than once. I think she's jealous that while Chris has been away, I've become more involved in Dahlia Lane's day-to-day operations. I think she was also jealous of my friendship with Travis."

"Oh," I said, "I'm so sorry for your loss. I didn't know you two were close. Jessie told me the first day I met her, something was going on with her brother," I said as nonchalantly as possible, stepping next to an open-weave rattan room divider. "Do you have any idea about what?"

"No. Wish I did. He'd been out of town for a couple weeks. Only came back a few days ago."

"I'm sure once Jessie gets ahold of her fiancé and he returns to East Hampton, it will lift her spirits. If that's possible," I said.

It might have been my imagination, but I thought I saw Emilio clench then unclench his fist before he said, "Well, she has me until then." He quickly changed the subject when he noticed me looking at him. "Did I mention I'm hungry? Let's get the show on the road."

"Okay. Okay," I said, laughing and throwing my hands in the air. "Almost finished. Something seems off in this room and I need to figure out what."

"Looks perfect-o as usual," he said, scanning the space.

Glancing toward the large front window, I saw my mistake. The rod to the sheer white floor-length curtains was too low. A small room makeover mistake. I should have placed the rod closer to the ceiling. I went to my tool box, got out my screwdriver, then dragged the stepladder over to the window.

Emilio got up and stepped over to me. "Can I help? The sooner we get this done the sooner we can eat. I'm starved. Skipped breakfast. I went over to Dahlia Lane Farms to pick up my camera and tripod."

I put one foot on the ladder, then turned to him. "And—"

"And what?"

Moving the curtain rod to the ceiling could wait. "You run into anyone? Jessie?"

"I did see her. Or should I say, a ghost of her. If you think I have dark circles under my eyes, you should see hers. I feel so helpless. She said she hasn't been able to get ahold of Chris to tell him about Travis."

"Well, she seems to have a good friend in you. I'm glad you're close."

Emilio didn't respond.

"I met Bryce and Kayla yesterday on my way out of Windmill Cottage. What do you think of them?"

"Slow down, Meg. Now I see why you had me come here. It wasn't for free labor, you would've been fine without me," he said, glancing around the living area. "Though, I commend all your choices. You made this tiny cottage seem so much larger."

"Thanks," I said. "It's all smoke and mirrors—but mostly mirrors. So what do you think?"

"I just said, you're doing a great job."

"Not that. What do you know about all the people at Dahlia Lane? Are you close to any of them besides Jessie and Travis?"

"Still the inquisitive one, aren't you?" he said. "Kayla the intern is a sweetie. A little timid. But she tries to please Jessie. Lauren browbeats her constantly. From what I've seen, Bryce's bark is worse than his bite. He told me Conrad took him in after his father went to prison for some kind of Ponzi scheme. He lives over Dahlia Lane Farms' barn. Does odd jobs and security." He hesitated. "Conrad has always been friendly. Putting it mildly, Lauren and I don't get along. I don't trust her. She's constantly undermining Jessie when she should be kissing Jessie's Birkenstocks for bringing her back into the fold."

I gave him a sideways glance. "Where do Lauren and Conrad live?"

"Before they married, Conrad lived in Southampton. Now they live in Lauren's farmhouse. The property borders on Dahlia Lane's. When Jessie's grandfather passed, he left his estate to his two sons— Jessie's and Lauren's fathers. The land was split in half. Jessie's father started Dahlia Lane Farms. Lauren's father, Lavender Fields. Per Travis, Lauren's father made bad investments and sold off every parcel, except a five-acre lot that has the farmhouse. Conrad paid the back taxes and mortgage after Lauren was forced to file Chapter 11. Soon after, there were wedding bells."

"How about Conrad and Travis? Did they get along?"

"I'd say Conrad and Travis were close. Lauren and Travis—oil and water."

"Why?"

"I was privy to a few scenes before Lauren was allowed back into the company. I overheard Travis telling Jessie not to have anything to do with her. I think Travis keeps, I mean kept, Lauren on a short leash. Keep this on the QT, but Travis told me the only fight he ever had with his sister was about bringing Lauren back into Dahlia Lane Enterprises. Jessie didn't feel she had a choice but to give her a role at Dahlia Lane after Lauren and Conrad got married."

"Hmmm," I said, sitting next to him.

"What are you hmmm-ing about?" Emilio asked, taking my chin in his hands and turning my head so I could meet his hazel eyes.

"Can't a girl hmmm for no reason? I'm just thinking that my dislike of Lauren is warranted. What exactly *is* Lauren's role?"

"Got me," he said, shrugging his shoulders. "Seems like every task Jessie gives Lauren, she passes on to poor Kayla."

"How long has Kayla been an intern?"

"About a month or so. And no, I don't know much about her. Although—"

"Yes-s-s?"

"I once saw Travis comforting Kayla. It looked as if she was crying. I have a feeling he's the one who brought her into Dahlia Lane."

"Do you think they were dating?"

"I don't think so. I guess we'll never know."

"Unless we ask her," I said.

"You know, another thing just came to me," he said. "Jessie once asked me to go to Dahlia Lane's business office to see if Travis was there. She needed to get his approval on something to do with the shops at the hangar. Instead of finding Travis, I found Kayla. She acted pretty squirrely, said she was looking for the day's recipes for *Jessica's Table*."

"What's so weird about that? I've seen her with the recipes."

"I've worked with Jessie in her design studio/office. It's in the farmhouse. I know that's where she prints anything Kayla might need. Travis's business office is next to the studio kitchen. Conrad used to share it with him. Now Conrad has his own office at Dahlia Lane Shoppes at the Hangar.

Emilio gave me a questioning glance. "Meg, what's up? Why are you grilling me? Speaking of grilling, a grilled cheese, tomato and bacon sure would hit the spot. That and an entire pot of road tar coffee."

I smiled. "I'm not grilling, more like lightly sautéing. Last question, then I'll go into overdrive so we can get to Mickey's lickety-split."

He crinkled his brow. "Get on with it."

"Conrad. What's his and Jessie's relationship?"

"Conrad was good friends with Jessie and Travis's father before he passed away. Conrad has been with the company since its inception."

"So why the heck did he marry Lauren?"

"That's the million-dollar question. One I don't have an answer to."

"Big age difference between them."

"Thought you said last question."

"I just want to get a pulse on all the players," I said, looking away. "Like I said. From meeting Lauren just twice, I don't like the way she seems two-faced when it comes to Jessie. She talks behind her back, then a second later is stevia sweet in front of her. Is it jealousy, I wonder? Or does she view Jessie as competition for Conrad's attention?"

"I think it's both. And I think Lauren wears the pants in her relationship with Conrad. As I've said, I've been privy to a few of their whopper fights. Or should I say, Lauren railing at her husband for some reason or another. He seems to take it like a champ. He's a better man than I."

He looked off in the distance and continued, "When I was at the farmhouse for the *Dahlia Lane Journal* shoot last month, I overheard them arguing. Only this time it was Conrad who was angry with Lauren. His face was so red, I was worried he was going to have a heart attack."

"Interesting."

"You're just a little gossip hound, aren't you?"

"Ruff. Ruff."

"Well, I only caught the tail end of Lauren and Conrad's argument. I got the feeling it had something to do with money, or lack of money. As in Lauren spending too much, and something about

Travis finding out about something. Conrad said they had to do something before everything imploded."

"Wow. Imploded is a strong word to use. How about Lauren? Is she involved in the business side of Dahlia Lane?"

"I highly doubt it. I don't think Travis would let her get involved. Especially after she bankrupted Lavender Fields."

"How about Chris Barnes?" I asked. "How does he get along with Lauren? Is he as hilarious as he seems on TV? How long has he been gone? Do you think Chris and Jessie are as madly in love behind the scenes as they are on-screen?"

"Yes, he's hilarious. Travis, Chris and I have gone out to Stephen Talkhouse a few times for some brews and music. Chris is just as affable as he seems on TV. I have no idea about Chris's feelings for Lauren. He's been away for six weeks. I've had Jessie all to myself."

"Emilio Costello! Do you have a crush on Jessie? Are you blushing? I can't blame you. She is pretty awesome."

"Of course I do," he said. "But I never had a chance. She only has eyes for Chris. They wouldn't be engaged if they weren't in love. Right?"

"Are you asking or telling me?"

He smiled. "Speaking of Chris, when Lauren came back to the company, she kept flirting with Chris. Throwing herself at him every chance she had. It didn't matter if Jessie or Conrad was in the room. Then something changed. Before you ask, I have no idea what."

"Even more interesting is this," I said. "I saw Lauren run into Pete Moss's arms as I was leaving Dahlia Lane the other day."

"Really? That's bizarre. Pete's an okay guy. A little on the weird side. Talks to plants and trees."

"And you don't?" I said, laughing. "I've even named a few of mine."

"Didn't you say you live alone with a cat? Maybe you need to get out more if you're talking to plants."

"Funny."

Emilio searched my face. "All kidding aside, is there something you know that I don't about Travis Sterling's death? Did your dad or Detective Shoner find out something you're not sharing?"

I paused, thinking about how I could get Emilio to help me find out what was going on at Dahlia Lane, without telling him what my father just told me about the hit-and-run.

Then it came to me, a way to illicit Emilio's help. "Bryce told me someone is leaving threatening notes around Dahlia Lane. Did you know about this?"

"No, that's crazy. So they're worried this person might be dangerous? Who are the notes addressed too? I never heard Jessie mention anything."

"I don't know," I lied. "There's no signature. So far, from what I've been told, nothing violent has happened."

"Hmmm."

"Now you're hmmm-ing," I said.

"It is a little creepy. I'm surprised no one's told me. I can't imagine anyone having any reason to threaten Jessie."

"I agree."

"If they were meant for Lauren, which seems likely, I wouldn't want Jessie to get caught in the crossfire. Thanks for telling me. I'll be ever vigilant. At least till Chris returns."

"Seeing you're friends with Jessie, maybe you could bring it up?" I said.

Then I had the same thought I had earlier. Were the notes being sent by Travis and someone, namely Lauren, shut him up? I glanced over at Emilio. At this point there was no need to involve Emilio in my hypothesizing. Like Patrick said, if Travis's hit-and-run was committed by someone at Dahlia Lane, I had to keep Emilio in the suspect pool.

I sighed. "Well, if we ever get a chance to go back to work at Dahlia Lane, we'll need to keep our eyes and ears open. Even though I've only just met them, I don't want anything to happen to Jessie or anyone else."

"Agreed," he said vehemently. "And you mean, *when* we go back. Not if. Jessie told me this morning she wants us to meet her tomorrow morning at Shoppes at the Hangar to help her with a few things before the grand opening Saturday. Said I should bring my camera and equipment."

"Why didn't you lead with that?" I said, laughing. "That's good news." I felt my heart pitter-patter. "What time?"

"Seven in the morning. She also had a strange request. She wants your father to come along. Something about Kayla needing him."

I laughed, then explained what happened yesterday while we were at Dahlia Lane's studio kitchen.

The next hour was spent putting the final touches on the cottage, which included Emilio helping me to raise the curtain rod to the ceiling. For all of Emilio's complaining about why he was there, his input and photographer's eye had been priceless.

Happy about what we'd accomplished, I said, "I think our job is finished."

"Finally. I'm starving."

"That's so funny, I had no idea."

"Ha-ha," he said, following me to the door.

I grabbed my tool box, opened the door, then ushered him out.

Before following him onto the porch, I took out my phone and shot a quick photo. I sent the photo to Elle with the words *Cottage number one of twelve. Fini!*

After I stepped out and locked the door, I stood on the porch and looked down the line at the other eleven cottages. Each cottage had a small covered porch with a porch swing. The cedar shake cottages were all painted white, but each one had different-colored shutters and front doors in hues that blended with the forest landscape. The pine scent was intoxicating in the summer heat.

The first time I'd seen the run-down motor lodge, Elle had taken me to the edge of the property and said, "Look, they will have their own babbling brook." I'd leaned down to put my ear to the water and heard a slight hum through my hearing aid. Elle had continued to tell me that back in the 1940s, the motor lodge was an escape for families leaving the hot summer concrete of New York City. I'd never asked her what she'd paid for the property, but I could guess. Thanks to her Great Aunt Mabel, Elle had been left with a sizeable inheritance.

"Ready to help me with our last chore?" I called out to Emilio. "It will only take a minute. Scout's honor."

"Okay, I'm timing you," he said, looking down at his watch. "If you don't feed me, I turn into a gremlin."

"What a sissy," I said, walking to the back of my woody. I unlatched the rear door and deposited my tool box. "I've decided to give each cottage its own name." I held up a small sign with the words *Serenity Cottage* stenciled in the same pale robin's egg blue as the cottage's shutters and front door. "Patrick trimmed this piece of wood from my stash. I salvaged it from a junk pile next to the old Long Island Rail Road tracks. I also found . . ." I stopped talking when I noticed Emilio's eye roll. "Okay. Okay. You're hungry."

After helping me secure the sign to the lamppost, Emilio said, "Well done, Ms. Barrett."

"Thank you, Mr. Costello."

"So when do I get to meet the great Patrick Seaton? I'm a big fan of his thrillers."

I looked at him. "I'll try to get him to come to your exhibit, but with his writing schedule and his mother in town, it might be hard."

"Why the frown?" Emilio asked.

My mind replayed this morning's awkward scene at Patrick's cottage. I told Emilio about Aurora Montague. "Truth be told, she scares the daylights out of me."

"Well, once she gets to know you, she's gonna love you. Everyone does."

"Thanks for the vote of confidence. But I'm not so sure." Then I confided in him about the tragedy that took away Patrick's wife and child.

"Yeah. I heard about that. But it was a while ago, right?"

"Right. Here I go talking about my love life when I've never asked you about yours."

"Nothing to talk about," he said. "A broken engagement, like yours, only I was the one cheating."

"Emilio! That's not like you."

He grinned. "Not cheating in the biblical sense. I was consumed with work at the magazine and my own ego. It was my fault she broke it off. She wanted to have children right away. I wasn't ready. Or financially secure. Hey, let's vamoose."

"Let's," I said.

"You can tell me more about the great Patrick Seaton and how you two met."

"Okey dokey."

If I'd told Emilio my first meeting with Patrick was exchanging dead poets' quotes in the sand, he probably wouldn't believe me. But the long and short of it started with me finding a quote by Emerson in front of Patrick's cottage — *Sorrow makes us all children again, Destroys all differences of intellect.*

Thinking of Patrick reminded me of the text I'd received saying dinner was on.

As I walked away from the lamppost, my knees felt like they might buckle at the thought of dinner with Patrick's food critic mother.

Thank God my father would be there to smooth the way.

At least, that had been my hope.

Alas, best laid plans and all that . . .

Chapter 15

Patrick, my father, Aurora and I waited at Pondfare's packed bar for our table. My father was his most charming. I had high hopes he would be the perfect foil for the immediate tension I'd felt between Patrick and his mother. It was so thick you could cut it with one of Pondfare's ceramic steak knives

Aurora seemed totally enamored with my father's attention, but not enough to keep the evening from going off the rails.

She started by insisting on changing tables, not once but three times. I'd never seen Patrick's jaw clenched so tight. During our appetizers, each time Aurora said something negative about Michelin-star Chef Patou's cuisine, I had to calm Patrick by grabbing his knee under the table and squeezing. I was sure when he woke up tomorrow morning he'd have a whopper of a bruise. The evening went downhill after that.

Patrick's mother had something snarky to say about each course — a passive-aggressive way of critiquing her dishes. For every two good things she'd said, she'd slip in a bad. Or vice versa. She sent back her salad and main course, but not until she'd consumed three-quarters of each. Who sends back a salad? On top of that, Aurora had no qualms about sticking her fork in Patrick's food, taking three or four bites, then turning her nose up. *Glad I didn't order that* was just one of her lovely comments.

So it hadn't been a huge surprise when Chef Patou's wife and sous chef Bella pulled me into her busy kitchen to show me a glossy hardcover book. The cover of the book featured a close-up of Patrick's mother sitting at a table in a bistro-style restaurant. She held a (pitch?) fork in one hand and a knife in the other. Someone had taken a black Magic Marker and graffitied horns to the top of her head and a mustache above her glossy red lips. The book, *A Guide to Fine and Not-So-Fine Dining*, by *NYT* food critic Aurora Montague, was centered on the silver platter in front of her.

Yikes.

At least now I had an inkling of why Patrick had never mentioned his mother. Not only had Aurora written a poor review of Pondfare in her book, she'd also written an even worse review of his deceased wife's sister's restaurant, Sarabeth's by the Bay. The copyright on the book had been four years ago—around the same time Patrick lost Catherine and his daughter. I had a suspicion that Aurora's bad restaurant reviews were only the tip of the iceberg in her and Patrick's *Titanic* of a relationship.

After thanking Bella for showing me the book and promising we were on our last course, I made my way back to the table, dragging my heels like a prisoner walking the green mile to the electric chair. Obviously, Patrick's mother's book hadn't been able to sway customers with discerning palates away from Pondfare's Michelin-star cuisine. The packed crowd in the waiting area proved my point.

Halfway to our table, I spotted a familiar face at a corner table partially hidden by a ficus tree.

It was Kayla, the intern from Dahlia Lane.

Small world. Well, not that small. Montauk's Pondfare was a top-rated restaurant in the Hamptons.

Kayla was seated with an older woman whose back was to me.

More as a ploy to take a breather from Aurora's antics, I thought, *Why not go over and say hi.* So I did.

It took a moment for Kayla to recognize me.

Once again, she looked like she'd been crying. Smudges of mascara gave her racoon eyes. "Hi, Kayla," I chirped. "I see we share the same taste in restaurants."

"Meg, right?" she said, forcing a smile.

I nodded my head.

"Meg, I'd like you to meet my mother, Gayle."

"Gayle, my pleasure, Meg Barrett," I said, reaching out my right hand. She gave my hand a gentle squeeze.

Mother and daughter shared the same mocha skin and dark intense eyes. "Nice to meet you, Meg," she said.

I moved out of the way of a server carrying a huge platter of at least two-pound lobsters, then said, "I bet you're very proud your daughter is doing such a great job working at Dahlia Lane Enterprises."

"She's what! Is this true, Kayla?" Gayle managed to choke out before leaping up from her chair. I had to grab the back of it to keep it from crashing to the floor. She took one last look at her daughter, quickly grabbed her small handbag from the table and took off for the exit.

Kayla looked like she'd just been tased with Bryce's stun gun. "Oh, no!" she whimpered. "I must go after her." She pushed the table forward and jumped up. With an open mouth, I watched her diminutive frame weave in and out of the throngs of people at the restaurant's entrance.

What the heck did I say?

When I returned to the table, my father raised an eyebrow, then nodded toward Kayla and her mother's empty table. I shrugged my shoulders, then sat down next to Patrick. By Patrick's frown, I knew things hadn't improved with Aurora.

"Mother, I'm sure Jeff doesn't want to hear any more about your second husband and the reason you got divorced."

Aurora said with a sniffle, "We all make mistakes, son. I'm sure you've made a few." Then looking at my father, she added, "You know what I'm talking about, don't you, Jeff? Patrick told me you're recently divorced. It's not for sissies. That's for sure."

"I'm sure no one wants to hear about it," Patrick said, grabbing my hand under the table. "Let's change the subject."

Aurora ignored Patrick, then said, "Jeff, I'm sure Meg told you about my son's wife and daughter." She gave me a sideways glance.

"Yes. He knows," I said.

Even though the room was loud with laughter and chatter, for a few minutes no one at the table spoke. Then we were saved by the waitperson delivering our final dessert course.

To ease the still palpable tension, I told Patrick and my father about Emilio's photography exhibit tomorrow at the Green Room Art Gallery. "I'd love for you both to attend. I went to a few of his installments when I worked at *American Home & Garden*. He's truly talented."

"I'd love to," my father said.

"Me too," Patrick echoed. "From everything you've told me, I'd like to see his work. Maybe—"

Aurora broke in, "Of course, I'd love to join you too, Meg. Patrick, you know how involved I am in the arts." We watched her take out her phone, her pointer finger hovering over what I assumed was her calendar. "What time does it start?"

Patrick spit out a mouthful of blueberry crème brûlée (the only thing Aurora didn't send back). "Mother, I thought you were leaving in the morning."

"Oh, darling. Are you trying to get rid of me? Why did you think that?"

"Uh, you told me," Patrick answered.

"I just talked to my agent. She booked me a gig to do a freelance article for the *Daily News* on the grand opening of Dahlia Lane Shoppes at the Hangar. An article on my personal impression from a foodie's point of view."

"Isn't the *Daily News* a New York City paper?" Patrick asked, looking as dumbfounded as I felt. "What do they want with the Hamptons?"

"You are so funny, darling. Almost every Page Two article in the *Daily News* is about something going on in the Hamptons."

"You mean the gossip page," he said. "Meg is working at Dahlia Lane. I won't have you ruining anything with your insensitive reviews."

"My reviews aren't insensitive. They're honest."

"Isn't that why you got fired from the *New York Times*? Because of all your negative *in*sensitive restaurant reviews? Every fine dining establishment in Manhattan, Brooklyn, Queens and the Bronx banded together and refused to let you within ten feet of their restaurants. Even food truck owners have your face plastered by their serving window in case you show up. You're persona non grata in New York City. Actually I'm surprised you aren't also blackballed on the entire Eastern Seaboard."

"You're making things up, Patrick," Aurora said, glancing at my father. "The reason the *New York Times* let me go was because of ageism. They hired some ingénue to take my place. I'm sure I'll win the lawsuit, ye of little faith. Maybe I'll get enough in the settlement to buy a place here in Montauk."

I had just taken a sip, more like a gulp, of chardonnay. It went down the wrong pipe, as my mother used to say, and I started coughing. My father stood to give me the Heimlich but there was no need. The look on Aurora's face scared me enough for me to stop mid-cough. She'd be great to have around when I got the hiccups.

"Meg, I'm surprised you drink alcohol," Aurora said, opening another vein. "Because of poor Catherine and Lucy. I hope you're not driving tonight."

Patrick put his arm around my shoulder. "Mother, stop. Leave Meg alone. It's me you're after. I'm asking you to walk away from anything having to do with the Hamptons. And you know why."

"I tell you what," she said, looking over at my father. "I promise I won't write anything negative about Saturday's Fourth of July grand opening at Dahlia Lane Shoppes at the Hangar. I'll have you know, I'm a big fan of Jessica Sterling. So no worries. Plus, I'd like to get to know your new girl here better. And, of course her delightful father. I assure you, I won't make waves."

"No, just a tsunami," Patrick mouthed in my direction.

"I promise, my little Paddington bear," Aurora said, reaching across the table and squeezing Patrick's wrist. He tried to look away, but when he saw her huge smile, for just a second the corners of his mouth turned up.

I wondered if we might all get along, after all, my misgivings for naught. I just needed to focus on this sweet side of her. Right now, she surely looked sincere in her affection for her son.

Then Aurora said, "Jeff, what do you think of your daughter's one-woman interior design business?" Then she looked at me. "What did you say, dear, you use for inspiration in your teensy cottages—old stuff? Even curbside trash?"

"Well, I mix it up a little," I said. "Old, new, whatever works. I like to upcycle—"

She cut me off. "Save the planet? How charming. Maybe you could get a job with one of the larger, more established firms. Job security is important," she continued. "You can't depend on my son's money, even though he's quite wealthy from all his bestsellers and screenwriting. However, you'd never know it by the way he lives in that little beach shack of his."

Patrick's cottage was the furthest thing from a shack.

"Why don't you let me help you, Megan?" she said, reaching her hand across the table for me to take. "I do have a few legitimate interior design contacts in the Hamptons."

I read Patrick's lips when he said under his breath, "I doubt it."

"I heard that, darling," Aurora said. She pretended to be hurt by sticking out her bottom lip. "We don't want to make a scene, do we, son?"

"I never make scenes, Mother. That's your specialty."

Aurora glanced over to my father, then shrugged her shoulders. "Kids. They can be very ungrateful."

Until the check arrived, no one spoke. Patrick put down his credit card and said to the young waiter, "Thank you. You've done a great job."

"I hope those dishes I've sent back aren't on the bill," Aurora snapped in the waiter's direction.

Patrick held his hand in front of her face like a Stop sign. "Enough."

A few minutes later, as we were saying our goodbyes to our friends, Chef Patou and his wife Bella, I knew Patrick and I were thinking the same thing—*We owed the couple big-time because of Aurora's behavior.*

Chapter 16

Friday morning I woke to the vibrating alarm clock under my pillow. Jo was snoring, so I'd crept toward the French doors, opened them and stepped onto my bedroom's small crow's nest of a balcony, overlooking the Atlantic.

There was no chance of a peachy sunrise. Dark clouds covered the horizon and the coastline was thick with an opaque mist that carried the scent of salt and briny seas. Not even the bad weather could dissuade me from the excitement I felt at meeting Jessie, Emilio, and my father at Dahlia Lane Shoppes at the Hangar.

Forty minutes later, I was sitting in my car in the huge empty parking lot on the north side of the hangar, my thoughts straying to last night's disaster of a dinner at Pondfare.

Suddenly there was a loud rapping on my driver's-side window, distracting me from my not-so-fond reminiscing.

My father opened my car door and I stepped out.

"How long have you been here?" he asked. "You said seven, right?"

"Just a few minutes. I was too excited, can't wait to see inside. Do you think I need an umbrella?"

He looked up at the gloomy sky. "Definitely."

I opened my back door and grabbed my umbrella, then we started toward the hangar's entrance. A white cottage butted up against the goliath building. Over a navy-and-white-striped awning there was a sign that read *Welcome to Dahlia Lane Shoppes at the Hangar.*

"I guess we're the only ones here," he said.

"Good. Let's explore the grounds before anyone arrives. Though, Jessie might already be inside. It's possible she walked here. She told me there's a brick path that leads from Dahlia Lane Farms to the hangar."

"I assume you don't want to talk about last evening. Especially seeing tonight is Emilio's gallery opening and your future mother-in-law plans on coming."

"Hardy, har, har. You've got that right. I don't want to talk about it. I haven't had a chance to chat with Patrick to get more info on their relationship. Strained relationship, I should add."

"Well, reserve judgment. Things and people aren't always black

94

and white. There's always a backstory."

"I will. Though she really knows how to get under a person's skin. New subject," I said. "Did they find Travis's phone? I thought maybe when they moved his car it was underneath?"

My father rubbed the stubble on his chin. "No. I talked to Arthur late last night. No sign of it."

"Could it have fallen into the water?"

"No. The parking lot wasn't that close to the water. I suppose it's possible someone found it and didn't know Travis's body was in the seagrass. If it wasn't for Springer—"

"Springer?" I said.

"The woman's dog. Travis could've been laying there for hours. We now know around what time Travis Sterling was hit based on his sister's phone call and when the woman and dog found him. Unfortunately, there were no traffic cameras near the parking lot. It's all back roads."

"I assume there were other parked cars at the diving site besides his Escalade," I said.

"Yes. Two. Arthur's checked the vehicles and their owners. Plus, it's doubtful someone would hit Travis, then park their car afterward in the same lot as the hit-and-run."

"You never know. You've told me over and over again how devious a murderer can be. Maybe they hit him, parked their car, then went back into the water in their diving gear, creating an alibi. Anyone at Dahlia Lane into diving like Travis was?"

"Wow. That's a little out there. Even for you, my crazy daughter. I will say, I doubt anyone else thought of that scenario but you. One thing you've forgotten. The tire tread marks in the dirt at the back of the Escalade. It was one of the first things Arthur's team did, make a cast. The cars in the lot weren't a match. But good thinking outside the box," he added.

As we walked, I thought about Jessie's brother. It seemed he was very involved in the creation of the Shoppes at the Hangar. I said, "It's been haunting me that the last thing Travis told his sister was he was coming to talk to someone here at the hangar. I'm sure it will be a no-brainer for East Hampton Town PD to trace Travis's recently called phone numbers without having his phone. But what if he'd sent a text to this mysterious person? Could they trace that as well?"

"No-brainer? Yes, they can. But it will take time. It's not like you see on TV."

I stopped walking and looked at my father. "So your theory is, the driver of the car hit Travis, then took his phone."

"It's leaning that way."

"Shouldn't you call Arthur for an update? Maybe he sent out a team to Dahlia Lane to talk to Bryce about the threatening notes?"

"I think Arthur has enough on his hands without me hounding him every five minutes. I'll check with him this afternoon. Only on one condition."

"What's that?"

"Take a breather. Isn't this"—he spread his arms wide—"something you've been dreaming of seeing for a long time?"

"Yes, but—"

He cut me off. "Of course you can always keep your eyes and ears open. Just like I will be doing when I'm with Kayla."

"Kayla. Oh, yeah, there's something going on with her too."

"Seriously, that sweet thing."

I told him about her and her mother's reaction at the restaurant and what Emilio told me about her and Travis and how he found her in Travis's office. "Maybe you can find out what's bothering her. I can tell she really likes you," I said, adding a wink.

He grinned. "She's a little young for me."

"You'd be surprised at some of the couples I see walking the Hamptons streets. Lots of older men and young women. Not many the other way around, though. It's not fair."

"What are you complaining about? Patrick's your age."

"Maybe he'll trade me in for a newer model in ten years?"

"No more negative Nancy-ing."

"Agreed. I can't wait to see inside the hangar. Look," I said, pointing, "there's Emilio now."

We watched Emilio park his bright orange hybrid Kia between my father's Explorer and my woody.

"I'd love to see the property before we go inside." I waved my hand, and Emilio started toward us. "Maybe Emilio can quickly show us around before Jessie show's up."

Fifteen minutes later, Emilio not only gave us a quick tour but also shot a few photos as he went, promising to share them with me so I could show Patrick.

Surrounding the hangar were winding paths with park benches and statuary, a huge pond with lily pads and koi, and gardens filled with tamed, but not too tame, colorful wildflowers. A small red barn housed goats and other farm animals for children to interact with.

Emilio told us a dessert food truck would be set up next to one of the covered picnic areas on the east side of the hangar. "I recently got to taste one of Jessie's blueberry-bacon donuts — to die for," Emilio said. "No one cooks like Jessie."

Near the end of our tour, Emilio led us to a large soundstage fronted by a grassy lawn for concert seating. "What do you think? Pretty cool, huh? Travis told me this is where they're going to have fireworks tomorrow evening. A big-name local band is supposed to show up. I know from watching all the preparation going into Dahlia Lane Shoppes at the Hangar, Travis and Jessie put their heart . . . and soul into this project." Emilio paused at the word *heart*, no doubt thinking of Travis's death.

Our last stop was in front of a white picket fence lined with dahlias. Beyond the fence was an iron and glass greenhouse. Hanging over the door to the greenhouse was a green and orange wood sign displaying the words *Peter Rabbit's Garden*.

Emilio opened the gate and we followed him inside.

"This was one of Pete's ideas," Emilio said, pointing to the neat rows of vegetables and herbs. "A harvest-your-own vegetables garden for adults and kiddies."

"Oh my gosh," I said, "this garden puts my small herb garden to shame. And that greenhouse is to die for. Dad, you know how much I love old structures. Especially greenhouses and glass conservatories."

"Yes, like your hidden glass folly, aka interior design studio," he said. "Your love of all things old and weathered is something your mom passed down to you."

I met his eyes, thinking of my mother's antique shop near Henry Ford's Greenfield Village in Michigan. The place where my love of nostalgia and vintage décor began. *Every piece tells a story,* she would say.

Emilio took a few photos, then said, "In the winter months, Jessie plans to fill the greenhouse with potted Christmas trees. And Travis said Pete Moss wants to hold seminars in the warmer months for the children on eco-friendly ways to save the planet."

My father pointed to a shed next to the greenhouse. "If this Pete wants to practice what he preaches, that gallon of weed killer and pesticide next to that shed should be exchanged for something less toxic. I have a few suggestions for a replacement that works just as well without using glyphosate."

All this talk about Dahlia Lane's master gardener reminded me about the romantic embrace I'd witnessed between Lauren and Pete on Wednesday. After I told my father about it, he just raised an eyebrow.

"Lauren's a flirt with everyone," Emilio said. "Everyone but Travis."

"Does that mean you too?" I asked.

"Around the time Lauren came back to Dahlia Lane, right before her marriage to Conrad, she started flirting with me," Emilio said, not looking happy in the least. "She wanted me to plead her case to Jessie about letting her be cohost of *Jessica's Table*. When I explained to Lauren that I'd mentioned it to Jessie in front of Travis, and Travis immediately put the kibosh on it, she wanted nothing more to do with me. Lesson learned. She was just using me. I swear I wasn't attracted to her, just trying to help Jessie's cousin. When you first see Lauren and immediately notice her resemblance to Jessie, you think aside from the flashy way she dresses, she'll be as sweet as her cousin. As I discovered, they couldn't be more opposite."

"Ditto," I echoed, a tad too vehemently.

Emilio smiled. "I was there when Jessie offered Lauren a chance to assist her and Chris in working on a fixer-upper project at a local community center in Riverhead. At first Lauren accepted. Then, when she found out it wouldn't be televised on *Dahlia Lane Home Makeover*, she pulled out. Unlike Jessie, Lauren doesn't have an altruistic bone in her body."

I'd wanted to ask Emilio why Conrad couldn't talk Jessie into giving his wife a bigger role in the company, but that's when I saw Kayla charging toward us.

Once inside the garden gate, she stopped next to my father, bent to catch her breath, then said, "Oh, there you are, Jeff! I told Jessica about your invaluable help the other day. She wants to know if you could come over to the studio kitchen again to help me make this—"

She handed my father a large recipe card. "It's for tomorrow's grand opening."

"Seems easy enough," he said, looking down. "Strawberry and blueberry sweet cheese tart."

"I thought the same thing when Jessica showed it to me," Kayla said, gasping for breath. "But that was before she told me we need to make forty *dozen* mini versions. I need to pass them out tomorrow at the entrance to Dahlia Lane's restaurant." Frowning, she said, "Mrs. Kincaid said she would help, but of course she handed the whole thing over to me at the last minute."

My father bowed and said, "It would be my pleasure, chef." Then he raised an eyebrow. "Forty dozen, huh?"

"It's okay if you can't help me," she said, her eyes looking feverish in her small face. "Bryce offered, but—"

"No problem. Let's get started," he said.

All Kayla did was nod her head in my direction, then look away. Was she embarrassed about last night's scene with her mother? It seemed it was a night of mothers—one I would also like to forget.

Chapter 17

Emilio and I watched Kayla and my father take a path that snaked its way to the north side of the hangar.

When we turned toward the main entrance of the hangar, someone in a golf cart was heading in our direction at breakneck speed. As the vehicle approached, I saw Pete Moss at the wheel. His ears must have been burning.

He braked inches from us, his dark brown eyes magnified behind round wire-framed glasses. "Oh, Emilio, it's you," he said. I was worried—"

Emilio introduced me.

Pete extended his hand. As came with the job, he had dirt under his fingernails—organic soil, as he always directed viewers to use on his Dahlia Lane Network gardening segments. For some reason, I couldn't picture Lauren being attracted to him, even though he was a fabulous gardener and had a huge following, which included myself.

"Worried about what?" I asked, thinking of the threatening notes. Did he know about them? More importantly, did Jessie?

He looked at me suspiciously. Had he remembered I'd seen him and Lauren in a passionate embrace? "Oh, nothin'. Just thought someone was fooling around in my garden. I'm here to make sure everything's battened down. Looks like a terrible storm's brewin'. Not a good omen for tomorrow. I can't believe Ms. Sterling's still going through with it."

To break the awkward silence, I said, "That's quite the leather garden holster you're wearing. I love to garden. But I wouldn't know what half those things are used for."

"Is that the Hermès insignia?" Emilio asked.

Pete hopped out of the cart and proudly jutted out his right hip. "A gift. Every master gardener should have one. You never know when you might need to test the soil, dig up an errant root or do a specimen cutting."

I thought, only in the Hamptons would someone give a designer gift from the expensive Hermès brand. In all fairness, as Elle had schooled me, the Hermès company started out as French harness and saddle makers. Now they were more known for their handbags, such as the Kelly bag, named after Grace Kelly, no less. And naturally, Elle had a couple vintage Kellies in her handbag closet.

There was an awkward pause. Emilio finally said, "Well, Pete. We'd better get inside before it storms."

"Oh. You're going inside? Ms. Sterling's waiting for ya?"

"Yep," Emilio said, looking toward the garden enclosure. "We enjoyed looking around. I'm sure, no matter if the weather's good or bad, tomorrow will be a huge success."

"Don't count on it," Pete said, as a gust of wind blew up what little hair sprouted from the top of his head. Between his hair and his wide-eyed stare behind thick lenses, he looked like he'd just seen a ghost. He hopped back in the golf cart and pulled away. I couldn't help but think something was different about Pete.

Then I got it.

During our conversation, Peat Moss Pete hadn't graced us with one of his fabulous smiles. Was his jolly screen persona an act? Or, like the rest of us, was he devastated by Travis's death?

"So what are you waiting for?" I said to Emilio. "Let's get inside before I hyperventilate from all the anticipation. What exactly does Jessie need help with? I'm willing to do anything, even clean toilets, if it means getting a sneak peek inside the hangar."

Emilio laughed. "So impatient. I thought living out here in paradise you'd calmed down a little."

"Oh, I'm very chill. I'll have you know I walk the beach and meditate every morning. You can't tell me you're not excited to see inside the hangar."

He gave me an evil grin.

"You brat," I said, lightly punching his arm. "You've already been inside."

"Once. And it was a month ago. Actually, Travis gave me a tour." He broke my gaze and looked away.

"It's so tragic," I said. "I hope Jessie can make tomorrow's grand opening the best ever, if only for the sake of Travis's memory."

"I'll fist bump you on that," Emilio said.

And we did.

"Are things always this volatile around here?" I asked Emilio. "Jessie seems so down-to-earth and laid-back. That's not the case for some of the others at Dahlia Lane. What do you know about Pete? He seems different in person than on camera."

"I really don't know him that well. But you're right there's something off about him. I can't put my finger on it. I don't think Travis cared for him that much. But he has a big following. I'm not into gardening, so I haven't watched any of his segments on the Dahlia Lane Network. I don't think Travis had much contact with him. At least not from what I've seen. Bryce, Conrad's nephew/ security guard and Pete seem pretty tight. An odd pair if ever there was one."

Not any odder than Pete and Lauren, I thought.

Emilio suddenly stopped short. He took his phone from his pocket and looked down. "Jessie wants us to meet her at the hangar's side entrance. Follow me." He took my hand in his and we started walking at a brisk pace.

I glanced at Emilio. I really, really wanted to share with him what I knew about Travis's death. Emilio, Elle, and I had been great friends when we worked together at *American Home & Garden*. But as Patrick mentioned, that was a couple years ago. As I've learned the hard way, how well do you really know another person? *Nah*. What could Emilio's motive be? Until proven otherwise . . . he was officially off my suspect list.

"Hurry, you guys," Jessie called as we got closer.

"Coming," Emilio shouted, then half pulled, half dragged me toward her.

When we reached her, I was stunned at how ethereal Jessie appeared. Ethereal, a word you might find in the Willkie Collins book *The Moonstone*. She wasn't dressed like the Lady in White, but she was wearing an ankle-length, pale blue floral gauzy dress that danced around her slim figure in the hot breeze.

As soon as we were face-to-face, there was no mistaking the toll her brother's death had taken on her. It was there in the eggplant-colored circles under her red-rimmed eyes. It was there in the slump of her shoulders. She appeared frail, her tanned face ashen. It was as if she'd aged a decade since Wednesday.

"Thank you for showing up," she said, giving us a weak smile. "I wanted to get photos of the interior for *Dahlia Lane Journal*. Travis did a video the day before he—" Her voice trailed off. "Our employees and staff show up at noon for a dry run. I was so impressed at how the two of you worked together at the windmill. Thought you might play off each other by choosing the best vignettes for the magazine. Sadly, my heart just isn't into it. Still, it needs to be everything my brother envisioned."

"Of course," Emilio said, "I would be honored to take some photos."

"Anything to help," I added.

"Lauren is against me opening tomorrow—even Conrad. Of anyone, I thought Conrad would understand why I need to do this on schedule." Turning to Emilio, she said, "Lauren's been antagonistic about almost everything I do recently. I believe she blames me for her failure with Lavender Fields. But I can't fathom why Conrad wouldn't want us to open. As head of our financial operations, he's been doing a great job. He's the one who procured all the local products for the shop, with Travis's blessing, of course. I just know in my gut, Travis would want us to go forward."

Emilio took her hand. "Don't worry, Jessie. You have every right to honor your brother's wishes. Meg and I aren't against you. And I'm sure Chris supports you in your decision."

"I finally got ahold of him," she said with a quick smile. "He was devastated about Trav—" Her voice broke off. "He won't be able to get a flight back to the States until next week. But he told me he knows Travis would want me to open on the date we picked."

"No worries, Jessie," Emilio said. "We're here to help. No matter how long it takes. Right, Meg?"

"For sure. And, Jessie, my father is over at the studio kitchen with Kayla, so no worries there."

As if she got a burst of energy, Jessie put an arm around each of us. "We've got this, team."

A zigzag of lightning stabbed the dark sky. Thunder followed. I felt more than heard it.

As Pete said, I hoped it wasn't a precursor to tomorrow's festivities.

I know what superstitious Elle would say, *Run for the hills.*

Chapter 18

The heavy door slammed shut behind me, echoing in the huge space. Jessie startled from the sound. I followed her and Emilio to the center of the hangar, trying to catch my breath as I twirled around. What I saw was beyond anything I'd ever envisioned—a theme park for cozy home addicts. Seating areas, potted plants and live trees surrounded us. On each of the two longer walls there were four white mini cottages. "Oh-h-h, it's magnificent," I said, mentally salivating at the sight before me.

While Jessie and Emilio looked on with huge smiles, I ticked off the names of the shops one by one. "Dahlia Lane Cooks, Dahlia Lane Paper and Books, Dahlia Lane Woodworks." I wiped away a tear at the one. "Dahlia Lane Gardeners Market, Dahlia Lane Aromatique, Dahlia Lane Pet, Dahlia Lane Clothing Supply, Dahlia Lane Antiques & Vintage Marketplace."

On the south side of the hangar was a huge white fresh-flower stand with *Dahlia Lane Blooms* stenciled in black.

On the north side of the hangar was a cottage storefront spanning half the width of the hangar. The sign simply said *Dahlia Lane Home.* Next to it was Dahlia Lane Homestyle Eatery. I'd read it was Dahlia Lane's first attempt at opening a sit-down restaurant. If it was successful, Jessie planned to open others. Which I was sure it would be.

Ugh. Did Patrick's mother really have to write about the Dahlia Lane Shoppes at the Hangar experience? Or had she made it up? If it was true, I hoped what she said about being a fan of Jessie's was true also. She certainly didn't seem too enamored with me.

Wiping away negative thoughts about Aurora, I glanced up at a glass ceiling the size of a football field. Suspended from aluminum rafters were gigantic prism lanterns. Suddenly, the glass ceiling above the rafters began to slide open, exposing a gloomy sky.

"Oh, Jessie, this whole space is unbelievable!" I said, feeling like I was eight and it was Christmas morning. "So much work and planning must have gone into it."

"I couldn't have done it without Travis," Jessie said. "My only caveat was that all the products come from local vendors. Even the food for the restaurant. Travis also hired only locals to work in the shops. It was his idea for the retractable skylight. Chris and his crew built the storefronts from my sketches. I can't believe how wonderfully it all came together."

"Don't leave yourself out, Jessie," Emilio said. "I know this whole vision was your idea. You told me when you bought the property you vowed not to tear down the hangar because of its World War Two significance for the community. You sure made good on your promise."

I noticed Jessie wasn't paying attention to Emilio's praise.

She swayed slightly. "Sorry, Emilio. I'm feeling a little woozy." Then she added a laugh. "I'm sure skipping breakfast didn't help. I just need to sit for a minute."

Emilio grabbed her elbow and guided her to a wood bench. She grabbed the arm of the bench and slowly lowered herself down.

"Can I get you something? A water?" I asked.

"No worries, Meg. I'll be fine in a minute."

"Deep breaths," Emilio said, sitting next to her. Then he jumped up. "I think I have a water bottle in my gear. Don't move."

Jessie laughed. "I won't. By the time you hand me the water, I'll be fine."

Emilio went over to where he'd placed his backpack on the cement floor. He bent down, unzipped the top and rooted around for the bottle. "Oh, look," he called over his shoulder. "I even have a protein bar."

"See," I said. "It's all good."

Jessie's face looked anything but good. "Who am I fooling," she mumbled. "Maybe I'm making a mistake, going through with the opening. I can't believe he's gone. What kind of monster would hit him without calling 911? The police told me his phone is missing. How is that possible? We'd just talked. He seemed upset about something before he left to go diving. I had a feeling it had to do with the opening. He told me heads were gonna roll. He never used such language—he was always soft-spoken and the first to find a compromise. Foolishly, I told him we would discuss it all later. We were a team. That later never happened. Now I feel guilty. Why didn't I stop him from leaving and find out what was wrong?"

I knew it was a rhetorical question, but she searched my face for an answer, then continued, "Knowing Travis, he was trying to protect me from something."

Or someone, I thought, as Emilio came back and handed her the water bottle and bar.

Had Travis been ready to tell his sister about the threatening notes? I was dying to see what was written on the others, wanting to confirm that only the letter *L* was at the top of each one. Bryce had no qualms about sharing information about them in front of complete strangers. So Jessie must know. Just another thing to add to her stress.

Emilio sat next to Jessie. "Let's focus on today and tomorrow. Everything else can wait. Soon, Chris will be here to comfort you."

"What about me and Con?" a female voice said from the shadows. "You couldn't have done any of this without us. You know we're here for you, Jessica."

Was Lauren listening this whole time?

Her high-heeled sandals made Clydesdale clip-clopping sounds on the cement floor as she approached us. Today she wore a white cropped T-shirt with a large gold DG logo across her chest. The prism lights caught the sparkle of a diamond piercing at her belly button. Her skintight black jeans also featured mini gold DG logos. The top and the jeans screamed *Look at me, I'm wearing Dolce & Gabbana.* Her outfit wasn't vintage Dolce, like Elle might have hanging in one of her room-sized closets. The reason I knew it wasn't vintage had to do with the hang tag sticking out from the back of Lauren's T-shirt. I couldn't read the price she'd paid, but I could see the initials CZ.

CZ was a luxury brand boutique in East Hampton. Once, I'd stepped inside and was immediately offered a glass of chardonnay. After I couldn't find anything under five hundred dollars—and that was for a twelve-by-twelve-inch polyester scarf—I'd chugged the wine and exited.

"What are you doing here, Lauren?" Jessie said. "I don't remember giving you the security code."

Lauren stepped under the open skylight. "Oh, cuz, of course you did. Remember that time Bryce let me in. I still think this is a bad idea. We should postpone." She stepped closer to Jessie. "Have you looked in a mirror lately? You look terrible."

"Thanks," Jessie said.

"Cuz, I have a feeling something awful is going to happen if we open. The astrological charts don't lie." Lauren looked from me to

Emilio. "I'm sorry, I'm worried about you. You look like death warm—" She didn't finish her sentence. "I insist we postpone the opening. For your own sake. I couldn't live with myself if you had a breakdown or something. I think Trav would've agreed. I want to move into the farmhouse until after the funeral. No arguing." She put her hands on her hips and focused her ice blue eyes on Jessie.

"We'll talk about it. But I'm not letting my employees down or all the local entrepreneurs who've curated so many wonderful products for our shops."

Lauren walked up to me, so close I could smell the coffee on her breath. "What the heck is she doing here?"

I wondered when she'd say something.

"I needed some help," Jessie said.

"And you went to strangers, instead of family. I don't think you're thinking straight."

"Of course I'm not thinking straight," Jessie said. "My brother is dead."

"What about Con? You've always listened to him in the past. He doesn't think it's a good idea to open tomorrow, either."

"I'm not changing my mind," Jessie said firmly. "You were supposed to help make the tarts. Kayla said you refused. Claims you had something more important to do."

"Oh, Kayla did, did she. She told me she could handle it. It's a good thing I won't be doing a review of her internship."

"You're as good of a cook as I am," Jessie said in a slightly softer tone. "You say you want to be included in segments on *Jessica's Table*. If that's true, then you need to step it up. Travis agreed."

"You're still punishing me for leaving Dahlia Lane. I thought you wished me luck when I opened Lavender Fields."

"I did," Jessie said, seeming weary of the sparring.

"Then how come you wouldn't float me a loan?"

"That wasn't my decision. That was—"

"Your brother, I bet."

"No, actually, it was Conrad who said to hold off."

"You're lying. My husband wouldn't do that."

"It's all in the past," Jessie said. "Let's move forward. Now's not the time for us to argue. Remember, I did let you take my place in the *Jessica's Table* episode yesterday."

"I thought the segment turned out perfectly," Lauren said.

Jessie's eyes filled with tears. "I haven't seen the tape yet. But you're right. I'm sorry. I appreciate you taking over. Lord knows, I couldn't do it."

"No thanks to that Kayla. Another thing you should do, fire her. She's like a scared little rabbit." Lauren patted Jessie on the shoulder. "For once, I wish you would listen to me."

"Kayla's not going anywhere. Look around, Lauren," Jessie said, throwing her hands in the air. "Does it look like we aren't ready?"

"Well, if you are, then what do you need these two for?"

Awkward.

Lauren didn't wait for Jessie to answer. "Opening so soon after my cousin's death is disrespectful to his memory. People will think our family is cold-blooded."

At the word *cold-blooded*, I thought about the person who'd mowed Travis down. That was cold-blooded.

"I'm not postponing the grand opening. I know what my brother would want, so please don't push it. I'm begging you."

Not giving up, Lauren said, "At least wait till Chris is here. I bet he doesn't want you to open."

"You're wrong. He supports my decision one hundred percent."

"Of course he does. He hasn't had to do any of the grunt work."

Jessie's cheeks pinked. "He never planned on being here for the opening. He's filming the Habitat for Humanity project for a two-hour special on *Dahlia Lane Home Makeover*.

"Okay, don't say I didn't warn you. I guess I should go check on the little child and her tarts."

"No need," Jessie said. "Meg's father is helping her."

"Say what?" Lauren turned, then snarled in my direction. "You've got to be kidding."

I just shrugged my shoulders and mouthed, "Sorry."

"By the way, Jessica," Lauren said, smiling, seemingly happy to drop her next words. "Conrad needs to speak to you. He mentioned something about an electrician and some kind of code enforcement issue."

"What?" Jessica looked panicked. "Where is he? Are you serious?"

"As a heart attack. Want me to handle it?" Lauren said sweetly.

"Would you?" Jessie asked.

"Anything for you, cuz."

Lauren started toward the back of the hangar, heading in the direction of the restaurant.

"Oh, Lauren," Jessie called after her. "I do have one favor. Tomorrow, can you please wear something from my clothing line."

Lauren stopped short and turned. "Of course. I just love the farmgirl *Little House on the Prairie* look. I'll even steal a pair of mud-caked cowboy boots from your closet. Tootle-loo."

Until she disappeared into the shadows from whence she came, no one said a word. Then Emilio snapped to attention. "We should probably get crackin'. You said the sales help is coming at noon. I better get more lighting equipment from my car," he said, looking up at the dark sky.

"I'll help you," I said.

"And I need to have a conversation with Conrad," Jessie said. "I don't understand why he's changed his mind about the opening. Plus, Travis told me we were all set when it came to passing Suffolk County code enforcement."

Emilio turned to Jessie. "Maybe Lauren's lying. It wouldn't be the first time."

"I don't want to think she'd go that far. But you can see how she can wear you down." Jessie looked toward where Lauren had appeared, then disappeared. "Since the day she and Conrad met, it's as if Lauren has some kind of hold on him. There's something else Travis brought up the last —"

She left the words unsaid and started walking in the direction Lauren had taken, then stopped, turned and waved to us. "Thanks again, you two."

We waved back.

"Things just keep getting weirder and weirder around here," I said a few minutes later. "One good thing, Jessie doesn't seem as shaky as she was before Lauren showed up. She seems more determined than ever to make tomorrow a success. I hope Lauren doesn't sabotage her efforts."

"Remind me not to go into business with my relatives," Emilio said.

"It's not always a disaster. Jessie and Travis sure appeared to have a close relationship. Look at the dynasty they've built."

"And then there's Lauren," Emilio said.

Indeed, I thought, grabbing my umbrella and following him to the exit.

Chapter 19

"So where should we start?" I asked Emilio.

"Let's start with the small shops and work our way to Dahlia Lane Home. How about we go in order, starting with Dahlia Lane Cooks."

"Good idea. You know what our working together reminds me of?" I said, walking toward the first shop on the west side of the hangar.

"What?" Emilio picked up his equipment, followed me and stopped in front of the Dahlia Lane Cooks display window.

"Reminds me of when we first met at *American Home & Garden*. Back when I was a lowly locations editor. I believe our shoot was on Long Island. Locust Valley, if memory serves."

Emilio grinned. "Oh, yes. It was before you rose to power as editor in chief."

"And you, as the magazine's big-shot visual director."

Emilio grinned. "I remember it well. I'd be in charge of getting the test shots before the actual day of shooting, so you'd know what props to bring. What I loved about working with you," Emilio said, adjusting his tripod, "you always took time to discuss the lighting. We were a creative team working together. Like Batman and Robin."

"Batgirl and Robin," I said with a laugh. "We could read each other's mind. Then, before we even set out, you'd come with me to the magazine's prop room and I'd choose what items fit the home and property—books, a myriad of vases, faux veggies and fruits, platters, extra-large glass canisters prefilled with grains, pastas, or cookies, different-sized baskets that would hold flowers, umbrellas, kids' toys, books, kitchen and entertaining linens, bed linens and pillows. Or anything else I needed to match the owner's aesthetic. If the prop room didn't have what was needed, I'd go out and buy items using *American Home & Garden's* generous prop budget. I do miss that."

Emilio laughed. "It does sound daunting, now that you mention it. You had to be a producer, photo stylist, and writer. Do you miss it?" he asked.

"Working for someone else? Nope. I'm happy with my one-woman show. But it sure helped me to have a discerning eye when decorating my cottages. Looking back," I said, smiling, "I think being editor in chief might have been easier than being magazine editor. I wouldn't trade a second of it. The only thing I would change was having Michael as my boss."

"And your fiancé, I bet."

"Oh, yeah."

"That's why you made such a good boss. You were understanding about all the things that could go wrong with your magazine editors, and you always cut them a break."

"Aw, shucks," I said. "And you were just as kind to the photographers under you. We were the dream team. Elle included."

"I'll high-five you on that one."

We slapped each other's hand.

"Ready to get started?" Emilio said. "We have a lot to cover before noon. Let me get a shot of the Dahlia Lane Cooks window display, then we'll go inside the shop."

"Sounds like a plan," I said, peering through the window. "I'm so glad Jessie trusts me to help do this. I bet you said something."

"Nope," he said. "She knows a good fit for her team when she sees one."

After Emilio finished with the display windows, we went inside Dahlia Lane Cooks. Following a dozen oohs and ahhs, most of them coming from me, we got to work. Despite not being a cook, I was still able to drool over the way someone had styled the large rectangular wood farm table in the center of the shop. The whole vibe was of an outdoor summer evening dinner party.

A sheer off-white delicate lace tablecloth was draped asymmetrically over the top of the table. There were four wood chairs on either side of the table, in two different styles. Under white china dinner plates with a raised lacy rim were burnished brass chargers. A wineglass and water glass, in two different styles of stemware, were at each place setting. No matchy-matchy in this display. Pale rose linen napkins were left un-ironed and draped across each dinner plate. On top of each napkin was a single dahlia stem.

A patinated brass pot in the center of the table held lifelike artificial flowers. Whoever styled the centerpiece knew to keep the arrangement lower than eye level to encourage across-the-table conversation. Surrounding the centerpiece were slim brass candlesticks.

At each end of the table were huge statement stoneware vases holding tall faux flowers, including pink dahlias, which looked so lifelike I bent down to sniff them. Next to the stoneware vases were wood risers holding rustic-looking cutting boards. One held a fake wheel of Parmigiano-Reggiano and faux grapes. At the opposite end of the table, next to the stoneware vase, the cutting board was topped with a pale green blown glass water pitcher with a long, fused-glass pink and green stirrer. Next to the pitcher were a couple of fake lemons.

"Wow! This table setting is exquisite," I said. "The way I would describe it for a magazine spread would be—Cool summer wildflower chaos. Do you need me to point the knife on the cutting board away from the camera?"

"You remembered *American Home & Garden*'s rule," he said. "Never take a shot of a knife pointing directly at my lens. So my answer is yes. Just point the tip a bit to my left."

After I did, I asked, "How about you, Emilio? How would you describe Jessie's tablescape?"

"Like everything Jessie touches, I would call it perfection."

"You would, would you, Emilio?" someone said from behind me.

I turned to see Conrad Kincaid standing in the shop's open doorway.

Chapter 20

"I was looking for Jessie," Conrad said, stepping inside. "She texted she wanted to see me. Do you know why? Hope nothing's gone wrong." He looked nervous, his eyes searching the shop's interior like he expected Jessie to pop up from one of the large copper bouillabaisse cauldrons like a jack-in-the-pot.

Emilio was in the middle of shooting a close-up of a stack of hand-carved wood dough bowls.

Conrad came and stood behind him. "Oops, you better take off that sticker. We don't want any prices in the *Dahlia Lane Journal* shots. Might scare people away."

"I got it!" I said, jumping into action. I figured if Jessie ever hired me for another Dahlia Lane assignment, I'd better keep in Conrad's good graces. Lord knew, I would never fill that slot with Lauren. I peeled the sticker from the side of the bowl and moved it to the bottom, where it wouldn't show up in the photo, noticing the price was eighty-five dollars. Not terrible for a hand-carved item. I knew from watching Patrick in his workshop, the time, not to mention all the stages a piece had to go through before it was finished, would add to its price.

"Thanks," Conrad said, narrowing his brown eyes at me. "I don't think we've formally met." He reached out his hand, and I shook it. His palms were damp and there were beads of sweat on his forehead and upper lip. "Conrad Kincaid."

"Nice to meet you, Mr. Kincaid."

"Conrad, please. Mr. Kincaid is what they call my father."

"I'm Meg Barrett, Jessie hired me to—"

"Assist Emilio here," he said, patting Emilio on the back so hard he almost dropped his camera. "Right, buddy?"

I didn't want to correct him that I hadn't been hired to assist Emilio, but Jessie.

"I don't want to disturb your work. I'm just confused about why Jessie said to meet her here, and she's nowhere to be seen. I guess we got our wires crossed. I'll head back to Dahlia Lane Home and see if she's there."

"I think Lauren told Jessie there was a problem with the electricity not being up to code," Emilio said.

"That's strange," Conrad said. "I don't know what that wife of mine is talking about. It's some kind of miscommunication, I'd bet. Not surprising with everything going on, especially what happened to Travis. You wouldn't happen to know if Jessie might have changed her mind about opening tomorrow? What's your opinion, buddy?" he said, looking over at Emilio. "I know you care about Jessie. Maybe you could sway her to hold off on the opening until after Travis's affairs are settled. I mean, at least until after his celebration of life."

Lauren must have made up the whole code enforcement scare to worry Jessie. Another check against her. Then I had another thought: what if I was wrong about Lauren? Could she be scared about opening because of the threatening notes?

Emilio looked at me before speaking. "I don't think she'll change her mind. Jessie said the shop clerks are coming at noon to get familiar with the merchandise."

"Well, if you see her, please tell her to call me. I need to tell her something important that might change her mind about tomorrow."

Say what? I thought.

"Does it have anything to do with the threatening notes Lauren is receiving?" Emilio asked. "Are you scared something bad might happen tomorrow?"

Conrad opened his mouth wide, then closed it. "How did you hear about that?" he asked. "Yes. Lauren has been getting threatening notes. I don't know how you heard about them. But I think it's time Jessie knows. My wife didn't want her to worry. Nor did I."

"Wouldn't it be better if Jessie knew?" Emilio said. "What if she's receiving her own notes and didn't want to worry anyone."

"You're right," Conrad said. "I'll tell her. I'm sure she'll cancel the opening. It's for the best. If you see her, tell her I'll be in my office."

"Will do," Emilio answered.

After he'd gone, Emilio said, "I hope you didn't think I was throwing you under the bus. I think Jessie should know about the notes."

"I agree. I just hope behemoth Bryce doesn't come after me for spilling the beans. Maybe once Jessie hears about the threats against Lauren, she will cancel," I said.

"I know Jessie," Emilio said, "I doubt she'll cancel. Especially at this late date."

Suddenly we heard Conrad shout, "What idiot left the skylight open!"

Emilio and I ran out of Dahlia Lane Cooks and saw Conrad charge toward the side door, where we'd entered with Jessie. He grabbed a remote off a ledge and aimed it at the ceiling. The skylight closed with a swoosh.

Conrad looked over at us, his face flushed. "Sorry, I didn't mean to call Jessie an idiot. She's been forgetful lately, another reason I don't think we should open tomorrow. There're too many moving parts" — he pointed to the ceiling — "for her to handle."

Emilio and I stood mute. I couldn't think of anything appropriate to say, so for a change, I kept my mouth shut. Up until now, I thought of Conrad as a congenial, caring person. Especially the way he was with Jessie in the Tulip Room. But his reaction to the open skylight was another reminder — first impressions aren't always the right impressions.

Chapter 21

At eleven thirty, Jessie met up with us in the last shop to be photographed, Dahlia Lane Clothing Supply. Emilio showed her some of the shots from the other nine shops. She seemed pleased but lacked her usual exuberance when viewing Emilio's photos.

"You sure you're happy with what we've done?" he said, obviously picking up on the same vibes I had.

"Yes. Yes, I am. I'm just really tried. I don't know why. I've been dragging all morning. Well done, you two. I seem to be saying that a lot lately."

"Maybe you should see your doctor," Emilio said. "Or at least have your blood work done."

She waved him off. "I'm fine. Meg, you have a sticker on your dress." She came over and peeled it off.

"Oh, I'm so sorry," I said. "I had to move some of the stickers so they wouldn't show up in Emilio's photos."

"No worries," she said, looking down at it. "I don't think it came from a clothing item. All I need to do is scan the barcode and we'll find the missing item. Conrad spent months setting up the inventory for the shops at the hangar. Come, I'll show you."

We followed her out of the shop to the long line of granite register and wrap counters. She pulled out a handheld reader and scanned the tag. Suddenly, her eyes welled with tears. She opened her mouth to speak but nothing came out.

"Jessie, what's wrong?" Emilio asked, putting his arm around her shoulders to keep her from crumpling to the floor.

"The tag is from Dahlia Lane Woodworks," she mumbled.

Emilio looked over his head at me and nodded. "Meg will put it back where it belongs."

"Travis didn't make all the wood items in the shop," she said. "But he made the prototypes, then Conrad found local artisans to recreate them."

I held out my hand. She placed the large sticker on my palm like it was a fragile piece of glass. "It's from one of the three-legged wood stools."

"I remember exactly where they are," I said. "I'll be right back."

"Thanks, Meg," Jessie said with relief, her shoulders softening.

I understood how hard it would be for her to step inside Dahlia Lane Woodworks. I thought back to after my mother passed, how it took months before I could step inside her shop, Past Perfect. Her aura was there. In every corner, every tabletop vignette, every dusty book in the floor-to-ceiling bookcases. The scent of her signature perfume was faint but still strong enough to hit me like a brick with the reminder she was gone forever.

As I made my way to find the unstickered stool in Dahlia Lane Woodworks, I felt an electricity in the air, almost a happy buzzing. The shopkeepers and employees were streaming in by the dozens. The interior of the hangar had come alive. I couldn't wait to come tomorrow as a customer. I already had my eye on a few things in the Dahlia Lane Antiques & Vintage Marketplace that would go perfectly in my next mini cottage at the motor lodge.

As I browsed the shop windows on my way to Dahlia Lane Woodworks, I heard a commotion near the entrance to the hangar. Conrad and Pete were standing in front of the Dahlia Lane Blooms flower stand. They were in a heated conversation. Conrad's cheeks were only a shade lighter than Pete's. Both had clenched fists. Conrad stepped closer to Pete, got inches from his nose and shouted something. Pete took a cowering stance and tried to walk away. Conrad grabbed him and spun him around. I couldn't make out any of Conrad's ranting, but I was able to read Pete's lips when he said, "You owe me big-time." Conrad put his hands on Pete's shoulders and started shaking him. Had Conrad found out his wife and Pete were having an affair? Or was it something else? Was Conrad accusing Pete of sending the notes to Lauren?

"Threaten me and this birdy may just sing," Pete said.

Immediately, Conrad lowered his hands.

Now it was Pete's turn to get aggressive. He gave Conrad a hard push. If not for the bench behind him, he would have fallen to the concrete floor. For being a small guy, Pete had no trouble holding his own. Pete then said something through gritted teeth I couldn't make out. Conrad turned and stomped away in my direction.

I quickly shifted my gaze, put my head down and scurried toward Dahlia Lane Woodworks.

As I entered the shop, I was greeted by a smiling young male clerk wearing a Dahlia Lane apron. After we got talking, I found out why he looked so familiar. David was the grandson of the Kittingers, the owners of the very first cottage I decorated after opening Cottages by the Sea.

I explained to him why I was there.

"It's extremely sad, isn't it?" he said. "I was a huge fan of Travis Sterling. He actually hired me. I sure hope they catch the person who hit him. I dabble in woodworking, but nothing like Mr. Sterling. When I saw they were hiring, I was the first in line. It's the perfect summer job until I go back to NYU for my architecture degree."

"We're fellow alumni," I said, raising my hand for a high five.

He slapped my hand, then grinned. He had the look of a surfer, with his lean physique, sun-highlighted light brown hair, and tanned body. Actually, he looked a bit like a young version of Patrick, who was also a surfer. Patrick would love this shop. One entire wall held a tall wood cabinet with apothecary-type drawers filled with hardware. On top of the cabinet was a sign on an easel that read *Hand Forged*. I pointed and said, "A lost art, if there ever was one."

"Yes, not many blacksmiths around anymore," he said with a grin. "I'm sure going to be happy working here. Have you been hired to do some of the interior design, like you did at Gram and Gramps's?"

"No, I'm just helping Jessica Sterling with a book she's doing on the windmill she renovated."

"Oh, I saw it from the road driving in. Next summer, I'm interning for credits with a historical architectural firm in Sag Harbor. The same one who worked on the restoration of the Dahlia Lane windmill. I'd die for a look inside. Maybe you could arrange that for me, seeing I'm a fellow NYUer."

Knowing Emilio and Jessie were waiting for me, I told David, "I'll see what I can do, fellow NYUer. I just have to place this sticker on one of those stools over there."

I glanced down at the large sticker with the Dahlia Lane logo, and below it the words *Handcrafted in the USA* and the price—one hundred forty dollars. After I found the stool without a price sticker, I placed it on one of the stool's three legs, just like its siblings.

"I guess that does it," I said, walking to the shop's open doorway. "David, please tell your grandparents Meg Barrett says hi."

"Will do," he said, picking up a pair of lath-turned wood candlesticks. After examining the price on the bottom of one, he turned to me and said, "Will I see you tomorrow? Gran and Gramps are planning on coming."

"Wouldn't miss it for the world," I said.

When I got back to where I'd left Emilio and Jessie, they were gone. I asked a bouncy young girl dressed in laid-back Dahlia Lane-style clothing, with a name tag that read *Brittany*, if she'd seen Jessie. She pointed in the direction of Dahlia Lane's restaurant.

"See that hallway to the right?" she said, flipping her long auburn hair off her shoulder. "Mr. Kincaid's office is the first door on the left. She might be in there." Then she asked, "You don't know when the employee meeting will be, do you? I'm so excited. I have to pinch myself that I'm working here."

I told her I wasn't sure, but if I saw Ms. Sterling, I would find out.

So far, I was impressed with the staff, making me confident tomorrow would be a big success.

As I walked toward the restaurant, I kept scanning the hangar for Emilio and Jessie. As Brittany said, I found a door with a *No Admittance* sign on it. I knocked. Surely the sign was for customers, not those like me, employed by Dahlia Lane Enterprises. No one answered, so I turned the knob and pushed open the door.

I hit something solid and looked up. Déjà vu. Guess who? "Bryce," I said, "sorry about the door thing." *Again.*

He glared down at me. "You should be," he growled. "Whatya want?"

I pushed past him, not an easy feat, and stepped into the large space. "I'm looking for Ms. Sterling and Emilio."

From the corner of my eye, I saw someone else was in the room. Conrad was sitting with his back to me at a desk topped with dozens of file folders. His right arm was raised, and he held one of those self-inking stampers in his hand. He let the stamper drop to the desk, then spun around in his chair, sending me the same look the not-so-friendly giant just did.

"I, uh, uh, was looking for Jessie and Emilio. They told me to meet them back at Dahlia Lane Home, but they're not there."

Conrad took two folders and shoved them into the desk's bottom drawer. After two attempts, he managed to get the drawer closed. Then he stood and faced me.

"You want me to escort her out?" Bryce said, turning to his uncle, then back to me. "I don't know where Emilio or Jessica is, but Kayla just told me your father, the cop—"

"Retired homicide detective," I added, looking for a reaction from the both of them.

Both kept their poker faces.

"Well, he's finished helping Kayla and he's gone home. I saw him on one of the new cams I've installed," Bryce said, standing up taller—if that was possible. "Where you should be."

"Bryce. Bryce," Conrad said, his frown gone, replaced with a smile that showed perfect white teeth. "Forgive my nephew." He stood and walked toward to me. "Ms.—"

"Meg." I must not have made much of an impression if he forgot my name in the space of an hour.

"Meg," Conrad said. "Have you checked the kitchen studio? My wife is there doing some kind of taste test."

The last place I want to be, I thought. And most likely why my father left as soon as he could. "Oh, okay. How about Emilio? Do you know where he is?"

"I'm sorry," Conrad said. "I don't. If you'll excuse me, I have to get back to work." He looked over my head and said, "Bryce, I need you to make sure things are going smoothly out there. No sticky fingers with the staff. Jessie should've been her by now. She knows we have a group meeting for the staff. I hope she's up to it. I haven't been able to catch up with her, and I hope she's feeling better than last night."

"I did notice she seemed a little unsteady earlier," I said.

"Really? That's not good. Not good at all." He was either a fabulous actor or he was concerned. "Maybe I should go over to the studio and see for myself." He looked down at his Rolex. "But I better stay here in case I have to start the meeting without her."

"I could get her and bring her here. It's raining pretty hard out there," I said. "I know where the studio kitchen is."

"You do?" Conrad asked, surprised.

Bryce looked away. He didn't want his uncle to know he'd allowed me and my father in the studio on Wednesday.

"I'll bring her back for the meeting," I said. "Maybe I'll see Emilio too."

"We don't need you," Bryce said, taking a step closer to me. "I'll go."

"No, Bryce. Let her go. I need you to gather up everyone for the meeting."

"Great," I said with a smile. "Do you also want me to ask Mrs. Kincaid to come with us for the meeting?"

"No," Conrad said, a little too strongly. "Just Jessie."

"What are you waitin' for?" Bryce said, opening the office door.

Before Conrad changed his mind, I bolted out.

I realized I volunteered to get Jessie without knowing how to get to the studio from the hangar. It was still storming outside, so walking wasn't an option. I grabbed my umbrella by the side door where I'd left it this morning and waited for Bryce.

He came lumbering out of the office. "What are you still doin' here? You heard my uncle. Get movin'."

"One small question," I said. "How do I get to the studio from here?"

He glanced around the hangar. "Come quick, I'll show you the shortcut."

He led me toward the front entrance, through the white cottage attached to the hangar that appeared to be Dahlia Lane's welcome station. I grabbed one of the maps of the property to show Elle.

"I said, get movin'. Don't be taking anything."

"You know what, Bryce," I said as we stepped onto the small porch. "I think we need to start over. You have the wrong impression of me. All I care about is helping Jessie and making her dream come true. I'm sure you feel the same. Kayla said you are a softy deep down."

That got him. He blushed. "She did, did she."

With his pink bowed lips and cheeks, he looked like a Macy's Thanksgiving Day Parade cartoon of a bald Betty Boop. His tone softened. "Just follow the road to the west of the hangar. You'll need the code to get through the back gate."

"No need. Jessie gave me the codes."

"I wish she didn't do that. With the creep writing those notes, the codes can't be given out willy-nilly."

Willy-nilly?

"How could I be the one sending the notes? I just started here on Wednesday?"

"Just sayin'," he said. "It's my job on the line as head of Dahlia Lane security."

"May I ask a quick question?" Before he answered, I said, "Does Ms. Sterling know about the notes?"

"Not your business, nosey lady. I'll handle this jerk. Stay out of it," he grunted, then looked out to the parking lot, where the rain was coming down so hard I worried it might break the glass skylight inside the hangar.

As I opened my umbrella, I heard his booming voice in my left hearing aid. "And don't mention to my uncle that I told you about the notes. Or else I'll —"

"Promise. My lips are sealed," I said, cutting him off. My first instinct was to turn and challenge him. I wouldn't be bullied. Then I thought better of it. Taking the meek approach might pay off in our future interactions.

If Jessie didn't know about the notes, it was high time she did.

Forewarned is forewarned . . .

Chapter 22

When I walked into the studio kitchen, Kayla was cowering in the corner. Jessie was sitting at the counter with her head in her hands. Lauren was in the middle of lecturing Kayla about the poor job she did cleaning up.

All I could focus on were three commercial baking racks on wheels holding rows and rows of sheet pans, topped with perfect-looking mini tarts.

Meg to the rescue. "Oh, it smells glorious in here. I sure hope I get to do a taste test."

Lauren spun around. "You!"

"Yes, me," I answered. "Your husband sent me to pick up Jessie and bring her to the hangar. It's time for the staff meeting."

"He did what?" Lauren glanced at her gold and rhinestone-bedazzled phone on the counter. "Why didn't the big jerk text me?"

"Heck if I know," I said, walking over to Jessie, who was still hunched over, holding her head in her hands. I gently put my hand on her shoulder. "Are you okay, Jessie?"

She lowered her hands and braced them on the countertop, then attempted to straighten up. "I'll be fine in a few minutes."

"You've been saying that for the past hour," Lauren said. "You should be in bed. Look at the weather out there. What if it's like this tomorrow? No fireworks. No concert. You say you want to do this for Travis. What would Travis say about you pushing yourself? He'd want you to go rest. I'll go over to the hangar. Just tell me what you were going to say at the meeting and I'll tell them. Remember I had a large staff at Lavender Fields. I can handle it."

Jessie looked at her. "I can do it. I just need a minute." She stood up from her stool and took an unsteady step toward me, then another. She looked like she was walking the thin white line in a sobriety test and failing miserably.

Before I could reach her, Kayla hurried over and grabbed Jessie's elbow, then led her back to the stool. "Ms. Sterling, I think you should see a doctor."

Jessie smiled. "Kayla, I told you to call me Jessie. I'll be fine." She swayed backward against Kayla's hip. "Well, maybe not," she said.

Lauren stormed up to her. "Give me your notes for the meeting and let the intern take you into the farmhouse and stay with you until I get back. You need to rest. I'll telephone my concierge doctor and have him come over. If you insist on opening tomorrow, you need to be feeling strong enough to do it."

For some reason, Jessie looked at me. She appeared even paler than this morning.

"I think it's a good idea," I said.

"Okay, I give in," Jessie said. "But, Meg, you give Conrad Travis's notes for the meeting. Kayla, you've done enough. Or should I say you and Meg's father have done enough. Go home." She turned to Lauren. "You come with me to the farmhouse. That makes more sense. I just need some restorative green tea and I'll be right as rain." Thunder boomed either as an exclamation point or a warning.

"Are you serious? You don't trust me leading the meeting with Con?"

I couldn't resist saying my next words. I looked at Lauren and said, "Conrad was very clear, he doesn't need you at the meeting."

Lauren stormed up to me. "What the hell! We'll see about that!"

"Don't shoot the messenger," I said, throwing my hands in the air.

"It has nothing to do with trust, Lauren," Jessie said. "Conrad can handle it. And Meg can get the meeting notes and bring them to the hangar. Kayla's done enough." Just arguing with Lauren seemed to give Jessie more strength. "Kayla, please show Meg where Travis's office is. They should be in the printer tray."

"Will do, Jessie," Kayla said, giving Lauren a defiant look. "Come on, Meg."

"Feel better, Jessie," I said as we went out a different door than I came in.

Before the door closed, I thought I heard Jessie say in a loud voice with an edge to it, "I don't need you staying at the farmhouse. I'll ask Wilhelmina to stay the night." I started walking down the hallway and realized Kayla wasn't next to me. I glanced back and saw she had her ear to the door. I raised my eyebrows and gave her a questioning look. She put her finger to her lips.

Go, Kayla. Better she translate the now heated conversation between Jessie and Lauren than me trying to listen. The problem I had when trying to listen through a closed door was the ear-splitting feedback I might get from my hearing aid, muffling the conversation inside.

Two minutes later, Kayla walked away from the door. "They're gone," she said. "They went out the other door. We better hurry to the office." She grabbed my wrist and led me down the hallway to a closed door. She opened it and we stepped inside. Kayla went over to the copy machine and grabbed the papers for the staff meeting, and said after a long exhale, "That was eye-opening."

"Go on," I said.

"You'll never believe it."

"Try me."

"First, I need to know you won't tell Lauren what I'm telling you."

"Don't worry. I'm totally on team Jessie."

"Me too," she said with a huge grin. "Jessie told Lauren the day before Travis died, he came to her and showed her proof Lauren had opened numerous credit cards in the company's name and was using them to spend outrageous amounts on luxury goods like jewelry and designer clothing."

I wasn't totally surprised. It validated what I'd seen when I'd gone through Lauren's handbag.

"What was Lauren's response?" I asked.

"She said to talk to Conrad, he's the one who gave her the cards."

"That's it?" I asked.

"Something else . . ."

"Yes-s-s?" I wondered if she could see the foam forming at the corners of my mouth.

"Lauren went ballistic over this one. Jessica said she's decided not to fill Travis's position in the company with Conrad and plans on restructuring Dahlia Lane after she and Chris are married. One last thing. When Chris returns, he's moving into the farmhouse."

"So, for a recap, Lauren is not a happy camper."

"No, and it couldn't happen to a better person," Kayla said with an evil smile. "What goes around comes around. Karma's a bitch."

She grabbed an empty folder from the desk and put the notes for the meeting inside, then handed them over.

I took the folder and said, "Thanks. I better get back to the hangar. I assume I'll see you tomorrow."

"Oh, yes, I'll be there. Crack of dawn. It's so sad Travis won't see the hangar's success. He was such a lovely, caring man. From my first day here, he was so welcoming and well—kind." She swiped at her eyes to stop the tears.

"I really wish I could have met him," I said. "I better take these over to the hangar before the meeting starts. Hope you're going home, like Jessie said."

"I will. First, I want to finish washing those two bowls in the sink as ordered by Lauren. Though I don't think I'm scared of her anymore. I'm pretty sure Jessica, Jessie, will have my back. From that conversation I just heard, Lauren's days are numbered. Oh, and please thank your father for helping me. Jessie wanted me to give him this." Kayla reached in her pocket and handed me a Dahlia Lane gift card. "I forgot with all the drama when Lauren came into the kitchen. Your father couldn't leave fast enough. I don't blame him."

"Wow. Five hundred dollars. I'm sure he'll think it's way too much."

"Jessie said he can use it everywhere, including online, the shops in the hangar and Dahlia Lane Homestyle Eatery."

"Nice," I said. "He'll be so happy. Thanks, Kayla. I better run. Chin up, buttercup," I added, thinking about last night at Pondfare, when a teary-eyed Kayla chased after her mother because I'd blabbed Kayla was working at Dahlia Lane. *What was that all about?* "Look," I said, pointing out the office window, "it's stopped raining. A good omen if I ever saw one."

"Let's pray it stays that way for tomorrow and Jessie is feeling better," Kayla said wistfully.

From her lips to God's ears, I thought, waving goodbye and heading for the door.

As I passed the farmhouse on my way to my car, I saw a woman exiting, a leash in each hand and a bulldog at the end of each leash— Boo and Ridley. I felt relief Wilhelmina was at the farmhouse to help Jessie.

I waved. She waved back. I thought about going over and talking to her, but I had important papers to deliver to Conrad. Plus, I had a great idea on how to do some sleuthing with the help of my buddy Georgia.

If my father and Doc wouldn't take me, I'd bet Georgia would . . .

Chapter 23

"So, Georgia," I said to my septuagenarian friend and proprietress of Montauk's the Old Man and the Sea Books, "did you hear about Travis Sterling from your boy toy, Doc?"

From the wing chair next to me, she peered over her book. "Boy toy? Ha! Well, I guess he is ten years younger than me."

"You'd never know it," I said, looking over at her short gray hair and athletic physique, knowing one of her secrets to her youthful appearance was her ten-mile-a-day bike rides to the Montauk Point Lighthouse and her healing custom-blended teas.

"Yes, I heard. Terrible. Terrible. A hit-and-run," she said. "I can't remember that ever happening in Montauk. And during tourist season, for gosh sakes."

"Well—"

"Before you ask," she said, cutting me off, "I know you probably think his death wasn't an accident. It's just part of your nature."

"Based on past experience," I said, giving Tabitha the tabby a good scratch behind the ears, "I was thinking, seeing Patrick is holed up in his writing cave and my father, well, you know—he probably wouldn't. And Doc definitely wouldn't—"

"Wouldn't what? Spit it out, girl. What do you need? Because I don't think you came here to pick up a book. Although, I did get in that Longfellow compendium you ordered for your next Dead Poets Society meeting."

Once a month, over fabulous meals and good wine, a bunch of us would meet with other classical poetry lovers, including Patrick and Georgia. "Longfellow has always been one of my faves," I said.

"Mine too."

"I probably don't need the book. I'm sure you know more about Longfellow than the author."

"I know Henry Wordsworth is the only American to be honored at Westminster in London. There's a marble bust of him in Poets' Corner, along with other famous authors and poets like Browning, Chaucer and Dickens. And did you know, Henry was quite the polyglot," she said with a smile. "Fluent in eight different languages."

"See," I said. "Who needs that book."

"We both do. I'm planning on finishing it before our meeting on Tuesday. Patrick's hosting, right?"

"Yes. At least before his mother showed up."

"Do tell," Georgia said. "I reiterate, why are you really here? I know that look in your eyes."

The Old Man and the Sea Books was my favorite port during a storm—and there'd been quite a few whoppers. Before answering her, planning to choose my words carefully, I glanced over at the small fireplace in front of me. In the cold months, there was nowhere I'd rather be than sitting in a wing chair next to Georgia, her two kitties sleeping in their beds by the fire, while a blizzard raged outside. During the warm months, instead of a crackling fire, Georgia had a copper tray resting on the fire grate topped with remote-control flickering candles—creating the feeling of cozy without the heat of a fire. The old converted fishing cottage had a back room filled with used books, some rare, but most well-loved and well-read. Needless to say, the back room was my favorite place to browse.

No matter the season, the bookshop was my touchstone. A place to kick off my shoes, boots, or sandals, while ignoring whatever Mother Nature was doing outside.

"I just want to go see where the hit-and-run happened," I said. "I thought you might want to take me. Living here all your life, you know all the back roads."

Before she could protest, I filled her in on everything happening at Dahlia Lane, along with what I'd just learned from a quick phone call I had with Emilio. He'd found out Jessie had no clue about the notes and immediately went in search of Bryce. So that meant Lauren was the only one receiving threats. If Travis had also been targeted, we'd never know.

"Who's Emilio, again?" Georgia asked.

After explaining my connection to Emilio and telling her about tonight's gallery show, I said, "You and Doc should come."

"You know, we just might. I love to see new artists. Maybe he could put some of his pieces in here. I only display local artists, and now that your friend's moved to the Hamptons, he would qualify. But from what you've told me about your suspicions of Travis Sterling's death, shouldn't Emilio be on your suspect list?"

"You sound like Patrick. Wait until you meet him. Everyone loves

Emilio."

"I trust your instincts. So I'd love to see his exhibition."

"So-o-o, what do you think about going to the scene?" Tabitha opened her mouth and yawned, followed by a loud meow. "See, Tabitha thinks we should go. Either that or she wants this chair for herself."

Georgia took a minute before responding. Instead of giving me a warning to stay out of it, like Elle, my usual partner in crime, would, her wise gray eyes twinkled in delight. "What are you waiting for?" Georgia said. "Let's hit the road. I've been wanting to see the new steps they built going down to the *Culloden* wreck site. Oh, and can we stop at the *Amistad* Memorial? I haven't seen the new plaque they erected." Georgia was an expert on all things Montauk—scratch that, the Hamptons. She was a third-generation East Ender and a member of the Montauk Historical and Preservation Society.

She stood and deposited Mr. Whiskers, who'd been snoring on her lap, onto the rug.

"Don't you have to wait until five to close?" I asked.

"Pshaw. The perks of being a bookshop owner. I can set my own hours. Plus, we'll only be gone for an hour, tops."

That was easy, I thought.

Almost too easy.

Had Doc shared something with her he hadn't with me?

A few minutes later, as we whizzed by Montauk's Fudge 'n Stuff, Rockin' Retro Gifts, and Blissful Bites Bakery, I wished Georgia's restored early-model Jaguar convertible had a strap to hold on to. "There's no hurry," I said, regretting not wearing a headband to keep my hair out of my eyes. As Georgia idled the Jag before turning left onto Edgemere, I glanced to my right at Catch of Day's plate glass window with a faded sign—*Wanted, Piano Player who can Shuck Clams*. The restaurant reminded me that I hadn't filled Georgia in on food critic Aurora Montague. So I did.

"That's quite a story," she said as we headed north toward the bay. "His mother sounds like a piece of work. I do remember about four years ago, someone claiming to be a food critic came into the bookshop and demanded I carry her book. I told her I'd look into it. When I had a sample sent to my Kindle, I knew there was no way I'd carry such a book with such negative connotations. Even if Ashley,

Patrick's publicist, had begged me, I probably would have only ordered one copy."

"Well, from what I've seen, Patrick wouldn't want the book in the Old Man and the Sea either."

"That can't be the only reason they're estranged," Georgia said. "Patrick has a good soul. There must be more to it."

"I'm not sure. Sarabeth's, the restaurant of Catherine's twin sister, was also reviewed in the book. And not too kindly."

"Sarabeth's by the Bay in Watermill?" Georgia said, swerving to the right, hitting gravel, then pulling back onto the road. "Patrick's mother must be nutty. Besides Pondfare, it's one of the best restaurants in the Hamptons. Shame on her."

"Indeed," I said, worried I'd chipped a tooth as Georgia flew over the Long Island Rail Road tracks. About to protest she should slow down, I changed my mind, remembering tonight was Emilio's gallery show. I needed time to shower and change.

"Sure it's wise to have the top down?" I said. "Those clouds look ominous. Also, did you forget to tell me you were a qualifier in the Daytona 500."

"Funny. Thanks to a few tweaks from our Motor City duo, your father and Doc, my baby's running like a charm. And didn't you say you were in a hurry to get there and back?"

"Not if my life's in danger."

"Don't be a wuss."

Heading north, Georgia finally slowed when Edgemere Road morphed into Flamingo Avenue. Georgia took a left onto Culloden Place, then another left onto Blackberry Drive, a right on Pine Tree Drive, then a left onto Soundview Drive. When Soundview turned into a dirt road, I noticed a charming cottage set close to the road. In the front yard was a frolicking springer spaniel. Could it be the same dog that found Travis's body? I was betting it was.

"Georgia, stop!" Unlike what Elle would have done—that is, ask why—Georgia slammed on the brakes.

I jumped out of the car and ran toward the dog. He happily greeted me by springing up and pressing his two front paws on my chest. I guess that's where the "springer" moniker came from. An elderly woman came to the cottage's screen door. I waved, then walked up to her. "I'm sorry. I think we're lost. We're looking for the parking area for the *Culloden* dive site." It wasn't exactly a total lie, because *I* didn't know how to get there. Only Georgia.

Squinty hazel eyes behind thick-lensed glasses peered back at me. Instead of opening the screen door, she locked it. I couldn't blame her for being cautious. The area was very secluded. I'd thought I discovered every inch of Montauk. Apparently, I was wrong.

"I hope you're not one of those lookie-loos," she said. "Trying to get a thrill at seeing where that body was found."

I feigned surprise. "Body? What body?"

She unlocked the screen door, then stepped onto the wood-planked porch. "There was a hit-and-run a couple days ago. The poor man died. Turned out he was some kind of celebrity or something. Springer is the one who found him."

"Springer?"

"My dog, over yonder," she said, pointing.

"How tragic. So, I take it you were with Springer?"

"Unfortunately, yes. There was nothing to be done. I called 911 immediately."

"Did you see who hit him?"

She shook her head. "Sadly, no. And this morning's *Montauk Sun* says no one has come forward."

It wasn't until I felt warm breath on my neck that I realized Georgia was standing behind me.

"Sadie, how are you doing?" Georgia asked the woman. "I didn't know you lived way out here."

Sadie glanced at me suspiciously. If she knew Georgia, then she also knew Georgia would never get lost.

"I haven't seen you and Bud in the shop lately," Georgia said. "I just got in some vintage paperbacks. Bud's favorites—John D. MacDonald, a few Earl Stanley Gardners and a Mickey Spillane and the like."

Sadie's chin quivered as she looked at Georgia with teary eyes. "Bud passed last fall. His smoking finally got him. Lung cancer."

"Oh, Sadie, I'm so sorry," Georgia said, reaching out to pat her shoulder. "So you sold your oceanfront condo and moved out here?"

"I couldn't afford the condo fees. My unit sold for a million. We paid a quarter of that for it in the eighties. I found this little gem. It's close to the sound and perfect for Springer and me," she said. "It was a bargain, but there's lots of work to be done inside. It will keep me busy, now that—"

"Meg," Georgia said. "Give Sadie your business card. Meg decorates cottages. If you didn't want to hire her, I'm sure she'd give you a few pointers for free. If you need anything major, she also has connections to a family-owned construction team."

"That would be amazing," Sadie said. "Arthritis has its grip on these old fingers. They just don't work like they used to. It's hard to hold a crochet hook, let alone a paintbrush."

I glanced at her veiny hands and swollen knuckles. I could only imagine her discomfort. "Okay. I'll grab one of my cards from my handbag. Be right back." Turning to Georgia, I said, "Sadie was just telling me a tragic story about a hit-and-run. She found the body. Did you know about it?"

Georgia didn't miss a beat. "How terrible."

"Be right back," I said, stepping off the porch.

I took my time walking to the Jag, knowing Georgia could get more information out of Sadie than I ever could.

Chapter 24

After we said our goodbyes, we got back into the car and continued up Soundview. Georgia then made a left onto an unnamed dirt road. As we bumped along, hitting pothole after pothole, I realized how secluded the scene of Travis's hit-and-run was. No traffic cameras and no through traffic. The last traffic camera we'd passed had been in downtown Montauk. There wasn't a chance of getting the hit-and-run vehicle on camera.

"I sure am happy you know the way," I said to Georgia. "I never would've found it on my own. I knew I'd made the right decision in asking you."

"Here we are. Culloden Point," she said, grinding to a stop in the small dirt parking area. I was slightly disappointed there weren't any other cars in the lot. Who did I think I'd find? Travis's killer? Maybe. My father always liked to throw out the statistic that most arsonists and serial killers liked to revisit the scene of their crime. I guessed I was hoping the same held true for hit-and-run drivers.

I looked around. There weren't any cordoned-off areas, suggesting the police had finished here. And with this morning's rain, there weren't any tire tracks.

I got out of the car before Georgia turned off the engine.

Before looking for the spot where Travis's body had been found, I went to the top of the stairs and looked out at Gardiner's Bay and the Block Island Sound. Such a gorgeous view, it was unimaginable it was the same spot where Travis had taken his last breath.

Georgia came up next to me. She pointed to the water. "Even though this area is secluded and hard to find, if you're a diver, you know how to get here. The *Culloden* wreck site is protected by the National Register of Historic Places. Long Island's first underwater park. I've been down there a few times. Not much to see, but worth the dive."

I knew Georgia loved to kayak and surf, so I wasn't surprised she was also a diver.

"It's about one hundred fifty feet offshore," she said. "The British burned it at the waterline so the Patriots couldn't take it. Once you're underwater, it's hard to locate it. The best time to dive is after a storm. You need to look for iron rust stains in the sand. No treasure though, just canons and lots of rusted metal."

"No jewels like Captain Kidd buried on nearby Gardiner's Island?"

"No. But a pretty important site if you're into American history."

As we turned back to the parking area and the scene of the awful crime, I asked, "You wouldn't happen to know where my father and Doc were fishing when they heard the sirens, would you?"

"Oh, I can show you on the way out. It's a secret spot my grandfather used to take me to when I was a kid. I told Doc about it."

"Great," I said.

As we walked to the only grassy area to the west of the parking area, Georgia asked, "What are you hoping to find?"

It took everything I had not to tell Georgia about Travis's missing phone. I'd promised my father. And a promise was a promise. "I just want to look around. You never know. Did you learn anything from Sadie?"

"Not really. I know it affected her greatly. She puts on a brave front, but I know she's a big mush. She only reads romances, which makes it extra sad her Bud passed away."

"Did she try to revive Travis?"

"She said there was no chance he was alive. I didn't ask for any details. I didn't want to upset her. I'm sure Doc could give you a better picture from a coroner's point of view."

"Her cottage is right on the road. I wonder if she noticed any cars speeding away before she set out for her walk?"

"No. But she did say there's been some rowdy teens who come by after dark. They drive an old army green Jeep Wrangler. She said they have bonfires, party, blast loud music and drink beer at the bottom of the steps to the dive site. That's why Sadie and her dog were there that morning. She usually brings a garbage bag on her walks to clean up the mess they leave the night before."

"Hmmm, a Wrangler. I'll tell Arthur. Could it have been an accident and these teens felt guilty after they hit him and laid him in the seagrass?"

"I suppose," Georgia said. "But they wouldn't be partying in the morning, would they? Unless they slept on the beach."

We stopped in front of a trampled area of seagrass. "This must be the spot," I said, tiptoeing into the area. There wasn't any impression (or blood) where Travis's body might have been. The crime scene unit had been thorough.

"It looks pretty picked over," I said.

Disappointment washed over me. For Jessie's sake, I'd fantasized I could be a hero and find her brother's phone or some other clue to the guilty party of the hit-and-run.

"You never know. Nancy Drew wouldn't give up."

"That must make you Bess or George," I said.

She laughed. "George. Definitely George. I have an idea. Wait here."

Before I could ask what, she was already at her car. She opened the Jag's trunk, grabbed something, then jogged back to me. In each hand was one of those grabber-reacher things seniors use, or in my case, I use when my back goes out after lifting heavy furniture.

Georgia handed me one. "Doc and I use these when walking the beach to pick up trash. The claw end is magnetic to pick up sharp metal. Thought it would be good for separating the grass around the trampled area."

"Okay, let's go. Elle's picking me up at six thirty. I sure hope you and Doc can come to the gallery."

Fifteen minutes later, we'd come up with nothing but a couple of empty Bud Light cans and an empty pack of Marlboros—too generic to be considered a clue. Even for Nancy Drew and her sidekick George.

"That was disappointing," I said as we trudged toward the Jag, both dragging our grabbers behind us in the dirt. When we reached the back of Georgia's car, she popped the trunk. She put her grabber inside, then I handed her mine. "Look," she said, "there's something attached to the magnet part of the claw. It looks like a mini tent stake."

Georgia reached for it.

"Stop!" I said, startling her. "Don't touch it with your hand. It might be evidence."

"Good thinkin', Nancy," she said with a grin. "But at the moment, I don't happen to have an evidence bag."

I glanced inside her trunk and saw a beach umbrella inside its case. I reached in, took out the umbrella, slipped off the case and held it open. Georgia raised the grabber over the opening, then I clasped it from the exterior of the case, separated the metal pin-thing from the claw, then let it drop to the bottom of the case.

"Good thinking," Georgia said. "But you know, the chances it's related to the hit-and-run are slim to none."

"Drats," I said. "I should have taken a picture of it."

"That's easy. When you get home, transfer it to a clear baggie, then take a photo from both sides."

"What would I do without you?" As I got into the car, I thought, *At least I got to see where Travis was hit.* And one, possibly two, clues was better than none.

On the way back, Georgia showed me where Doc and my father had been fishing. It was only a short distance to the *Culloden* parking lot.

When we passed Sadie's cottage, she was sitting on the porch with a tall glass of iced tea in her hand. Springer was beneath her, resting his chin on Sadie's feet. We waved and she waved back.

Her house was so close to the street, I could see the lemon slices in her tea.

"Do we have time to see the new plaque at the *Amistad* Memorial?" Georgia asked. "I could take Highway 70 to Montauk Point State Parkway. I helped raise funds for it with a community book sale."

I glanced at my watch. "Sure. If I'm running behind, I can go out my kitchen door and yell over that I'm gonna be late. The advantage of having a best friend living next door."

"How's she doing, anyway? Any calmer?"

"I would say calmer from when we all went to dinner the other night. But still, very emotional. Maybe she's preggers," I said.

Georgia laughed as she turned onto Highway 70, "Preggers? That's a new one. She'll make a great mother."

"You're right, she will. You never wanted children?" I asked her.

"It wasn't in the cards. Plus, my ex-husband was a child, and I didn't have the energy for having another one. No regrets. Just that we didn't get divorced earlier. Robert was an energy vampire. A narcissist. It's kind of funny, seeing he's a psychiatrist. Maybe his clients sucked all his energy out of him, and that's why he had to be babied when he got home from the office."

Georgia was a private person when it came to her past. Even

though I counted her as a good friend, I hadn't known she'd once been married. I knew her philosophy was to live in the moment, no crying over spilled milk or bad memories.

"We only lasted three years. He wasn't a bad person, just not a giving person."

"Like Doc is."

"Doc is the kindest person I've ever met. It must have something to do with what he's seen as a coroner in Detroit. Or maybe he was born that way. Whatever the reason, I'm not complaining."

"And since you've been dating," I said, "he sure has become more adventurous in his old age. Thanks to you."

"The key to happiness, in my humble opinion, is being adventurous as you age and reading everything you can. You can quote me on that."

"I will, wise sage," I said as we turned into the lookout next to the Montauk Point Lighthouse.

Georgia parked and we both jumped out. We followed a path next to the lighthouse that ended with a large boulder. On the boulder was a brass plaque. "Do you want to do the honors?" I asked her.

"Sure," she said, then started reading. "Schooner *Amistad*. In 1839, illegally enslaved Africans subdued captors on ship, came ashore nearby, then jailed in Connecticut. Finally freed by U.S. Supreme court in 1841."

"I'm glad there was a somewhat happy ending to their story. But what a harrowing ordeal."

I glanced over at Georgia. Tears shined in the corners of her eyes. "I know I said you can't live in the past. But it's always a good idea to learn from historical events. Fighting for freedom from oppression of any kind is worth commemorating."

"Agreed. I'm glad we stopped here," I said, glancing over at the forty-foot flagpole next to me, flying the red, white and blue. "Tomorrow's the Fourth of July. The grand opening of Dahlia Lane Shoppes at the Hangar. You and Doc should come."

"Wouldn't miss it," Georgia said. "I hope it turns out as a wonderful tribute to Jessica Sterling's brother."

"It will," I said.

Will it?

Chapter 25

"I can't believe Arthur skunked out of coming to Emilio's show," Elle said as we passed by the Montauk farm stand. "Thanks for the produce, by the way. You do know my tastes. Although, for some reason I've thrown a hate on asparagus. Actually, my sense of taste seems off lately, not to mention smell."

I looked over at Elle at the wheel of her vintage aqua Ford pickup, wondering if her rosy cheeks over a constellation of freckles and her heightened sense of smell might mean the shots worked and she was pregnant. *Aunt Meg*, I mused.

Tonight, Elle's vintage ensemble included a sleeveless psychedelic-print swing dress, which I guessed was vintage Pucci (swing dress = pregnant?). She wore a sheer fuchsia scarf around her neck that displayed a huge aurora borealis brooch. I'd seen the brooch before. It had been worn by a model in one of Elle's vintage charity fashion shows. I also knew it was from the iconic fashion designer Schiaparelli, along with her matching borealis earrings and bracelet. It was surprising that today Elle only wore one brooch. As a rule, she never left the house without an eye-dazzling cluster of rhinestone pins affixed somewhere on her clothing.

Along with her antiques and vintage shop, Elle also inherited a huge nineteenth-century dental cabinet filled with priceless costume jewelry.

My dress was also vintage. A halter sundress Elle had gifted me on my last birthday. I thought the black-and-white print depicting 35mm cameras would be the perfect choice for Emilio's photo exhibition in Bridgehampton. Elle had insisted I borrow her chunky 1930s black-and-white Bakelite stretch bracelet. For earrings, she'd wanted me to wear Bakelite hoop earrings half the size of my head. I'd opted for my mother's pearl studs—thinking, let the dress and bracelet do the talking. Plus, I didn't want to take away from my best friend's magnificence.

"Why isn't Patrick coming with us to the gallery?" she asked.

"He insisted, as a favor to me, he'll bring his mother for a late appearance. He's gonna tell her the show starts at eight instead of six. I gave my father the choice of coming with us or Patrick. He chose neither. He's coming solo. Georgia and Doc might also come."

"From what you've told me about Patrick's mother, it sounds like a smart move by Patrick. Although I am dying to meet her."

I'd told Elle about our evening at Pondfare, half as a distraction not to discuss Travis Sterling's death in greater detail and keeping to my promise with Arthur not to upset is wife.

The East Hampton Town Police had released only a short statement, saying Travis had been killed by a hit-and-run, asking the public with any information or possible eyewitnesses to please come forward. So far that hadn't happened.

While the authorities were trying to keep Travis's death on the down-low, *Dave's Hamptons* had gone in the opposite direction. It was big news, not only because Travis Sterling was a quasi-celebrity but also because the Sterlings had been residents of East Hampton dating back to the 1700s. There was a whole exposé on how Jessica and Travis's great-great-grandfather had been one of the partners in Carl Fisher's proposed dream to make Montauk the Miami Beach of the North. Unlike Carl, Jessie's great-great-grandfather had pulled out before the whole venture, including the resort Montauk Manor and all Fisher's other enterprises, went belly-up. Kind of like Lauren's attempt at creating a Lavender Fields empire to rival her cousin's.

I hadn't had time to talk to Arthur about what Georgia and I learned at the site of the hit-and-run. After I returned home, as Georgia suggested, I slipped the metal piece we'd found into a clean baggie, took a few photos, then tucked the baggie in my handbag, planning to give it to my father later. I would also relay what Sadie told Georgia about the Wrangler full of teens who liked to party on the *Culloden* site beach.

As Elle inched the pickup through the center of East Hampton, we had plenty of time to people watch. The shady street was filled with strolling models, actors, celebs and multimillion and billionaires — most hiding behind dark sunglasses, stopping to perform double-cheeked air kisses when they met up with one of their ilk. There was a reason some called the Hamptons the American Riviera.

Speaking of celebrities, I'd once learned a lesson the hard way — it's taboo to bother the rich and famous in the Hamptons. Too gauche. I'd done it only once with disastrous results.

When I'd first moved to Montauk, I'd approached my all-time top movie-star crush in a Southampton gourmet market. It didn't end well. His security entourage nabbed me before I could even get an autograph. All I'd done was put my hand on his arm to get his attention. Security swooped in like a swat team from an episode of *Law and Order*. They only allowed me to leave the market after they took a photo of my driver's license, warning me, stay away — or else. I wasn't about to stick around for the *or else*.

My celebrity crush just stood there like a big oaf. And *poof!* No more celebrity crush. Proving once again you can't judge someone by their outward appearances, or in this case, their movie roles.

"It's unbelievable Travis Sterling is dead," Elle said. "This time, instead of you or me, your father was at the scene. I think Arthur is holding back on sharing details with me. I think I scared him the other day when I had one of my crying fits. It was over spilled milk of all things."

I glanced over at her and saw she was wearing a smile. I grinned back. "I thought you were lactose-intolerant?"

"Funny. I'm not lactose-intolerant. My quart of nightly pistachio ice cream is proof. I can't wait to see Emilio. What are the chances we would all be living in the Hamptons?"

"Chances are pretty good. Amagansett is only about eighty miles east of Manhattan."

"True. Is he the same old Emilio?"

"Definitely," I said. "He did warn me his photography had changed from when we used to go to his exhibitions."

"I loved his pop-up exhibits. Especially that one in Cobble Hill, where he spent six months visiting a nursing home, photographing elderly residents. On each huge print would be one face —"

"I remember," I said, interrupting her, "The photos were in black and white except for the eyes and lips. Emilio tinted them in color. To the right of the photos was a white placard with the title of each piece."

"Yes, my favorite was One Zero Four," Elle said. "The subject's age. I could've stayed forever just staring into all those beautiful wrinkled faces. Each line and wrinkle told a tale, a roadmap of a life well-lived."

I glanced over at her as we picked up speed. "Oh, no. Why are you crying?"

"They were all so magnificent."

She was right. Changing the subject once again, I said, "Well, his new photography must be pretty good if he got into the Green Room Gallery. A slew of provocative artists has shown there. I read in *Dave's Hamptons* half of the proceeds will go to charity."

"Once, I loaned out some of my vintage clothing and jewelry to a fashion photographer who shot photos of models emerging from time capsules."

"Elle, now why are you crying?"

"You can never go back, can you?"

"Go back where?"

"In time."

"Why would you want to?"

"I don't. It's just so sad that you can't."

"Hey, why don't you pull over and I'll drive. Hard day at Heron's Roost?"

"Don't you know it," she said, wiping her eyes with a floral hankie she'd stuffed in her bra.

"Elle, everything is fine. I'm fine. You're fine. Patrick and Arthur are fine. Remember that dream you told me about? Where we're all around the dining room table at Heron's Roost for Thanksgiving? Well, that day is almost here. As soon as I finish the Dahlia Lane Windmill Cottage book, I'll be out there to help you. Oh, did I mention Jessie Sterling said she wants to meet you? She's even found things for Windmill Cottage she bought from Mabel and Elle's Curiosities. So focus on that, Missy. No more tears unless they're tears of happiness."

"I've missed you," she said, and the tears started again.

"I'm right here."

Elle laughed. "These are happy tears, silly. Tell me more about Dahlia Lane Shoppes at the Hangar," she said, accelerating once we'd finally gotten through East Hampton.

"Oh, I'll leave that as a surprise. You're going tomorrow, right?"

"At least for the concert and fireworks," she said. "Arthur has to work."

"You could come with Patrick, his mother and me."

"His mother? No, thanks, I'll pass. Even though it's a holiday, I need to do some things at Heron's Roost. Arthur promised to pick me up, then we'll go to the shops at the hangar together. So what do you think about Travis Sterling's death? You're the first one to—"

"Hey, Siri," I said into Elle's phone, which was attached to the truck's air vent, "play Motown." Four songs later, including my all-time favorite, "You're All I Need to Get By," where Elle sang Tammy Terrell's part and me Marvin Gaye's, we reached the outskirts of Bridgehampton.

My mission was accomplished—distracting Elle from talk about Travis's death.

"Finally," Elle said as we inched our way toward the center of Bridgehampton. "Too bad Arthur couldn't have loaned us an East Hampton Town PD helicopter. We would've been here an hour ago. I'll be happy after Labor Day, when we get the Hamptons back."

Elle made a quick right into a small alley, nearly mowing down a teen who was walking with her head down, eyes fixed on her phone.

"Yowza!" Elle shrieked, slamming on the brakes.

The girl went around the pickup. Then, without looking up, she gave us the middle finger.

"Oh, no," Elle moaned. "That might be my daughter one day."

"No daughter of yours would be that disrespectful," I said as Elle continued at a slow crawl down the alley, stopping when we reached the entrance to a public parking lot.

"I'm not talking about her rude gesture," Elle sniffled. "I'm talking about my son or daughter getting hit by a car because they're looking down at their phone, not paying attention. I'm gonna make a terrible mom. If it ever happens."

"It's gonna happen. And you're going to be a wonderful mom. And Arthur a wonderful dad."

"You're right. How about you? Don't you want to be a mom? You're not getting any younger."

"Whoa, buddy. Baby steps."

"Exactly. That's what I'm saying. We both need baby steps in our lives. How about Patrick? Does he want a child—oh, I'm sorry. See, I can't keep my filter on anymore."

Distracting her from going down the what-if rabbit hole, I said, "By the time your kids are teens, they'll probably implant their phone screen onto a pair of contact lenses. They already have glasses that do that."

"That doesn't sound safe, either!"

"Look over there," I said. "There's a spot next to Emilio's bright orange Kia."

Chapter 26

When we walked inside the small gallery space, we found ourselves shoulder to shoulder with the Hamptons art crowd. Most were dressed in light cottons and linens, the air scented with expensive perfume. A model-type female server handed me a glass of champagne. Elle waved the glass away (another clue to her condition?).

"I can't even see Emilio," Elle shouted over the din of the crowd. "Do you see him?"

I scanned the room. It was so sardine packed, I not only couldn't find Emilio, I also wasn't able to glimpse any of his art.

Finally, I spotted him in the northwest corner of the open space. "There he is," I said to Elle, pointing to where Emilio was encircled by a gaggle of females.

When I'd worked with him at the magazine, his boyish good looks always turned men and women's heads. It appeared that hadn't changed.

Elle grabbed my wrist. "Come on."

By the time we reached Emilio, my champagne flute was empty. Not because I drank the champagne, but more from all the jostling and shoving as we made our way across the gallery.

Elle and Emilio exchanged hugs and kisses, but there was no chance of reminiscing, because Emilio was soon pulled away by a female gallery assistant wanting him to talk to a potential client about one of his photographs.

Before Emilio got buried in the crowd, he glanced back at us and smiled. Knowing my ability to read lips, he mouthed, "Sorry, we'll catch up when things calm down. I'll meet you outside."

I gave him a thumbs-up and said to Elle, "Let's go see what everyone's raving about."

This time it was me who took Elle's wrist and pulled her toward the nearest wall. "Pregnant woman coming through," I said. "Give her some room."

"Meg!" Elle protested, digging in the two-inch heels of her vintage sandals.

"Look, it's working," I said as the crowd parted.

We stopped in front of a six-foot photo. "Boy," Elle said, "Emilio was right in saying that his style has changed. I think that winged thing is giving me the evil eye."

The large photograph showed a black-and-white close-up of a stone-carved mythical creature jutting out from the roof of an abandoned building. "Something about it is beautiful. Majestic. Powerful. Almost protective," I said. "Once when we were coming home from location on an *American Home & Garden* shoot, Emilio pulled over on a side street in the worst part of Brooklyn. Then, he got his camera from the back of the van and photographed this horned creature at the top of an old crumbling brownstone."

"A gargoyle?"

"That's what I thought. No, this one was part animal and part human, peering, or should I say leering down, at us. Maybe that's where he got his inspiration for the show?"

Before I could discuss more about the photograph, an obnoxious, seemingly entitled couple shoved their way between us. This time, it was Elle who said to the woman wearing a black large-brimmed sun hat and dark sunglasses, "Watch it. You don't want to be shoving a pregnant lady. Come on, Meg."

Instead of apologizing, the woman gave Elle a scathing look that resembled the grimace of the creature on Emilio's photo.

"Look," I said, not even having enough room to point. "There's an opening in front of the fourth image."

"Say what?" Elle shouted into my right hearing aid. "I can't hear a thing."

"Welcome to my world," I shouted. "Let's go outside and take a breather. We'll come back when the crowd thins." I grabbed her hand and we headed for the door.

Just as we were going out, my father was coming in.

"You might as well come out with Elle and me," I said.

He glanced around the gallery. "Good for Emilio. A packed house," he said, then followed us out the door.

Once outside, the three of us sat on a park bench in front of the gallery. Compared to inside the gallery, the eighty-degree temperature felt like a cool breeze.

"I should have called and told you to come later," I said to my father.

"That wouldn't work," he said, raising an eyebrow. "Isn't that when you told me Patrick and his mother are coming?"

"True," I said.

"She can't be that bad," Elle said, clicking her tongue. "After all, she gave birth to wonderful Patrick."

"Not bad, just high-maintenance," I said.

"Maybe she was having an off day."

My father winked at me. "You're so right, Elle. Meg, you should give Aurora a second chance."

"In that case, Dad, if you feel that way, you should definitely wait around for Patrick and Aurora. Give Aurora a personal tour of Emilio's photographs. Put your money where your mouth is."

If looks could kill. "Touché, daughter."

"I'm parched," Elle said. "I could go for a cold drink."

"Want me to go inside and get some champagne?" I said, standing up.

"Sure. Make sure it's cold."

Darn. I'd been testing her. Elle wasn't pregnant, just hormonal. She'd never drink if she was.

"Dad, want anything?"

"No, I'm good. I'll save your seat. I see people eyeing it."

Inside the gallery, I was happy to see the crowd was thinning. I slithered between a couple of elderly women in pearls arguing over which was better—the American Ballet or the New York City Ballet. When I finally made it to the front of the bar and was ready to order, I got an elbow in the nose. Someone holding an empty wineglass had reached in front of me.

"Another red, buddy boy," the guy demanded. "And is there any way you can get your security team to get these paparazzi clowns off my back?"

"How do you know they're here for you and not Emilio Costello?" I asked a bit snarkily from under the guy's armpit.

"Who the hell is Emilio Costello?" he said, lowering his arm.

"The artist of the exhibit you're here for." Then I said to the bartender, "Two champagnes, please."

I glanced over at the rude guy to see his expression. Smiling, he said, "Put them on my tab. Or would you rather go out for a drink? Somewhere quiet, perhaps?" Then he put his hand on my shoulder.

"The drinks are complimentary," the bartender said.

147

I looked the rude guy in his pale blue eyes. "Even if they weren't complimentary, I can get my own drink, thank you very much. And no, I will not go out for a drink with you. Another thing, don't ever put your hands on me."

He looked around nervously to see if anyone overheard, and a lock of blond hair (professionally highlighted?) fell in front of his right eye. "Do you know who I am?" he said, sticking out his muscled chest.

"No clue," I said. "Maybe you should show me your driver's license so I can take a photo of it. If you ever bother me again, I want to be able to keep you in my crosshairs in case I need a restraining order."

Talk about an incredulous expression. In all his years of stardom, I'd bet no one talked to him like I had. It felt great to get revenge for that scene long ago in the market, when the jerk's security entourage pounced on me after I'd laid *my* hand on his arm.

While Hollywood's number one or two top box office star looked on, the bartender handed me two champagne glasses. I turned and headed for the door. If I'd been wearing a long scarf, I would have whipped its tail in his face. With a self-righteous bounce to my step, I made my way outside.

It's true, karma is a bitch, I thought, remembering Kayla's words about Lauren.

When I reached the park bench, I saw Emilio was there with his arm around Elle's shoulders. All three were laughing about something.

"What's so funny?" I said as my father patted the bench between him and Emilio.

"Just talking about old times," Elle said, her face all aglow. "Emilio was just about to explain the thought behind his exhibition."

"Emilio," I said, sitting down, "it's wonderful from what little I could see. You must be so happy about the turnout."

"Happy and overwhelmed," he said.

"Quite a departure from your elderly faces series," Elle said.

"Not really, when you think about it," Emilio said. "The heads of grotesques tell a story, just like the faces of centenarians."

"Grotesques?" I said.

"Grotesques are the common term given to stone or marble carved figures attached to the façades of buildings."

"Like gargoyles?" Elle asked. "Bet they were used to scare away the devil."

"In some cases, yes. Most served a practical purpose. They were used as a rainspout for runoff water pooling at the top of buildings. That's why many have open mouths. Elle, you're right about the history of grotesques. In twelfth-century Europe, grotesques became the norm for the outside of churches and cathedrals. The hope was they would scare the pagan population into turning to Christianity, making the masses feel safe once they stepped inside and were surrounded by sculptures of saints, cherubs, and angels—a place of safety from evil forces. They were making a promise, come inside and evil won't follow. The different styles of grotesques used over the centuries were a signpost of the time period in which they were created. For example, my Green Man, did you see him inside the gallery?"

"Sadly, or happily, in your case," I said to Emilio, "we could only get close enough to see one of your pieces. What does the Green Man look like?"

"He has rich renaissance ivy foliage coming out of his ears and mouth. You can't miss him. He's half lion, half man. The ivy was meant to show the synthesis of man and nature. A common theme dating back to the Roman Empire. But in my research, it wasn't until about ninety years ago that the Green Man was seen on the façades of buildings.

"No, that wasn't the one we saw," Elle said. "We saw a goat-horned man."

"Emilio," I said, "I noticed all your grotesques were on façades of crumbling buildings in run-down neighborhoods. Like back in the day when we stopped in Brooklyn so you could take some pictures."

"Surprised you remembered," Emilio said with a grin. "I've always had a fascination with decaying buildings."

"Meg and I are big fans of architectural salvage," Elle said. "What are you trying to convey in your photographs?"

"Decay and opulence. Light and dark."

"Like the shadowing in the goat-man photo," Elle said. "There are lots of grotesques in the Harry Potter movies."

"You're right," I said. "I read J. K. Rowling had a bachelor of arts in the classics. There are tons of mythical creatures, half man, half animal, in classical literature. At least from what I remember from my English classes at NYU."

"Exactly," Emilio said.

"I once went to a retrospective of photojournalist Margaret Bourke-White at the Detroit Institute of Art," my father said, turning to Emilio. "One of the photos was from the 1930s. Margaret was sitting on one of two stainless steel gargoyles on the sixty-first floor of Manhattan's Chrysler Building while it was still under construction. Breathtaking exhibit. Margaret even named the gargoyles Min and Bill. They were meant to represent the hood ornaments on Chrysler automobiles."

"Yes. I'm a big fan of Bourke-White's photography," Emilio said. "Min and Bill were functional waterspouts. That photo of her sitting on Min, or was it Bill?" he said, laughing, "was first shown in *Look* magazine, an iconic shot of modern architecture with a touch of medieval. She was the first American female war photojournalist. The first journalist to enter the Soviet—"

A tall, elderly, well-dressed man with a red scarf around his neck walked up to us. "Emilio! There you are! Your admirers are awaiting you. I've already sold two of your photos. You'll never guess who bought them."

Emilio introduced us to the Green Room Gallery's owner, Cabot Harrington. Cabot made quite an impression. I didn't know if it was because tomorrow was the Fourth of July, but he was a doppelganger for Uncle Sam, right down to his tall lanky body and his white goatee. All that was missing was his star-spangled hat and red bow tie.

When Cabot mentioned the name of the celebrity who bought Emilio's work, I almost fell off the bench. Maybe the jerk was humiliated after our tête-à-tête and bought pieces of Emilio's art to show what a big man he was.

"But now, I have Mrs. Caruthers asking about the goat-man."

Emilio said to the three of us, "I better get inside. Please stay after the show if you can, I'll give you a private tour."

"But what if you sell out before then?" Elle said, adding a pouty bottom lip.

"Don't worry," Cabot said, "we just mark the work sold. The buyer comes back at a later date."

After they walked away, I glanced down at my watch. "I hope Patrick arrives after our tour. I think he and his mother should get their own private tour."

"I'll second that," my father said. "In fact, I think I will try to go inside right now and take a gander. I'm glad Emilio gave us a tutorial. I'm excited to see his work."

"I think I might go with you, Jeff," Elle said.

"I'll stay here," I said, searching the grassy area. "Be on the lookout for Aurora."

"Meg, really?" Elle said, clicking her tongue. "She's Patrick's mother. It seems impossible she's that bad. Don't you agree, Jeff?"

"Uh-h-h, yes. Well, she is a colorful character. I'll give you that much."

They got up from the bench. Elle put her arm through my father's elbow. As I watched them walk away, I realized how fortunate I was to have two such wonderful people in my life. And both living in what I now considered my hometown — Montauk.

After they disappeared inside, I scanned the crowd milling around the outside of the gallery and saw a familiar face. Kayla's mother from the other night at Pondfare. I jumped up from the bench and caught her before she stepped inside the gallery.

"Hi, there. You probably don't remember me. I'm Meg. I know your daughter, Kayla. We met at Pondfare."

Her smile morphed into a scowl. "Oh, I remember you," she said. "If you see my daughter, give her a message — all will be forgiven. But only if she leaves that horrid place." With that, she waved me away and went inside.

Holy Moses. That was weird. No way I would give Kayla that message. At least not until after the grand opening tomorrow.

What could be so bad about interning at Dahlia Lane? I thought. Bad enough to tear apart a mother and daughter. Before I'd come up to their table at the restaurant, they seemed to be getting along.

I had a terrible feeling I'd soon find out . . .

Chapter 27

After Emilio gave us a private tour of his work, I breathed a sigh of relief. Patrick had stuck to his word about waiting to bring his mother after the show closed. Speaking of mothers, I'd steered clear of Kayla's mother, watching her exit the exhibit almost as soon as she entered. If I wasn't mistaken, it looked like she'd been crying. I felt a yin-yang tug of wanting to solve the mystery of their falling out and how it related to Kayla interning at Dahlia Lane. Was it any of my business? No. That didn't mean I could let it go. Maybe Emilio would know something. I'd wait till tomorrow and ask him.

Georgia had showed up with Doc. A history freak, she loved the show and promised Emilio he should feel free to display some of his smaller works in the Old Man and the Sea. Georgia was a big supporter of local writers and artists. Before leaving, she'd pulled me aside and said, "Call me tomorrow morning. I might have something exciting to tell you without Doc around. It involves Travis Sterling."

I'd begged her to tell me now, but she'd said it would wait until morning.

Elle left at the same time as Georgia and Doc. I'd recruited my father, after much cajoling, to give me a lift home. He was right to think I had an ulterior motive. He'd know how to handle Aurora when she came. I'd bribed him with a quick recap of Georgia's and my trip to the hit-and-run site, promising if he dropped me at my cottage, I would turn over what we found in the grass where Travis's body was found and tell him about meeting Sadie.

Sure, I could have hitched a ride home with Patrick and his mother, seeing he lived a mile away. However, going with my father seemed a safer option.

"Meg, there you are," Patrick called out from near the gallery's entrance. Thankfully, the *Dave's Hamptons* crew left twenty minutes ago. Now there'd be no need for food critic Aurora to broadcast anything negative about Emilio's show.

Aurora had her arm through Patrick's. When they reached me, Patrick tried to shake her arm away. She wouldn't let him go. He leaned in with her still attached to his hip and gave me a long passionate kiss.

"Darling, such a public display," Aurora said. "I thought I taught you better."

Patrick remained silent but the bulging vein at his temple said everything.

"Aurora," I said, "so happy you made it." I went to her to give her an air kiss, but she backed away.

"Not much of a crowd," she said, glancing around. "Hardly worth coming. I should have stayed at Patrick's, resting up for tomorrow at Dahlia Lane."

I opened my mouth at the same time Patrick said, "Then let's do a quick stroll around, then I'll drive you back."

"I think I've seen enough," Aurora said, eyeing the print directly in front of her. "Bizarre subject matter."

"Not bizarre, Aurora," my father said, coming up from behind her. "Quite interesting, in fact. Come. I'll give you a private tour."

Father to the rescue.

After they walked away, I said to Patrick, "I want you to meet Emilio. Now that he's living in Amagansett, I hope you'll become good friends. But first let me show you his exhibit."

"Sure," he said. "Let's start at that one." He pointed to the opposite side of the gallery from where his mother and my father stood.

"Amazing," Patrick said ten minutes later. "You must love these. I know how much you're into architectural salvage, cornices and what-not."

"What not?" I said, laughing. "And here I thought you were just pretending to be interested when I went on about Elle's and my fixer-upper projects. Don't you think Emilio's grotesques almost seem alive?" After I explained to Patrick what a grotesque was, I said, "I'm not sure I'd want one hanging in my bedroom. But in a modern loft in the city, one of these would be perfect."

"I think at a smaller scale, I could see one in my attic office."

"After the success of this show, I'm sure Emilio will make smaller prints. Just tell him your favorite. I overheard someone say they came because of an e-blast from Ashley's publicity firm. Please thank her."

"I will. She wanted to come but couldn't find a sitter," Patrick said. "She also said she sent out a social media press release for the show in the online version of *Dave's Hamptons.*"

"That explains the great turnout. Though I think after this one, Emilio won't need much more publicity."

"Let's just hope my mother doesn't blow it with her big mouth," he said, frowning. "And I'm worried about tomorrow."

Patrick glanced over at Aurora. "She's never been this bad. I'm sorry. Uh-oh, here she comes." He grabbed my elbow and steered me away. "Meg," he said in a super loud voice, "didn't you want me to meet Emilio? I'm truly a fan. Let's find him."

Emilio was in the gallery's office, sitting in a chair next to a glass desk, holding a sheet of paper in his hands. His smile was as big as one of his six-foot-wide prints.

Before introductions could be made, Aurora burst into the office. "I'm ready to go home, Patrick. I've seen enough."

He gave her an incredulous look. "Don't be so rude, Mother. Meg was just about to introduce us to the show's artist, Emilio Costello. I'm sure you'd love to commend him on his successful show."

She reached out her hand in Cabot's direction. "Nice to meet you. Now can we go?"

"I'm sorry, madame," Cabot said, "I wish I could produce such wonderful works of art, but I'm not Emilio Costello. That genius is sitting right in front of you."

Emilio stood up. "Patrick, it's so nice to meet you. I'm a big fan of your books. I assume this is your lovely mother, Aurora, who Meg has told me so much about. I hope you enjoyed the show?"

Aurora frowned in my direction. "It was too dark for my taste." Then she grudgingly said, "But I could see how some could like it."

"Oh, and how was that, Mother? You could tell by all the sold signs on Emilio's work? It's amazing that with every slightly positive thing you say, there has to be a big negative."

"Patrick! How can you be so cruel? And in front of perfect strangers."

"Emilio, I loved your show, and I hope now that you've moved to the area, we can all get together." He turned to his mother. "I'll be waiting in the car."

Patrick went over to Emilio, shook his hand, blew me a kiss, then left the office.

Aurora stood there with her mouth open, tears welling, her cheeks flushed.

She glanced at me, then flew out of the office.

"I better go follow her," I said to Emilio and Cabot. "Sorry."

I found Aurora in my father's arms, sobbing. "I'm such a terrible mother. I don't blame him for hating me," she said between gulps of air.

My father looked over her head at me and said, "I'm sure that's not true, Aurora. We all make mistakes as parents. I know I have."

She must not have known I was behind her because she kept talking. "I'm afraid your beautiful daughter will take him away from me, just like Catherine did. Doesn't he understand that after my second husband left me, I had to make a living the only way I knew how. The masses thrive on negativity. Just look at social media. No one took me seriously at the paper until I started writing snarky reviews. I love food. Always have. Especially my son's. I've gone too far, now. I'm a bitter old woman who doesn't deserve a second chance —"

"Now, now," my father said as I backed away and slipped out the door to find Patrick.

He was sitting in his Range Rover with the engine running. I opened the door and got in the passenger's seat. His face showed obvious relief when he saw it was me, not his mother.

"You okay?" I asked.

"I'm fine," he said with a smile. "I have a big favor to ask. Do you think you could bring her to the Dahlia Lane shops grand opening, then I'll meet up with you later? I'll owe you big-time."

"Sure," I said, shaking inside at the prospect. "Just don't be late."

"Maybe it's too much for you to handle. I have a morning conference call with my agent and a film producer who might want to buy the rights from my last book for a possible Netflix film. I don't want my mother in the background butting in."

"Of course I'll take her. And congrats. That book will make a great movie. Tough day?"

"I'm sorry if I overreacted. She just knows how to get to me. She wasn't always like this. Not when my father was alive. She remarried soon after my father died. Her second marriage was a disaster. She married a Manhattan restaurant owner who cleaned out all her bank accounts, CDs and retirement account. Then he took up with the restaurant's twenty-something sous chef. After the divorce, her food critic columns changed. I mean, she's always been high-maintenance, but also had a soft side. She knew when she'd gone too far and would always apologize. When I was young, she always encouraged me to write and truly loved my father. She's a gifted writer when she uses it for good."

"Like you," I said quietly.

"She turned her gift into a sword when she got a job as a food critic. I think her bad restaurant reviews had nothing to do with the food. She was just writing them as a form of punishment. An ode to her cheating restaurateur ex."

He was silent for a minute.

I took his hand in mine. "Don't give up hope." Then I told him about what I'd just overheard between my father and Aurora.

"I have been pretty hard on her. When her book came out with the bad review of Catherine's sister's restaurant, I went ballistic. Then after the accident, I was in a dark place. I blocked her number and changed mine. Moved to my cottage and sulked and grieved. Until I met you. I think you saved me."

As we kissed, I held back tears. After breaking apart, I said, "Maybe your mother needs saving now. Just talk to her. What can it hurt?"

"Maybe you're right. Things couldn't get worse."

Chapter 28

Saturday morning I wanted to start my day right. There was no better way to greet the sun than on my beach, sitting on my favorite boulder, which Patrick called my mermaid throne.

What made this particular morning even more special wasn't that it was the Fourth of July, or even the opening of Dahlia Lane Shoppes at the Hangar—it was the Longfellow quote I found in the sand when I reached the bottom of my steps.

> *Look not mournfully into the past, it comes not back again.*
> *Wisely improve the present, it is thine.*

Of course, I read into the quote's deeper meaning. What I gleaned was Patrick and Aurora were making positive strides in their relationship.

The weather was perfect for the opening at the hangar. I'd promised Patrick I would pick up his mother at seven thirty. I'd be lying if I said I wasn't apprehensive about the car ride to East Hampton. People don't change their colors overnight. But there was always hope.

After twenty minutes of mediation, I got up, blew a kiss to a circling seagull and started toward the steps leading to my cottage. Halfway there, my phone vibrated. I'd made it a rule never to bring my phone with me in the mornings. I'd preferred it to be just me and the sea.

This morning was an exception for a good reason—I was waiting for that important call Georgia had promised.

Shielding my phone from the now bright sun, I glanced down.

It was her.

"Georgia." The call went to my hearing aids. Another rule I usually adhered to, never wear hearing aids during my morning sojourns on the beach. "What is it?" I asked. "What did you want to tell me? I hope it's good news."

"I was thinking about our visit yesterday. And then it came to me. Sadie."

"Yes? Sadie. What about her?"

"She has a video doorbell. I heard it make a noise from inside her cottage when I came up behind you on the porch. Think how close her cottage is to the street. The only road leading to the *Culloden* parking lot."

"Holy moly. You're so smart! She might have footage of the car leaving the parking lot during the estimated time of Travis's hit-and-run. Genius!"

"Well, we don't know for sure what kind of video her particular model records. But it's sure worth a try. Tell your father or Arthur. I know it goes without saying that no one should mention this to the public. It would put Sadie at risk. I worry she's all alone out there."

"Of course. Any chance you want to go with me and Patrick's mother for a sneak peak of Dahlia Lane Shoppes at the Hangar before it opens?" I went on to tell her about last night and what I'd overheard from Aurora.

"Don't worry about being alone with her," Georgia chastised. "Remember, both of you love Patrick. It will all work out."

"I hope so," I said with a sigh.

"Sorry, I can't join you. This is one of the Old Man and the Sea's biggest days. After I close, Doc and I will be there at the hangar for the concert and fireworks. Wouldn't miss it."

After I said goodbye, I took a few minutes to reframe the rest of the day, repeating a mantra in my head as I climbed the steps to my cottage, *All is well. All is well. The present is thine—*

After showering, putting my hair in a ponytail and applying sunscreen and light makeup to my face, I went to my small closet, looking for something to wear. After piling a dozen combinations that didn't seem to work onto my bed, I realized why I was having such a hard time. I was worried how Aurora would view me. "Meg Barrett, get a grip," I said out loud.

Jo meowed, then laid her fat furry body on the top of the towering pile of clothing, rendering them wrinkled and cat-haired. "You little brat!"

She looked up at me with an innocent eye, stretched, kneaded a T-shirt, then settled down for her morning nap.

I finally chose a sleeveless ankle-length cotton sundress with tiny red and blue flowers on a white background. Red flip-flops, because there was lots of ground to cover at the hangar. I was going for comfort instead of style.

When I got downstairs, I sent a quick text to my father about the video doorbell. I would let him mention it to Arthur, instead of me.

Before leaving the cottage, I grabbed my white straw sunhat and cross-body bag from the hat rack by the kitchen door and exited.

At seven twenty-five, nervous and panicked with anxiety, I pulled up to Patrick's cottage. Aurora was waiting outside. There was no sign of Patrick. Had I misread the Longfellow quote in the sand? I felt the beginning prickles of the Barrett blotches.

Without a word, Aurora came to the passenger's side of my woody and got in.

"You look lovely, Aurora," I said and meant it. She was also wearing red, white and blue. Classic white linen pants, a red linen blouse, and a red and blue silk scarf at her neck. "Though you might need a hat to protect you from the sun," I said. "Looks like a spectacular day for the grand opening."

"It surely does," she said with a smile as she fastened her seat belt.

A few minutes later as scenic Old Montauk Highway morphed into new Montauk Highway, Aurora said, "Meg, I owe you a huge apology."

I kept quiet. Waiting. It wasn't until we passed the farmer's market in Amagansett that she continued.

"Last night, I had a wonderful talk with my son. We both have four years to make up for. And I realize now I let my bitterness at my ex-husband consume me. The timing for my book wasn't the best, either. Patrick was furious with me for the review I gave Catherine's sister's restaurant. Then, only a few days later, the accident happened. The one time he talked to me, he wasn't making sense. He told me to stay away. I realize now it was his grief talking. I came to the funerals. My publisher put me on a thirty-state book tour. I know now I gave up too easily trying to contact him. I knew he was in a dark place. I should have insisted he see me. So I told myself I would see him when I got home from the tour. By then it was too late. I tried calling him after I returned to Connecticut. It went straight to voicemail. Then a few days later, there was a recording saying his phone was no longer in service. I took the train to Manhattan and found he'd sold his and Catherine's Soho loft.

"He'd moved and I didn't know where. He even changed his phone number. Then recently, I saw him mentioned in an article about the screenplay he was writing for a series to take place in the Hamptons. I contacted Catherine's sister, Sarabeth. She gave me Patrick's address—and, well, you know the rest."

I continued to listen. It made sense in a convoluted type of way. What I couldn't understand was why she waited so long to contact Sarabeth.

But it wasn't up to me to question her. It was up to Patrick.

She stared out the car window, then finally said in a whisper that even with my hearing aids I could barely make out, "Patrick told me that you've helped him deal with his grief. And if I wanted him in my life, you were a package deal. I think I was jealous of your relationship with my son. And I apologize."

I thought of Georgia's earlier words. "We both love Patrick," I said. "That's all that counts. Now let's have some fun. Wait until you see the interior of the hangar. It's amazing."

For the next ten minutes Aurora discussed a few of her favorite episodes from *Jessica's Table*. The conversation went so well that by the time I pulled into the parking lot of Dahlia Lane Shoppes at the Hangar, I felt like pinching myself. I crossed my fingers that this new Aurora would be the same one who'd write the Dahlia Lane article for the *Daily News*.

Chapter 29

The sun was shining, the temperature was in the upper seventies, and there was a light breeze. There was also a huge line snaking its way from the entrance of the hangar to the parking lot. The shops didn't open for another two hours. I considered going to the side entrance Emilio and I took yesterday and banging on the door till someone I knew let us in.

When leaving the Green Room Art Gallery last night, Emilio told me Jessie said we could come a couple hours early to the hangar, *not* wait in any lines, and promised to tell security ahead of time to let us in.

I hadn't heard from Emilio, even though I'd called him last night to see if he was happy about the gallery turnout and to find out what time he planned on being at the hangar. I'd also wanted to give him a heads-up I was bringing Aurora. At seven this morning, I'd sent another text—*Call me!* No response.

Before I could mention our VIP zip-line status to Aurora, she was already ahead of me, parting the crowd on her way to the entrance. When she got to the steps, she looked back at me and motioned for me to follow. Once she reached the security guard at the door, Aurora flashed him what I assumed was a press pass.

"Not fair," I heard someone shout. "We've been waiting here for hours."

I didn't recognize the guard. It wasn't Bryce, but by the size of him he could have been his cousin.

Once inside, I gave Aurora a quick tour of the interior of the hangar. So far, so good. There hadn't been one complaint or frown—only smiles and praise. I exhaled. Could it be true? That today would be a huge success on all fronts?

Even though the hangar didn't open until ten, all the employees stood ready at their stations, dressed in their Dahlia Lane-logoed aprons. The huge skylight was open, showcasing fluffy clouds and blue skies. The air inside the hangar was scented with floral and citrus notes, Dahlia Lane Farms' signature room and linen spray fragrance.

Dahlia Lane Homestyle Eatery didn't open until noon, but as we approached, a young woman was outside, posting the menu on a board by the door. Aurora went up to her and told her about her assignment, then asked if she could do a tour of the restaurant before it opened. "Just to get a first impression of the décor and kitchen setup," she said.

"I don't know," the woman answered. "I don't think anyone's inside."

"Surely the chef de cuisine is inside," Aurora said. "I know prep work must be in the making. It will only take a minute for me to pop my head in. I'm sure Jessica would let me. What do you think, Meg?"

"Uh, she might. Tell you what. I'll go look for her. Ask if" —I glanced at the girl's name badge—"Holly can let you in. Wait here. I'll be right back."

As a reward for Aurora's new and improved sunny disposition, I wanted to offer her carte blanche access to the restaurant. Partly as a test, and partly as a way to remain in her good favor.

I was stunned Aurora didn't put up a fight. She just smiled and nodded her head. "Sounds like a plan," she said as I went in search of Jessie.

Chapter 30

In front of Dahlia Lane Woodworks, I saw Conrad heading toward the front of the hangar at top speed. I could've charged after him and asked permission to enter Dahlia Lane's restaurant, but because of the scowl on his face, decided not to. Instead, I stepped into the shop. David was standing behind the woodblock counter with a huge grin on his face.

"I was going to ask if you were ready for the grand opening," I said, "but I can tell you are."

"I'm counting the minutes," he said. "Or should I say, hour and a half. I may have had too many cups of Dahlia Lane Farms dark roast coffee. I'm feeling jittery and anxious. I don't want to let Ms. Sterling down by screwing anything up."

"Not possible. You've got this."

"I'm here alone. But an hour after we open there will be three of us."

I kept to myself about the line outside, which most likely had doubled or tripled from when Aurora and I first walked in. "Hey, you haven't seen Ms. Sterling, have you?"

"No. Actually, I was hoping to. I want to wish her good luck. Not that she needs it. Mr. Kincaid was just here, doing an inspection. He seemed pretty nervous himself."

"Well, I'm sure you'll have a great day. I'll be back to purchase a few things." I glanced over at the cabinet holding the hand-forged hardware. I had an antique pine desk I'd been working on in my design studio that needed new old-looking hardware. I took one more glance around the shop, feeling a lump in my throat at the thought Travis Sterling would never see the fruits of his labor. Thankfully, Jessie would.

"Take care," I said to David, heading to Dahlia Lane Woodworks' door. I'd left Aurora waiting too long. Who knew what mischief she might be getting into?

"You too," David said. "Oh, wait, can you do me a favor?"

"Sure. What is it?

"Mr. Kincaid dropped this a few minutes ago. Do you mind giving it to him?"

"Of course not."

David handed me a folded piece of paper. I didn't look at it, just stuffed it in my handbag, anxious to get back to the restaurant and Aurora. "As soon as I see him," I lied. The last thing I wanted to do was talk to Conrad while I had Aurora in tow.

Five minutes later, I gave up. There was no sign of Jessie. But I did see Bryce and Kayla standing near the side entrance next to Conrad's office.

Emilio was also missing in action. Maybe he slept late because of his gallery showing. Though, I knew he was just as excited about today as I was.

I pasted on a huge smile and walked up to Bryce. "Bryce, can I ask a favor?" He looked down at me with his usual grimace. "Do you think you could let me inside the restaurant before it opens?"

"Uh, why should I?" he said. "What business do you have going inside?"

"Bryce!" Kayla said in a stern tone. "I don't see a problem. I think the door's probably open." She looked up at Bryce. "Didn't you tell me you saw Jessie go in there about an hour ago."

He shrugged his massive shoulders, then we heard a loud crash coming from inside Dahlia Lane Paper and Books. "What the hell!" he shouted, charging toward the shop.

"I think Bryce takes his security job very seriously," Kayla said with a smile. "Come. Let's go check out Dahlia Lane Homestyle Eatery. Maybe Jessie's still there. I need to ask her what time she wants me to pass out the tarts. I wheeled them all over last night and put them in the restaurant's walk-in.

We found Aurora sitting on a bench outside the restaurant, looking down at her phone. Her eyes lit up when she saw us.

"Aurora, I'd like you to meet Kayla, Jessie's intern. Kayla helps Jessie with the cooking and gardening segments." I turned to Kayla, trying to think of how to introduce Patrick's mother. I kept it simple. "Ms. Montague is writing an article on Dahlia Lane Shoppes at the Hangar for the *Daily News*. She wants to see the restaurant and kitchen before it opens. Maybe chat with the chef de cuisine."

Aurora stood, then held out her hand like she wanted Kayla to kiss it. "Charmed, I'm sure." The adage *a leopard can't change its spots* came to mind. Maybe this wasn't a good idea.

Kayla grinned and shook her hand. "How exciting to be a writer.

Though, I don't know if Chef Sully is in yet. The restaurant doesn't open until noon."

"Well, let's have a quick look-see, anyway. What do you think?" Aurora said, flashing Kayla a perfect pearly white smile before she turned toward the restaurant's main entrance.

Kayla only hesitated a moment before saying, "Sure."

We followed Kayla inside and waited until she found the light switch.

Once illuminated, the restaurant was everything I'd imagined it to be. Dahlia Lane's, or should I say Jessie's, signature homey and functional touches were everywhere. Teal glass vases filled with dahlias topped each natural wood four- and six-top table. Industrial brushed-steel chairs with sea green suede upholstered seats added a touch of modern to the eclectic décor. The walls were covered in large sepia-colored landscapes of Dahlia Lane Farms. In each landscape there was a pop of color. I had a feeling Emilio must have been the photographer.

I walked up to one of the photographs for a closer look. Kayla came up behind me. "Aren't they amazing. I don't know how she does it. Everything she touches is magic. The opposite of her cousin."

Turning to Aurora, I said, "What do you think?" I held my breath as she came up next to us.

"Very tasteful. I'm not surprised. Let's just hope the cuisine matches up to the ambiance," she said a tad arrogantly. I hoped that didn't mean she planned to stay until noon. I'd told Patrick I'd drop her back at eleven, after he had his business video call. Then tonight we would go together for the concert and fireworks.

"Oh, it will!" Kayla said. "You wouldn't believe all the top chefs Lauren forced Jessie to interview. Jessie passed on them all. Instead, she hired a local chef with no professional cooking school experience or Michelin stars."

"Bet Lauren wasn't happy about that," I said.

Kayla winked and smiled. "You got that right."

"Lauren?" Aurora questioned, examining the wineglasses hanging over the bar like she was a health inspector. *Was she looking for fingerprints?* Again, a warning bell went off.

"Lauren is Jessica's cousin," I said.

"Oh, wasn't there some kind of scandal with her?"

"Not a scandal," I said. "She just tried to start her own—"

"Copycat version of Dahlia Lane Farms," Kayla finished for me. "Lavender Fields went belly-up, bankrupt."

Aurora clicked her tongue in distaste. "Oh, yes. I—"

"Water under the bridge," I said, cutting her off. "Everything is good now."

Kayla gave me a raised eyebrow. All I needed was Aurora to mention Jessie's cousin's downfall in her article.

"So Kayla," I said, "tell us about Dahlia Lane's chef. You said he was local. Was he chef anyplace I might have been to?"

Aurora took a few steps toward the kitchen. "Why don't we just meet him or her in person?" she said, nodding toward the double swinging doors."

"Comfort Kitchen is the name of Chef Sully's restaurant."

"In Bridgehampton?" I asked. "I love that place. He makes awesome food. Comfort food that's good for you."

"How is that possible?" Aurora asked. "Never heard of Comfort Kitchen."

"It's only been around for about three years," I said. "So you probably wouldn't know about it."

Aurora startled, then looked away. By reminding Aurora about the time she'd been away from the Hamptons and her son, I'd just put my size eight foot in my mouth.

Luckily, Kayla broke the silence. "Just last week, I was one of the lucky ones to taste a sample of everything on today's menu. Travis—"

"Poor man," Aurora said. "So tragic. My son said no one's claimed responsibility for his hit-and-run?"

Trying to keep things on an even keel, I chirped, "There's a light on in the kitchen. Should we go check if Jessie or the chef is in there?"

I didn't have to twist Aurora's arm.

Like a bat outta—she went flying through the swinging kitchen doors.

Ten seconds later the screaming commenced . . .

Chapter 31

I grabbed Kayla's wrist and we sprinted toward the kitchen. When I reached the still-swinging doors, I said, "Wait here. I'm sure it's nothing."

Kayla just nodded her head and took a step backward.

Taking a deep inhale, I pushed against the doors and stepped inside.

Crouching on the floor next to Jessie's still body was Aurora. She held Jessie's limp wrist in her trembling hand. With tear-filled eyes, she looked up at me. "She's dead. Jessica Sterling is dead."

Jessie was lying facedown, her dark hair fanned around her. "Impossible," I said. "She can't be."

"There's no pulse," Aurora said.

"We have to do CPR. There should be a defibrillator in here somewhere," I said, frantically glancing around the kitchen.

From behind me, I heard Kayla scream.

There wasn't time for hysteria. I said, "Kayla, call 911 and find the defibrillator."

I got on my knees next to Aurora. "We need to turn her over." I pressed my hands against Jessie's left shoulder. Aurora put her hands on Jessie's left hip. Working together we flipped her onto her back.

Judging by the red bandanna tied around her neck, her swollen blue face and bulging *navy* eyes—there wasn't any need for life support.

Chapter 32

"Oh my God!" Aurora shrieked. "That's not Jessica Sterling."

"You're right," I whispered, "It's her cousin, Lauren." I knew if I relived the scene later in my mind, I'd feel guilty about the relief I'd felt that the dead — murdered — body in front of me wasn't Jessie's.

Lauren must have listened to Jessie's suggestion on how to dress for the grand opening. She was wearing something either from her cousin's wardrobe or Dahlia Lane Clothing Supply. The explanation for why we thought facedown Lauren was Jessie.

Now, the big question was, did someone purposely murder Lauren? Or was Jessie the killer's target?

There wasn't any time to work it out, because Kayla, soon followed by Conrad and Bryce, charged into the kitchen.

When Kayla glanced down at Lauren's still body, she choked back a sob before saying, "Thank God! It's not Jessie."

Conrad gave Kayla a scathing look, pushed her aside and sprinted toward us. He dropped to his knees and went to cradle Lauren's head. "What-t-t happened?" he moaned. His eyes met mine, then they trailed back down to his wife's bloated face.

On instinct, I said, "I don't think you should touch anything until the police arrive."

Now it was my turn to feel his anger. "I'll do what I damn well please. She's my wife." Tears coursed down his tanned cheeks. "Are you sure she's —" He reached to untie the bandanna at her neck.

"Stop!" I said. "You really shouldn't do that. The police will want the scene to be as untouched as possible."

Aurora put her hand on Conrad's shoulder. "I can confirm she's dead. I'm the one who found her. You can be confident, if I thought there was a chance she was alive, I would have performed CPR."

"Aurora," I whispered, "maybe we should wait outside for the paramedics and police."

A voice boomed from the direction of the swinging doors, "That's a good idea, Ms. Barrett." Arthur came over to us. "Everyone out. Please wait in the dining room."

"I'll do no such thing, Detective," Conrad said, standing up. "Someone just killed my wife. They could be out there right now."

"My team is stationed at the exits. None of your employees will be able to leave until their driver's licenses are scanned and phone numbers taken." Looking down at me, he said, "Why am I not surprised you're here."

I shrugged my shoulders in innocence, my emotions too tangled in the horror of it all to defend myself.

Arthur went to stand behind Conrad. "Everyone needs to step away from the body. I'll also need access to the hangar's security camera footage."

"Bryce is in charge of security," I said, nodding my head in Bryce's direction.

As far as I knew, Arthur and Bryce hadn't met. But it wouldn't be hard for Arthur to figure out just by his size and wide-legged military stance he was Dahlia Lane's head of security.

"Please go out and talk to Officer Martinez," Arthur directed Bryce. "He's stationed outside the restaurant doors. Show him your control room."

Seconds after Bryce left the kitchen, the paramedics charged through the swinging doors.

"Now the rest of you wait in the restaurant. I'll talk to everyone personally." Arthur narrowed his large brown eyes on me. "Especially you, Ms. Barrett."

Aurora glanced from me to Arthur, then back again, giving me a questioning look. I'd have to explain later about my relationship with my best friend's husband, who happened to be the chief homicide detective for the East Hampton Town Police Department. I'd also make sure not to share about all the past homicides I'd been involved in since moving to the Hamptons.

Oh, how I wished Patrick would show up and whisk Aurora away. And where were Emilio and Jessie? I didn't think my heart could take any more if something happened to them. "Come, Aurora," I said, gently putting my hand on her arm. "Let's let the professionals handle things."

Thankfully, she listened and got up without complaint. We stood, and I slipped my arm in hers. When we reached the swinging doors, I held one side open for her to pass through. She stopped and turned around. "I think you could have a better bedside manner, Detective. We're all traumatized. I'm the one who found her, and—" Before she went further, I gave her a little shove out the door.

So many things were spinning inside my head. So much so, I almost fainted at the sight of Emilio in the restaurant's dining room.

Jessie was noticeably missing.

Emilio was seated at a table for four with a young female officer. When he saw me, he jumped up from the table, ran toward us and took me in his arms.

All the while, Aurora looked on.

Emilio pushed back the hair by my right ear, then he whispered into my hearing aid, "They won't tell me anything. What happened?"

"Lauren's dead. Murdered." I felt Aurora's eyes on us. I struggled out of Emilio's embrace and choked back a sob, and said to him, "Jessie. Please tell me Jessie's okay."

Emilio looked toward the officer at the table. "Is it okay if I talk to my friend for a minute?"

Before the officer could answer, the doors from the kitchen opened and we watched Kayla enter the dining room.

"Kayla," Emilio said, "why don't you have a seat. You don't look too well."

"Neither do you," she said. Then under her breath, "It was awful, we thought it was Jessie. Who would do something so terrible? Where's Jessie?" Her eyes darted around the restaurant. "She's not here? What if someone did to her what they did to Lauren?"

"What did they do to Lauren?" Emilio asked.

"They choked her to death—"

"That's enough, young lady!" Arthur said, holding the door from the kitchen so Conrad could walk through. "No one is to discuss anything between yourselves. You," he said, pointing to Kayla, "sit here." He pulled out a chair for her at the nearest table. "The rest of you take a seat at your own table. I'll call you one by one." Then he looked directly at me. "No chatting."

"This is unconscionable," Conrad said. "We can't sit around. We have to find my wife's killer. And Jessie. Where is Jessie? She hasn't been here all morning."

"No more questions," Arthur ordered. "This is a homicide crime scene. And I am in charge." In a softer tone, he said, "Please take a seat, Mr. Kincaid. Everything that can be done is being done."

"Detective," Emilio said, "is it okay if I leave? I've already talked to Officer Rider."

Arthur looked to his officer.

She glanced down at her notepad. "We're all done."

"Okay," Arthur said. "You can leave, Mr. Costello. I know Meg, Ms. Barrett, has your contact info."

Aurora cleared her throat and lasered her blue-green eyes on me. I pictured her going back to Patrick and telling him that Emilio and I were in a romantic tryst. The least of my worries right now.

Emilio gave me a soulful look before moving toward the restaurant's exit. When he reached the door, he turned, looked at me, then mouthed, "Jessie's okay. She's in the hospital . . ."

The last word I read from his lips was *Poisoned!*

If Aurora hadn't been staring at me, I wouldn't have folded onto the restaurant's gleaming hardwood floor.

Chapter 33

Patrick picked up Aurora from the hangar as soon as she'd been questioned and released.

After Kayla left, so did Officer Rider. Leaving me, Conrad and Arthur in the restaurant.

"I need to leave," Conrad shouted at Arthur. "I need to tell Lauren's family about what happened. Make arrangements. Can't this all wait? And what about Jessie? Is she okay? I'll come down to the station later. Shouldn't you be out looking for my wife's killer? I need to send home my employees."

"That's already been taken care of," Arthur said. "My team, with the help of Suffolk County and the New York State Troopers, have everything under control."

As if he felt my eyes on him, Conrad spun around and faced me. "Why the hell is she here, anyway? This is personal family business."

"Ms. Barrett was the second person to enter the kitchen," Arthur said, loosening his tie. "Her eyewitness account will be crucial to our investigation."

"Let her go first, then. I would like to hear how my wife was found."

"Not an option," Arthur said, then nodded his head at me. "Ms. Barrett, please take a seat at that table in the far right corner. You, Mr. Kincaid, can follow me to the other side of restaurant. I promise, what we discuss will be out of *ear*shot."

Was it my imagination or did Arthur say the word *ear* louder than the rest of his sentence? To top that off, Arthur sat at the table first so he was facing me.

In perfect lip-viewing position.

Had Arthur placed his chair in my eyeline so I could learn what was being said without giving away police evidence? Was Detective Arthur Shoner finally thinking of me as an asset?

And what a lip-read it turned out to be. It took everything I had to keep from bouncing out of my chair and running over to make sure what I deciphered was correct.

In a platinum nutshell, I gleaned Arthur had been on his way to arrest someone for Travis's hit-and-run when he got the call from the 911 dispatcher. Which explained why he showed up just moments after Aurora found Lauren.

Arthur told Conrad there was video footage of Lauren driving her Mercedes away from the scene of the hit-and-run minutes after Travis's phone call with his sister.

Lauren had killed Travis.

Go, Sadie! And Go, Georgia for thinking of Sadie's video doorbell.

There was no reason to read Conrad's lips when he shouted, "What are you suggesting, Detective? That my wife ran down her cousin, then fled the scene! That's ludicrous. You're accusing my newly murdered wife of being a murderer? Have you lost your mind?"

Arthur kept his cool. "So, let me get this straight. You had no idea your wife hit Mr. Sterling, then fled the scene?"

"Of course not."

"Can you provide an alibi for Wednesday morning?"

"Yes, I can. I was here at the hangar checking in inventory for the opening. Do I need a lawyer?" Conrad asked, getting up from his seat. His eyes locked on mine, as if he'd forgotten I was in the room. He looked down at Arthur, who was still seated. "I'm leaving. Unless you want to arrest me? In that case—"

"Not at this time. I only came here for your wife," Arthur said.

"Where is Jessica Sterling?" Conrad asked again, glancing around the restaurant as if she might pop up from behind the bar. "She never showed this morning. I've been calling her. Oh my God. Did this maniac do something to her, too? You know my wife has, *had*, a stalker. Poison pen letters."

I gasped and about jumped out of my skin at the word *poison*.

Coincidence or Freudian slip?

"We do know about the letters. But, as of yet, we haven't seen one. Not that we haven't tried reaching Mrs. Kincaid. Maybe you could provide us with them. It would help our inquiries into your wife's death."

"Death!" Conrad screeched. "You mean murder, Detective. I'm not sure where she kept them. I'll check when I get home."

Try her handbag, I thought.

"We'll do the checking," Arthur said. "The judge signed a warrant to search your house and your wife's car. They should be showing up any minute."

"Shouldn't I be there?" Conrad asked. "Let me rephrase that. I insist on being there."

Arthur stood. He reached out and put his hand on Conrad's arm. "You are free to go. I'm not arresting you. You've had a shock. And, you're right. This isn't the time or place. I will be in touch. Later today. I'm sorry for your loss."

Conrad opened his mouth, thought better of it, then closed it. Silently, he strode to the door and knocked to be let out. An officer opened the door, then raised his hand up to keep Conrad back. Arthur nodded his head and said, "You can escort Mr. Kincaid to his car. Make sure he leaves the grounds."

Conrad pushed the officer to the side and walked through the door and into the hangar.

"Well, that was revealing," I said at the same time Officer Rider came flying through the door.

"We got him, Detective. And he's confessed to his part. They're waiting for you at the station."

"Who? Who do you have, Arthur?" I asked.

Instead of answering me, he said, "Officer Rider, get a statement from Ms. Barrett. Then let her go." With that, he left the restaurant.

There were so many things I wanted to ask him. Especially about Jessie's poisoning. Who confessed? Officer Rider had just said "We got *him*." There were three men at Dahlia Lane she could be referring to—Conrad, Pete and Bryce.

Had I forgotten anyone?

Yes, my subconscious answered.

Emilio . . .

Chapter 34

When I walked out of the deathly quiet hangar, my legs felt numb. I was barely able to propel myself forward from all the stress of the past couple hours. If I did fall, the plainclothes officer escorting me to my car would surely help me up. Right? With all the scenarios whirling around, not only my legs felt numb, but also my brain.

I tried to start up a conversation, even name-dropping that Detective Arthur Shoner was a friend, but the officer just followed behind me in silence. Maybe he was working a drug case as an undercover circus mime.

When we reached my woody, I shakily got out my keys, then hit the key fob to unlock the doors. That's when I saw it. Someone had left a folded piece of paper on my windshield.

I twisted my body to face Officer Mime, leaned my spine against the woody, then reached behind me, grabbed the paper, then stuffed it in the pocket of my dress.

I thought I knew who it was from.

Emilio.

All questions would soon be answered.

"Okay. Thanks for the escort," I said.

He just nodded his head and waited until I was inside my car.

I was dying to read the note. Instead, I waved and backed out. Glancing in the rearview mirror, I saw I was still being watched. I pulled out of the empty lot. Empty, with the exception of a dozen law enforcement vehicles. The same lot that was packed with cars looking forward to the grand opening that wasn't. I had half a mind to make a U-turn. Drive over to Windmill Cottage or the farmhouse to see if Emilio's car was there. But why would it be, if Jessie was in the hospital? Poisoned.

As I pulled onto the street that would lead me to East Hampton's Main Street, I noticed a golf cart, tipped over and lying on its side. From far away, I wasn't able to discern if it was one of Dahlia Lane's, but it sure looked like it. Strange that it was on its side like that. If I wasn't so exhausted, I'd drive up and look inside.

The adage *I'll sleep when I die* came to mind. Checking to make sure no one was following me, I veered off the road and pulled up to the golf cart.

I was right. The golf cart did display the Dahlia Lane flower and vine logo. Not only that, but hanging from a hook was Pete's Hermès leather garden holster. I knew not to touch anything. Did someone run him off the road? I thought, shivering.

I searched the area, which was easy to do because it was an open field. Thankfully, there was no dead body. Before getting back in my woody, I shot a photo of the golf cart and another with a close-up of Pete's garden holster, then sent them to Arthur. My job was done.

I got into the car and headed for home. Home. My favorite four-letter word.

As I passed through East Hampton, I realized I was jealous of all the tourists and summer people strolling the tree-lined streets, oblivious to the fact someone had just been murdered. Scratch that— two people had been murdered. My heart thumped when I remembered looking at Lauren, thinking she was Jessie. I needed to speak to my father. Needed him to make some kind of sense of it all. Per Arthur, Lauren had killed Travis. Emilio said Jessie had been poisoned. Was Jessie poisoned by the same person who killed Lauren? If that was the case, Lauren wasn't killed by someone thinking she was Jessie. And then there was the "him" that had been arrested.

In Amagansett, the tears started to flow. As soon as I hit Old Montauk Highway, I pulled into a secluded parking area overlooking a calm Atlantic.

Putting the car into Park, I pulled out the note I'd found on my windshield and unfolded it. As I thought, it was from Emilio.

> *Picking up Jessie soon from the hospital.*
> *Come tonight at nine to Windmill Cottage.*
> *Bring your father. We have a lot to show*
> *you. E.*

I would do everything Emilio asked, including inviting my father.

Did Jessie know who killed her cousin? The same person who poisoned her?

Maybe I was reading into things. Perhaps she'd been *food* poisoned. Ate a bad oyster or clam.

Now, all I had to do was keep calm and wait until nine.

Chapter 35

When I walked into my cottage, Jo just about tripped me, then made a mad dash for her food bowl. I smiled at the consistency of it all. It helped me to feel grounded after what happened at the hangar.

I glanced around my small, perfect (at least to me) cottage. I'd decorated it to feel cozy and safe. There was a handmade fluffy throw draped around the back of the love seat next to the fireplace, made by Georgia in shades of sand and sea. The Longfellow book, also from Georgia, was on the coffee table. The next Dead Poets Society meeting on Tuesday was supposed to take place at Patrick's. Longfellow surely had a few things to say about death — murder, not so much. He did write, "Into each life some rain must fall." Poor Jessie. I hoped after the news of Lauren, Jessie's fiancé would be on the next plane. Another Longfellow quote came to mind. *Be still, sad heart, and cease repining. Behind the clouds is the sun still shining.*

I prayed it would be so.

I wasn't in a hurry to get on the phone with my father or Arthur, begging them to fill in all the blanks regarding Travis's and Lauren's murders. All I wanted right now was to feed my cat, grab a bottle of water and sit on my deck. At nine o'clock tonight, I was sure all things would be answered. I needed to focus on the fact Jessie was coming home from the hospital, Travis's hit-and-run solved, and maybe Lauren's murderer caught.

Chapter 36

I pulled up to Windmill Cottage thirty minutes early.

It had been torture counting the minutes and hours until meeting my father. As a favor to me, Patrick was taking his mother to Sarabeth's. She wanted to make amends. A good sign. He'd listened to my version of what went down at the hangar. I was sure his mother's version was completely different. I'd also told him about the note Emilio left and about his request my father and I meet him and Jessie at Dahlia Lane. Since we still didn't know who killed Lauren, Patrick warned me to be careful. That was one reminder I didn't need. I knew from experience all the twists and turns a murder investigation could take. Deadly turns.

There was one good thing to look forward to later. Patrick promised after Aurora was tucked in bed, he'd walk up the beach and tuck me in as well. Silver lining if there ever was one.

I parked behind Emilio's Kia. The gates to Dahlia Lane Farms had been open when I arrived. Had it only been Tuesday that I'd been so excited about working for Jessie? There was a light on in Windmill Cottage, but I'd promised my father I'd wait until he arrived before going inside.

Suddenly, the sky exploded with fireworks. I'd almost forgotten it was the Fourth of July. I got out of the woody and hopped on the hood to watch the show. The fireworks were amateur at best. I'm sure nothing like what Jessie and Travis had planned for tonight, but still bright enough to light up the area by the gazebo.

Was I hallucinating? Were there two figures running across the lawn near the gazebo?

One of them was tall. Giant-size tall. Bryce tall. One of them was short, Kayla short.

I couldn't tell if Bryce was chasing Kayla or running with her.

I slid off the hood of my car and zoomed in their direction, happy I was wearing my running sneakers. "Wait. Stop!"

I tried to keep my eyes on them, but they disappeared into the darkness.

There wasn't a moon and the fireworks display had ended. The pair had simply vanished.

I had a flashback to another time when chasing someone didn't turn out as planned. Completely unlike me, I made a very mature decision. I turned back toward my car, where hopefully my father was waiting.

It was then that I felt it.

It knocked me to my knees.

My muscles convulsed in ropes of excruciating pain as the electrical current traveled up and down my spine.

I'd been tased.

"Bryce!" Kayla screamed. "Why did you do that! Are you crazy?"

"I did it for you," I thought I heard him say.

In a blur, I saw Kayla bend down to look at me. She said, "We have to get her inside. I don't want to run anymore."

Chapter 37

Once again, we were gathered in Windmill Cottage's Tulip Room. Bryce, Kayla, my father, Emilio, Jessie and me.

"It was me," Kayla sobbed. "I sent Lauren the letters. I was here a few minutes ago, trying to retrieve the last letter before the police found it and they falsely arrested me for Lauren's murder. I didn't kill her, I swear!"

Jessie was sitting across from me on an upholstered chair, her feet on an ottoman. Her face seemed washed of color, but her eyes were bright in her beautiful face. I could tell she'd been crying by the overflowing pile of tissues in a small wastebasket by her feet.

"Why, Kayla?" Jessie asked, her eyes searching Kayla's face. "Why would you send those letters to her?"

Kayla was on her knees, crouched next to Jessie's chair. Between sobs, she got out her story in short jerky bursts. "My father was Lauren's CFO at Lavender Fields Farm. Right before the business went under, Lauren blamed him for its demise. She lied, said he was cooking the books. She was the one taking money out of the business for her own use. Not only was my father innocent, he was getting ready to report what was going on to the IRS. She caused his stroke by warning him if he didn't keep quiet, she'd make sure he went to jail. Now he just sits there. No interest in anything. My mother and I—"

"Take your time," Jessie said, patting her on the shoulder. "Why didn't you just come to me—or Travis?"

"It was Travis who hired me as an intern. He found out what happened to my father and came to our house to talk to him. Travis also hired me to make sure Lauren didn't do anything to you, Jessie. He was worried Lauren was up to something with the business, like she'd done at Lavender Fields during the short time she owned it. Travis brought me in as an unpaid intern but was putting money in my bank account to help with our bills and medical expenses. We lost the house because of Lauren. Now we live in a one-bedroom rental. Travis wanted to make amends to my family for what Lauren did. But the notes were my idea. Mine alone. I couldn't stand what she'd done to my wonderful, loving father. I would never do anything physical to anyone. I swear."

No, but Bryce would, I thought, still feeling the aftereffects of my tasing. "I assume that until I blabbed," I said, "your mother didn't know you were working at Dahlia Lane. Is that why she was so angry with you?" I was lying on the love seat, feeling like my muscles and brain were made of Jell-O. Bryce kept sending furtive glances at my father, who was standing behind the love seat in protective mode.

Earlier, when my father heard me howl after being tased by Bryce, he came charging to my rescue. He gave Bryce a one-two punch that sent him to his knees. Just like Bryce had done to me with the Taser. No one hurt his little girl.

"Yes," Kayla said, wiping her forearm across her wet eyes. "After my father's stroke, when my mother found out Lauren was let back into Dahlia Lane, she wanted nothing to do with her or Dahlia Lane. That's why I couldn't tell them I was working here. It would kill my father. He's a bitter man, not the father I've known all my life. He used to be like you, Jeff." She looked from my father to Jessie, her eyes feverish in her small face. "Jessie, I swear, working with you was the best thing that ever happened to me. I just wanted Lauren to pay for what she did. I really did look after you. Plus, I wanted to help your brother because he'd been so good to us. I didn't kill Lauren."

"Damn right you didn't kill her," Bryce said. "You were with me all morning. I gave the police the footage of the restaurant's outside delivery door and the entrance from the hangar. It will prove we're both in the clear."

I got up on one elbow and craned my neck at Bryce. "Didn't you say you saw Jessie go into the restaurant this morning?"

"You did, Bryce," Kayla answered for him. "But now we know it was Lauren, not you, Jessie."

"She was dressed like you, Jessica," Bryce said.

That made Jessie stifle a sob. "For once she listened to me. Oh my God, does that mean I might have been the killer's target? I can't handle this. It's all too much. First my brother, now my cousin. Who would do this?"

No one answered. But I had a feeling whoever killed Lauren wasn't in this room.

"Did you see anyone else go into the restaurant after that?" my ex-cop father asked Bryce.

"No. But this morning Kayla and I were all over the place."

"Kayla," I said, trying to sit up. "You told me you went to the restaurant in the hangar last night to put the tarts in the walk-in fridge. Was anyone else there?"

"Yes. Chef Sully. He can vouch that I came and went. I didn't have a key, anyway."

"But Lauren did?"

"I have no idea," Kayla said, turning to Jessie. "If you want to arrest me for sending the notes, I understand."

"And if you want to arrest me," Bryce said, handing my father the Taser, "you can. I was only trying to protect Kayla."

"Bryce didn't know about the notes," Kayla said. "I only told him tonight, because I had to retrieve the last note I'd left for Lauren. I didn't want anyone to think I killed her."

My father glanced down at me. "Well, do you want to press charges against him for the Taser?"

"Not right now. But I think Jessie will agree: Kayla, you need to confess to Detective Shoner about the notes. And it will be better if it's before they find your prints and compare handwriting."

"Of course, I'll do anything. Please don't hate me, Jessie."

"I don't hate you, Kayla. If my brother wanted to help you and your family, then I will do the same. But for now, I need to process Lauren's death. If that's possible."

"I understand. I will go to the police right now and turn myself in," Kayla said. "Bryce, will you take me? I don't trust myself driving."

"If you're sure?" he said. "I hope you know what you're doing."

Before they left the room, Kayla came over to me. "Meg, I'm so sorry you got hurt because of me. When and if you forgive me, and I don't go to jail," she said, looking up at my father, "I'd like to make amends. And to you, too, Jessie."

Jessie just looked away, tears in her eyes. "We need time, Kayla."

Kayla turned to Bryce. "Please go to the car. I'll be right there. I want to share something with Jeff."

My father looked surprised but followed them out of the room.

"Do you really think she'll turn herself in?" I asked Jessie.

"She seems sincere. I know it was Travis who brought her to Dahlia Lane as an intern. If he was helping her family financially, then I think I should believe she'll talk to the police."

Chapter 38

My father came back into the room. I could tell by the set of his jaw he wasn't about to share what Kayla just told him. "So, Emilio, my daughter said you wanted us both to come here. Was it about the letters? And Ms. Sterling, Meg also said you were in the hospital because you were poisoned."

"I'm fine. Thanks to Emilio. He stopped by last night to see if I was all set for this morning at the hangar."

"Wilhelmina and I found her in the bathroom," Emilio said, looking over at her with affection. "She'd been vomiting all night and had bad stomach pains. She wouldn't let me call an ambulance, so I drove her to Southampton."

"Emilio stayed the night with me. They said it looks like I ingested some kind of poison. The results haven't come in yet, but I feel completely fine now."

"Did you inform the police?" I asked, feeling relief that Emilio had nothing to do with Lauren's death.

"Yes," Jessie answered. "Detective Shoner called to tell me about Lauren. So he knows I was in the hospital."

"So why are we here?"

"It's not about the threatening letters," Jessie said. "Although I'm glad that's cleared up. Last night before I got sick, I went into Travis's office and found the video footage he took of the shops at the hangar to put on our website and social media. I don't know how it all fits in now, but Emilio insisted I call you and show it to you and your father."

"Jeff, if you don't mind, please take a seat next to Meg," Emilio said, gesturing to the spot next to me on the love seat.

I managed to slowly sit up. My father sat next to me, took my hand and squeezed it. "How's my little troublemaker doing?"

I stuck out my tongue, then squeezed his hand back.

Jessie opened a laptop and handed it to my father. He placed it on the small table in front of us and tapped the screen's play icon.

The footage showed the interior of Dahlia Lane Woodworks. Near the end, Travis focused the camera on a stack of wood dough bowls. We watched Travis pick up one of the bowls and turn it over. The camera zeroed in on a small sticker. It read, *Made in China.*"

For at least five minutes, we watched Travis turn over every item in Dahlia Lane Woodworks. Before the screen went black, we could hear Travis say, "Conrad, you better have a good explanation."

"What am I missing?" my father said.

"Oh, you don't know, do you?" I said.

"Know what?" he asked.

"Everything being sold in Dahlia Lane Shoppes at the Hangar either had the Dahlia Lane brand or is handmade by local artisans. Those bowls are supposed to be hand-carved. Not mass-produced."

"And that's a big deal why?"

"For one thing, Jeff," Jessie said, "those bowls have a high price on them because they were supposed to be one of a kind. My brother assumed the invoices Conrad gave him were for handmade locally sourced products. He would cut a check and give it to Conrad to pay the vendors. I've had Emilio search Travis's office. We found this invoice," she said, waving a piece of paper in the air. "Then I made a call to the vendor. They had no idea what we were talking about. They never sent any of their products to Dahlia Lane. Initially, they said Travis personally contacted them and promised they would be one of Dahlia Lane Woodworks' suppliers. Then the next day a woman called from Dahlia Lane, saying they'd found someone else."

"You think Lauren is that woman?" my father asked.

"I think," Emilio said, glancing at Jessie, "Lauren and Conrad were scamming Dahlia Lane and keeping the difference between the invoiced price of goods and the overseas price."

"That's the problem," Jessie added. "We still don't know if this was Conrad's idea or somehow Lauren got him involved."

"Travis sounded angry with Conrad. Not Lauren," I said. "I remember those bowls mentioned on the invoice. In fact, I was in Dahlia Lane Woodworks this morning. David, the salesclerk, told me Conrad had been in and he dropped something. It's in my handbag."

My father got up and went to the credenza by the window. My handbag was on top. He brought it over and I searched for the paper. I'd completely forgotten to give it to Conrad. I dug it out and handed it to my father.

"Con's been with our family for years. His father and mine were best friends," Jessie said. "Now Lauren's dead. Murdered. It's too much to bear. Chris is trying to get a flight back. I've never needed him more."

I thought for a moment I saw hurt in Emilio's eyes.

Listening to her, I picked up on one thing. Jessie had no idea Lauren was the person behind the wheel of her brother's hit-and-run. When I'd called my father, we made a pact not to say a thing until we could find out who the "We've got *him*" person was that Officer Rider mentioned.

My father handed the paper back to me. It was an invoice. The company logo was the same as the one Jessie just showed us — The Woodshop. Only this one was for three-legged wood stools.

I handed it to Jessie.

"Oh, Con — what have you done?" she cried.

It was then that we heard the clang of the windmill's bell. A few minutes later, Wilhelmina stepped into the room. She went to Jessie and whispered something. I read her lips: "There's a detective waiting in the hallway. He wants to talk to you."

Jessie shook her head. "Let him in."

Chapter 39

"Ms. Sterling," Arthur said, "I hope you're feeling better. I wanted to come in person and fill you in on the latest developments in the case. There are quite a few. If you would like to wait until tomorrow, I would understand."

"No, Detective. Please tell me now."

He glanced around the room, raised an eyebrow in my father's direction, and said, "It might be better if we talk alone."

"I would like them to stay," Jessie said. "Have you found my cousin's killer?"

"No, but we're pretty sure we know who killed your brother."

Jessie looked at him in shock. "My brother? Are you saying the same person who hit Travis killed Lauren?"

Here it comes, I thought, remembering overhearing Arthur earlier telling Conrad he'd been on his way to arrest Lauren.

"No, it's more complicated than that—" Arthur mumbled.

"How can it get any more complicated?" Jessie said. "I've been possibly poisoned, my brother and cousin are dead, we've found evidence someone in my company has committed fraud, my intern was sending threatening notes to my cousin, and my head of security just tasered Meg."

Arthur looked over at me and I shrugged my shoulders.

"And I forgot to add," she said, "there's a chance whoever murdered Lauren might have thought they were murdering me!"

"Have a seat, Arthur," my father said. "I think we better take things one at a time."

"I prefer to stand, Jeff. But I do agree, we have a lot to talk about."

It only took about ten minutes for Arthur to share the news that Lauren had hit Travis with her Mercedes, called Pete Moss to come and clean up her mess and retrieve Travis's phone. He didn't say how he found out these things, but I knew it had to be Sadie's video doorbell.

The one thing Arthur didn't tell us was who killed Lauren. It couldn't have been Jessie or Emilio, because Emilio had stayed the night and this morning with Jessie in the hospital. Kayla and Bryce seemed confident the hangar's camera footage would prove their innocence in Lauren's death. Bryce had seen who he thought was

Jessie enter the restaurant an hour before I saw him and Kayla. So Lauren hadn't been dead long. It could have been Pete, because, per Arthur, he hadn't been picked up until after Lauren's death. And Conrad. Only a few minutes ago, Jessie had voiced, *Oh, Con. What have you done?*

I had a lot of questions and I could tell my father did too. But we would wait until we were alone with Arthur to ask them.

"Ms. Sterling, I've stationed someone outside your door," Arthur said. "Is this where you'll be spending the night?"

"No, I'll be in the farmhouse. Wilhelmina is staying there with me."

"When you leave, please take Officer Rider with you."

"Does that mean you think whoever killed Lauren was after me?"

"I don't have an answer for you right now," he said, "but your toxicology report just came back. You had glyphosate in your blood."

"Weed killer," my father said.

"Pete," I said out loud, looking at my father, remembering what he said about the weed killer near the shed on the grounds of the hangar.

Arthur turned to me, then back to Jessie. "I will know a lot more in the morning."

After that news, there wasn't much more to be said. Except one thing. "Arthur," I asked, "does Conrad Kincaid know all about Pete's arrest?"

"As a matter of fact, he does. I just saw him at the East Hampton station. He was there with a bondsman, paying Pete Moss's bail."

"Why would Conrad do that?" Jessie asked.

"I don't know. But I promise you, when certain results come in, I'll be making an arrest."

Chapter 40

Arthur, my father and I sat on my deck overlooking a black ocean. Above us, a black sky. Black, like Lauren's heart. But whose black heart had killed Lauren?

My father followed me home so we could make sense of everything. Our timing was perfect because Arthur was just putting the recycle bin by the curb.

Arthur confirmed the video footage from Sadie's doorbell camera had not only caught Lauren leaving the scene of Travis's hit-and-run but also Pete Moss arriving soon after Lauren left.

When we were at Windmill Cottage, we'd forgotten to tell Arthur about the faked invoices, so I gave him a quick recap. "I'll have Jessie send you a copy of the video Travis took, proving company fraud is involved. And now that we know Conrad's bailed out Pete, what are the chances the three of them were in it together? Pretty good, I think." I told them about the fight Pete had with Conrad at the hangar. "It was like Pete was holding something over Conrad's head," I added.

"I can't tell you what Mr. Moss said in his confession, but I will say there was no mention of Mr. Kincaid. Only Mrs."

"Oh, Dad, I almost forgot. What did Kayla tell you before she went to turn herself in?" I turned to Arthur. "She did go to the police about the threatening notes she was writing to Lauren, right?"

Arthur nodded his head as he looked at my father.

"With everything going on, I almost forgot. Kayla told me she'd caught Lauren crushing up some white pills, then adding them to Jessica Sterling's tea. It was the afternoon following the news of her brother's death."

"Wow," I said, thinking about the bottle in Lauren's handbag. "If she was willing to crush up a pill—she sure could add some of Pete's weed killer to Jessie's tea. Did you look at all the surveillance footage of the restaurant?" I asked. "The front door was open when Kayla brought us inside."

"It's being taken care of," Arthur said. He stood. "Meg, I do want to thank you for the photo of the golf cart. By the way, did you notice anything familiar in Mr. Moss's tool belt?"

"Not really," I answered. "Though I didn't look at the photo after I sent it to you."

I slipped my phone out of my pocket and searched for the photo. I enlarged it and saw what he was talking about. "Those metal pin-like pieces in the holster? They're just like the one we found attached to Georgia's grabber when we were at the *Culloden* parking lot. What are they used for?"

"They're called landscape pins," Arthur said. "Used to tie down tarps under the soil to prevent weeds from coming up. Mr. Moss must have dropped one when he moved the body. He's made a full confession of his own volition as an accessory to covering up the hit-and-run. However, please don't share any of this until I have a news conference in the morning."

"How about Travis's phone?"

"Did Pete tell you where to find it?"

"Mr. Moss said he gave it to Mrs. Kincaid. We searched her residence but didn't find it. Now, it's been a long night. And day," Arthur said. "No more questions. Elle is waiting for me. I still haven't told her about Lauren Kincaid's murder—I assume you haven't either," he said, cocking his head in my direction.

"No. She wasn't home when I came back from the hangar."

"Good," he said, heading for my deck's side steps. "As I told Ms. Sterling, I think in the morning we'll have more answers and be able to make an arrest."

After Arthur disappeared into the darkness, my father said, "I'm beat. You want me to stay the night?"

"Of course not. I'm fine."

"Says the girl who just got tased. Sure you don't want to press charges?"

"I will, if it comes out Bryce is guilty of something." I stood and gave him a kiss. "Thanks for saving me."

"Anytime, daughter. Anytime." He looked toward my cottage's French doors. "I think someone is waiting for you. And she doesn't look happy."

"Since when has Jo ever looked happy?" I said with a smile.

"Jeff," I heard someone call out as a form materialized at the top the landing, leading up from my beach.

"Patrick," I said. "It's you."

"Yes, it's me. Who else were you expecting? Everything okay?"

"Depends how you look at it," I said.

He came across the deck and gave me a kiss. Patrick must have tucked his mother in as promised and walked up the beach to my cottage—also as promised. I couldn't have been happier to see him.

"Did you do something different to your hair?" he asked.

I laughed. "Yes, a new beauty treatment. It was quite shocking."

"She got tased," my father said.

"What? Tased? You said you were going to be with your father."

"True, Patrick," my father said. "And her father told her to wait until I arrived at Dahlia Lane Farms. Didn't I, daughter?"

"Dad, you would've chased after them, too. I'm fine. It's Jessie I'm worried about."

"Chased?" Patrick looked from me to my father. "Someone, fill me in."

So my father did, doing a much better job than I could because of my fried brain.

"Okay, I'm clear on everything, except who killed Lauren? Was it Pete?" Patrick asked.

"Arthur promises he's close to figuring that out. And I'm happy to let him," my father said. "I'm gonna go now that you're in safe hands."

"Thanks, Dad," I said. "For everything."

"Thanks, Jeff," Patrick said. "Between the two of us, you would think we could keep her in line."

Usually I would protest, but my phone buzzed. I blew my father a kiss, then looked down at my phone. It was a message from Emilio. *I swiped Jessie's keys to the hangar. Meet me. Let's look for those real invoices. I don't trust Jessie with Conrad. E.*

In the past, bad Meg would have met Emilio on her own. Now, after making sure my father was gone, *good* Meg showed Patrick Emilio's text.

"I'm going with you," he said.

"What about Aurora? What if she wakes and you're not there?"

"That's the least of my worries. What if I wake up in the morning and find you're not here?"

Chapter 41

Because of my Taser hangover, Patrick drove my woody to Dahlia Lane Shoppes at the Hangar. It only took us fifteen minutes without traffic and driving ten miles an hour over the speed limit. In case we did get pulled over, I had to admit there was an advantage to having a neighbor and friend who was in the East Hampton Town Police Department.

When we arrived at the hangar, the gates were open. Looking ahead, everything was dark except for the solar lights at the entrance.

"Let's pull around to the side," I said, pointing. "That's where Conrad's office is."

"Okay. But how are we going to get inside?" Patrick asked.

"I've already texted Emilio. He'll be at the door."

"Sure we shouldn't call Arthur? Or at least your father as backup?"

"You're my backup. It's not like we're trying to catch a killer. We're just trying to find the original invoices that give Lauren a motive for killing Travis and possibly poisoning Jessie. She's dead, but it doesn't mean we shouldn't look for a motive. Plus, it might lead to her killer."

He grinned. "You just said we're not here to catch a killer."

Patrick parked next to Emilio's Kia. He got out of the car, came and opened my door and helped me out. "You sure you're up to this? It's not every day you get tased. Someday soon you'll have to tell me what it felt like. I'll use your description in my next book."

"Funny. Shush, I see the light from Emilio's phone. Let's hurry."

"Yes, ma'am." He took my hand and we hurried onto the path leading to the side door.

When we reached Emilio, we didn't say a word. The key was already in the lock. All he had to do was turn it. Emilio held the door for us, nodded at Patrick and ushered us in. Once inside, I saw a blinking keypad on the wall next to the door. Hoping the alarm code was the same as the gate code, I punched in the numbers Jessie had given me. We were in!

The interior of the hangar was eerie, to say the least. Looking over at the restaurant and picturing Lauren's body made it even more spooky. There were a few security lights on. I pointed to the short hallway where I knew Conrad's office was. I started toward it. Patrick and Emilio followed behind.

As soon as I put my hand on the door handle to the office, Patrick mouthed, "Let me go first."

It wasn't time to argue.

The door was unlocked.

He opened it.

Smoked billowed out.

"There's a fire," I whispered, stating the obvious.

Emilio pushed past me and Patrick.

"Don't go inside," I shouted to deafer ears than mine.

"Stay here," Patrick said. "I mean it."

I believed he meant it.

But I still followed them inside.

Chapter 42

One of the metal filing cabinet drawers had been pulled out and set on fire. The rest of the office seemed clear of any flames. Emilio grabbed a fire extinguisher hanging on the wall by the door and aimed it at the flames.

It was hard to see through the smoke, but I managed to make my way toward the back wall of the office, where I knew Conrad's desk was. When I reached the desk, I grabbed a letter opener and went to work jimmying the drawer that yesterday I'd seen Conrad stuff papers in.

It worked! I grabbed the two folders and turned around. Emilio had put out the fire in the file cabinet drawer.

"It's too late. They're all ash," he called out.

"These might be something," I said as I walked over and handed Emilio the folders.

"Where's Patrick?" he asked.

"I dunno," I said, looking around. "He couldn't have gone that far."

"Wait. Do you hear that moaning?" Emilio asked.

No. I didn't hear it, but I followed Emilio's eyes and took off for the north side of the office. Now that the smoke had lifted, I saw an open door next to a bathroom. "Emilio, you check the bathroom. I'll check inside here."

It was a supply closet. A dark supply closet. I stepped inside and tripped over a pair of feet. Size eleven feet. Patrick's feet. Grabbing my phone from my pocket, I turned on the flashlight and faced it downward. Patrick was lying on the floor. His forehead was bleeding and he was out cold. I got down next to him. His eyelashes fluttered, *thank God,* but he didn't open his eyes. I quickly dialed 911. Before I could send my location, I heard someone say in my left hearing aid. "Put the phone down."

I placed the phone on the floor, next to Patrick. I quickly stood and faced Conrad. It wasn't a big surprise to find him here. After all, it was his office. What was a surprise was the handheld inventory scanner Conrad brandished like a club. A dark substance that looked like gooey chocolate glistened on the end of the scanner.

Patrick's blood?

Chapter 43

"Why'd you kill your wife?" I asked, hoping there was an open line on my phone to the 911 dispatcher. Or at least, I prayed, Emilio was listening.

"Why would I do that?" Conrad asked. "Oh, maybe because I found out she killed her cousin in cold blood? Or perhaps it had to do with the fact she told me she planned on poisoning Jessie, so no one would ever find out about all the money, we, as in she, kept siphoning from the Dahlia Lane coffers? I couldn't let her continue. Someone had to stop her."

"Why didn't you stop her earlier? Before she killed Travis."

"Because I had no idea she'd go that far. I didn't know until after Travis's death—"

"You mean murder."

"I also didn't know Lauren and Travis had a huge blowout. He was going to turn us both in for fraud. Lauren followed him to the dive site. Where things got out of hand."

"That's an understatement if I ever heard one."

He laughed. "She said she did it for me. She did it for herself. Lauren tried to call me Wednesday morning, but I missed her call. I was waiting at the hangar for my meeting with Travis."

"So, once you did know Lauren was the hit-and-run driver, why didn't you just tell the police she killed Travis? Where does Pete Moss come in?"

"Pete's been in love with Lauren from back when she used to work at Dahlia Lane, before she started the disastrous Lavender Fields. Lauren used his love to her advantage. She'd laugh about him to me, saying we never knew when he might come in handy. Seems Pete wasn't *that* much in love with Lauren, because Pete recently started threatening that he'd turn us in." Conrad glanced around the office. Did he know Emilio had come in with us? I hoped not.

Conrad lowered his arm holding the scanner, then looked down at it like he didn't know how it got there. I took a step closer, and he raised it in the air again. "I don't want to hurt anyone."

Too late for that, I thought. I had to keep him talking until either Patrick came to, Emilio came to the rescue, or the police arrived. "Why do you think Pete confessed to everything?"

"I'm sure to save his own neck." He paused. "Pete told me he was worried Lauren would blame him for the hit-and-run. It would be a case of he said, she said. Pete told me when he was arrested, he had no idea Lauren was dead. I was Pete's one call from the police station. If I didn't bail him out, he would lie and tell the police I was the one who told Lauren to kill Travis. Plus, he has Travis's phone. Apparently, there's lots of bad stuff about me on that phone."

I felt something touch my left ankle. I didn't look down. I knew it was Patrick. Knowing he was okay, I felt more confident confronting Conrad. "Back to why you killed Lauren."

"She was taunting me. I didn't mean to. I only choked her to make her promise to stop with her plan to kill Jessie. I took it too far. Then it was too late." Conrad's hand started to shake. For a moment I thought he might drop the scanner. "Simply put, I killed Lauren so she wouldn't kill Jessie. Don't you see? I was protecting Jessie. Jessie is the one I should have married. Not her look-alike."

"Why didn't you just turn yourself in? Won't they be arresting you after they look at the surveillance footage from the restaurant's kitchen?"

"I thought about it. But Jessie still needs me. I need to turn things around. I deleted the video of me walking in and out of the kitchen. It wasn't that hard."

Behind Conrad's head, I saw Emilio peer around the corner from the open bathroom door. He put his finger to his lips and took a step inside the office. He was holding a tall metal toilet paper stand in his right hand.

I had to keep Conrad distracted.

But that wasn't an issue because Patrick had gotten to his knees and crawled over to Conrad. "Meg, run!" he shouted.

Patrick tackled Conrad to the ground in a stellar wrestling move. Emilio rushed over and finished the job by whacking Conrad with the toilet paper holder.

Good night, Irene.

Chapter 44

"I couldn't have done it without you, buddy," Elle said, glancing toward the rows of small cottages that once made up the Sea Breeze Motor Lodge.

"My pleasure. Look how happy everyone seems," I said. "Because of you, their lives will be changed in unimaginable ways."

It was Labor Day. The sun was shining, the humidity was low, and the temps were in the mid-seventies. Elle and I had stopped on our way to a Labor Day feast at Doc's cabin to help the new residents move into their forever homes. Not that they had many belongings. But thanks to Elle, each cottage not only had new linens, towels, cleaning supplies, dishes and glassware, but their fridge and cupboards were stocked with food and drink.

"I've talked to local hotels and restaurants in Montauk about hiring some of the women," Elle said as we walked toward her pickup. "Just about all of them are on board. One of the problems with getting help in Hamptons restaurants and hotels is there aren't many affordable housing options for seasonal workers."

"That's a great idea," I said.

Elle smiled, turned and gave one last look at the bustling scene. "We better get to Doc's before we're missed."

"Sorry Arthur couldn't make it."

"Part of the job," she said. "Heard you're bringing dessert. How did that happen? I could have made something."

"Oh, yes, between the Sea Breeze and Heron's Roost, you've had plenty of time."

"Were you supervised when you made your dessert?"

"Actually, I wasn't. Unless you count Charlie. I didn't want Patrick breathing down my neck. And, I have to say, it turned out darn good."

"How do you know? Did you taste it?"

"No. It looked too pretty to taste. I did take lots of photos."

"Hmmm, interesting."

"You can taste it first. I'm sure you won't be disappointed."

Elle raised an eyebrow.

"Patrick's bringing it to Doc's. He seemed pretty impressed when I showed it to him." I glanced at my watch. "In fact, Patrick should be at Doc's by now. He's helping my dad make bouillabaisse on the grill."

"That sounds ambitious," Elle said, "though if anyone could pull that off, those two master chefs could. You better stay away."

"Just get in the truck," I said.

She did as she was told.

Once we were buckled in, we hit the two-lane highway that snaked its way around Fort Pond Bay. Elle turned to me and said, "Did you hear the news? Dahlia Lane Shoppes at the Hangar is opening at the end of September. Jessica Sterling and her fiancé were in Mabel and Elle's last week. They told Maurice the good news."

"I heard. I'm so happy Chris has been helping her untangle the mess that Conrad and Lauren caused. Emilio and I are supposed to stop by next week to help her choose the best photos for the Windmill Cottage book. Maybe you could tag along."

"That would be *beyond* awesome," Elle said with a huge grin as she made a right onto a rutted road surrounded by dense pine trees. "Now I have you alone, I have a bone to pick with you."

I turned to look at her. "You do?"

"Now that I know about everything that went down at Dahlia Lane, I'm at a loss to know why neither you nor my husband told me about things as they were happening? I'm not a delicate Sevres china cup."

"Arthur forbade me."

"When did that ever stop you?"

"Well, it all worked out. My father told me DNA results came back from samples taken from under Lauren's fingernails. It matches the scratches at the back of Conrad's neck when he was booked the night of the, uh—"

"The night you, Patrick and Emilio almost died."

"I don't think any of us would have died. An inventory scanner isn't as lethal as some of the other times—"

"After that bash to his forehead," she said, "I bet Patrick would beg to differ. What about Pete Moss?"

"Oh, he'll be serving time. But not as much time as Conrad. Pete turned over Travis's phone to get a better sentence. What's on it might help Conrad get a worse sentence. Emilio, recording Conrad's confession, will be the final nail in Conrad's coffin.

"From what you told me, Conrad did save Jessica Sterling's life. Will that count as anything?"

"Doubt it. All he had to do was tell the police. Then Lauren would have been arrested for Travis's hit-and-run and Jessie's attempted murder. There's one good thing. The weed-killer dose in Jessie's system wasn't near enough to kill her. Lauren might not have gone through with it. Guess we'll never know."

"How about the intern?"

"No charges have been filed. And naturally, Jessie is still helping the family. Though Kayla won't be her intern. Jessie's kind, but not that kind."

"Well, next time, you better include me or else. Though, that won't be an issue because you'll be too busy helping me at Heron's Roost to get in trouble. Arthur will be happy about that. At least it is all solved," she said, pulling up next to Patrick's Range Rover. "I'll be honest. Between those hormone injections and the Heron's Roost renovations, I would've been too distracted, anyway."

"Exactly," I said.

Chapter 45

As we walked toward Doc's cozy little cabin, I marveled at how perfect it was. Two old wicker rocking chairs sat on the front porch. One for Doc and one for my father.

As I followed Elle inside, the old wood-framed screen door banged behind us in welcome. Every time I stepped inside the cabin, I felt like I'd walked onto the set of *On Golden Pond*. When Doc took an early retirement from the Detroit PD coroner's office, he'd bought the cabin, fully furnished, sight unseen.

The ceiling in the main room was unfinished, exposing wood beams and supports. Vintage books followed the perimeter of the main room. In order to pick one out, you needed a ladder. Old fishing rods (not the ones my father and Doc used — they were hi-tech) hung on the wall near the door. Kerosene lamps that looked like they'd come in handy for our next hurricane hung from hooks jutting out from the rough-hewn log walls. There was a worn sofa, rattan chairs with lumpy cushions and a game table with four chairs. A game of Scrabble had been paused in mid-play. As I passed by, it took everything I had to stop myself from adding the word *worsted* for a triple-word score. Because his smudged reading glasses where nearby, I knew the letters on the wood stand belonged to my father.

On the shelves next to the table were old board games and puzzles.

In other words, Doc's cabin stole my vintage heart. If I was decorating this cabin for a Cottage by the Sea client, I couldn't have done better.

"Whoa!" I said, approaching the open kitchen. "Smells good in here! Bet it's my lemon berry dessert. Patrick Seaton! I hope you put it in a warmed oven, as I instructed."

Patrick heard me from the back deck that overhung Fort Pond. He opened the sliding screen door and stepped inside. In one hand he held a ladle, in the other a Montauk Brewery Wave Chaser. He was wearing a white stained apron (fish guts?) that said *Reel Men Fish*.

I had a feeling the apron was Doc's and a tad on the sexist side. Then I changed my mind when I saw Doc's girlfriend pass by wearing a *Reel Women Fish* apron. Go, Georgia!

Patrick came up to me and planted a sloppy kiss on my cheek. "Of course, my little taskmaster chef. Your scrumptious dessert is warming in the oven."

"That's quite the adjective—scrumptious. Well, you just wait. It will be."

"I have no doubt," he said.

"It better be *lightly* warming, two hundred degrees, buster. I slaved over that dish." A complete lie. If cooking was this easy, maybe I would take a lesson or two.

"Come out on the deck," he said, grabbing my hand, "you have to see the pot of bouillabaisse your father is cooking. I'm pretty sure this dish will put him in the winning category on our competition scoreboard."

"Oh, I'm sure next time you'll come up with something just as fabulous." *And I would reap the benefits.*

I freeze-framed the scene. "Look around, it doesn't get much better than this. Does it?"

"You're right. But what about our trip to London and Cornwall? How does that rate on a scale from one to a hundred?"

"A zillion!"

Patrick laughed.

"What's so funny?" I heard a voice say from behind me.

I turned around. "Aurora," I stuttered. "How nice. I didn't know you were coming."

"I didn't either," Patrick said. "Not until this morning when she turned up at my door."

Aurora had left Montauk shortly after Patrick got walloped on the head by Conrad. Patrick said I was reading into it, but I knew Aurora blamed me for his injury. In a way, she was right.

"Meg," Aurora said. "Yes. I popped out to the Hamptons to attend this end-of-the-summer soiree. Isn't it a picture-perfect day?"

"Uh, yes. It surely is. You drove all the way from Connecticut? Or did you take the Block Island Ferry?"

"Oh, didn't I tell you?" Patrick said. "My mother's recently moved."

No, he didn't tell me. I felt the steam building from behind my hearing aids. I bit the side of my cheek and said, "Oh-h-h, how wonderful."

"Aurora, there you are!" Elle said, coming from the kitchen with a platter in one hand, cocktail napkins in the other. "Did you make these to-die-for pear appetizers?"

"Why, yes, Elle, I did," Aurora said, grinning. "Where do you think my son got his talent from? Me of course."

"Meg, you must try one," Elle gushed. "Delish."

I took a napkin, then a slice of pear topped with cheese and walnuts and stuffed it in my mouth, realizing afterward, as Aurora looked on, I probably should have broken it down to two bites. "Heavenly," I said, doing a hard swallow. "I would love the recipe."

Elle coughed and Patrick grinned. Traitors.

"Now that you'll be living in Manhattan, Aurora," Elle said, "you can come out here and share more recipes with Meg. Wouldn't that be great, Meg?"

"Manhattan," I repeated. *Not Montauk.*

"Yes, I got a little pied-a-terre near Gramercy Park. I've decided to retire from doing restaurant reviews and write a murder mystery. In it, there will be a certain cheating, sleazeball chef who gets his just desserts," she said, laughing. "Patrick's promised to help me plot out the clues and red herrings. I also plan on legally changing my name back to Seaton. Aurora Seaton."

"Patrick told me you were a great writer," I said.

"He did?" Aurora looked up at her son and grinned.

"I'd love to be your first reader," Elle said. "As you know, my husband is on the police force, and because of murder-magnet Meg, I've been privy to one murder mystery after another."

I shot Elle the evil eye. She just grinned back at me.

"Aurora, she's kidding. Right, Patrick?" I said, giving him the elbow.

"Yes," he said, "Meg's not a murder magnet, she just finds herself in a lot of sticky situations." He put quotation marks in the air for the word *sticky.*

I felt the Barrett blotches reach my cheeks. Luckily, my father called through the sliding screen door, "Dinner's ready, come and get it!"

Saved by the dinner bell!

An hour later, after an amazing bouillabaisse (with saffron!) served at a long table with bench seating and a sunset view of Fort Pond, it was time for dessert. I let Patrick dish out each serving, afraid my hands would shake too hard if I did it.

Mentally crossing my fingers, I looked from Georgia, to Doc, to Elle, to my father, to Patrick, and finally to Aurora as they each took a bite. Naturally, it was Aurora's face I fixated on.

"Uhm-m, Meg," Aurora said, her mouth full. "This is delicious. I must have the recipe!"

Hallelujah. She likes me. She really likes me. At least she liked my dessert.

"Jeff, what do you think about your daughter's dessert?" Aurora asked.

"Delicious. So proud of you."

Patrick squeezed my hand under the table. That was when I noticed the empty serving dish was different than what I'd used.

I whispered, "That's not my dessert, is it?"

Patrick turned to me so I could read his lips. "It's exactly like yours, except I used sugar instead of salt."

I could have gotten mad that he hadn't clued me in. But heck, glancing at all the smiling faces at the table, I let it go. Plus, it was Patrick's fault for the mix-up. Who kept a large canister of salt between their stove and the coffee maker?

Apparently, he did.

After the dishes were cleared and put in the dishwasher, Elle pulled me aside. "Come. I want to show you something."

"Okay."

She took my hand and led me to the front porch, motioning for me to have a seat on one of the rockers. She sat next to me. For a moment we sat in the twilight, watching fireflies dance through the trees, breathing in the scent of pine and happiness.

"Well, that—"

"Shush," she said, stopping me. "I need you to look at something."

"Of course—it's not bad, is it?"

She reached into her shorts pocket and took out something. Then handed it to me.

I looked down at a white wand that looked like a digital thermometer.

Even in the dim light, there was no mistaking the clear plus sign in the wand's window.

"Oh, Elle—"

"Yes, Auntie Meg?"

Recipes

Aurora's Baked Honey & Goat Cheese Pears

4 Anjou pears cut into ¼-inch-thick slices
1 tablespoon butter, unsalted and melted
1 teaspoon rosemary
1 round of Le Chevre or similar French goat cheese, sliced
Honey
¼ cup pecans toasted and chopped

Preheat oven at 425.

Line a baking sheet with parchment paper.

Spread the pear slices on baking sheet. Brush with melted butter, then sprinkle evenly with rosemary. Bake for 8 minutes. They can also be grilled.

Remove the pears from the pan and allow to cool slightly.

Transfer the slices to a serving platter and top with slices of goat cheese, drizzle with honey and top with pecans.

Jeff Barrett's Bouillabaisse

This spectacular and satisfying dish can be somewhat intimidating if you've never made it, but it's actually quite straightforward and relatively easy if you prepare and follow these instructions. A couple of rules for perfect bouillabaisse:

Always use seafood stock, preferably homemade as indicated here. Cook the seafood in the soup at the very end, then add them to the pot in the order given. *Do not overcook!*

Seafood to use without mussels or clams. Figure 8 ounces of seafood per person, total:

2-inch chunks of flaky white fish: halibut, cod, haddock, snapper, striped bass, etc. Any white, flaky fish; no dark fish!
Shrimp
Sea scallops
Clam meat, frozen

Start by making the stock:

8 cups water
3 bottles clam juice (at least 8 ounces each)
Shrimp shells
Any other fresh fish bones or lobster shells
Lobster base to add flavor
Carrots
Onion
Celery
Leek
Saffron
Herb bundle of thyme, bay leaf, parsley tied together with leek green
Piece of potato (pull out after 30 minutes, set aside to add to rouille)

Bouillabaisse:

Onion, chopped
Leeks, chopped
Fennel bulb, chopped
Garlic, chopped
1 cup dry sherry
A couple of tablespoons of Pernod (if you have it)
Crushed tomatoes, 15-ounce can
Salt and pepper

Rouille:

Cooked potato
Roasted red pepper
Saffron
Garlic
2 egg yolks
½ cup olive oil
Cayenne
Lemon juice
Salt and pepper
French baguette slices, rubbed with garlic, toasted and buttered.
Chopped fresh parsley as garnish

Simmer stock ingredients for 30 minutes; remove and reserve potato, then simmer for another 30 minutes. Remove bundle and strain stock into large pot or bowl and reserve; you should have about 8 cups.

In a large Dutch oven (such as Le Creuset or Staub), add 2 tablespoons olive oil and 1 tablespoon butter and heat on medium until butter just melts and starts to bubble. Add all chopped vegetables (except tomatoes) and sauté until cooked and soft but not brown. Add wine, and Pernod, and reduce. Add tomatoes and season with salt and pepper. Bring vegetable mixture to a boil, then add in the strained stock. Return to boil, then reduce heat to simmer for 10 minutes. Remove from heat and blend until smooth with immersion blender (or in a blender or food processor) and keep in Dutch oven until ready to cook seafood and serve.

To make the rouille, to the bowl of a food processor, add the cooked potato, garlic, roasted red pepper, a squeeze of lemon juice, and egg yolks. Process until smooth. With processor running, slowly add olive oil to create emulsion. Add cayenne, saffron, salt and pepper. Set aside.

When ready to serve, reheat the bouillabaisse until just simmering. Add the fish first, then the shrimp and scallops, and then the clams. Simmer no more than 7 minutes total. Turn off heat and check for seasoning.

To serve, place 2 baguette toasts at bottom of wide bowl. Spoon soup and seafood over toasts to cover with roughly equal portions of each seafood. Place a dollop of rouille on top and garnish with fresh chopped parsley. Serve remaining rouille on the table as a condiment.

Enjoy!

Meg's Super Easy Lemon Berry Dessert

4 ounces cream cheese (½ package)
¼ cup of lemon curd (if you can't find a jar of Dahlia Lane Farms lemon curd, feel free to use your grocery store favorite)
¼ cup sour cream
2 cups fresh raspberries
1 cup fresh blueberries
¼ cup packed light brown sugar

Adjust oven rack to sit seven inches below the broiler element.

Whisk together cream cheese, lemon curd and sour cream in a medium bowl until smooth. Set aside.

Scatter berries in a broiler-safe 9-inch ceramic tart or quiche dish. Spoon cream cheese mixture over berries and gently spread so the mixture covers berries completely. Sprinkle brown sugar evenly over the surface.

Place in oven and broil until sugar is bubbly and caramelized, 2–4 minutes.

Serve warm.

Meg's Guide to Common Interior Design Mistakes and How to Fix Them

Mistake: All the furniture in the room is hugging the wall.
Suggestion: Move the furniture away from the walls. Even if it's only a few inches. Perhaps put a table behind the sofa. Set up groupings of furniture so they are conducive to conversation. Not everything has to face the television.

Mistake: The TV is larger than the furniture below it.
Suggestion: Think outside the box on how to place the television. Even wall-hung televisions should have furniture below that is wider than the television. Measure the width of your TV before you buy new or vintage dressers or sideboards to go underneath.

Mistake: Furniture in the room is too large or too small.
Suggestion: Try to use furniture in scale. Your furniture size should be in proportion to the size of your room. Accessories and décor can vary in size.

Mistake: Small area rugs that only fit under the coffee table or dining room table.
Suggestion: Sofas and chairs should be touching the area rug and will make the room appear larger. Dining room chairs should be on the area rug, even when the chairs are pulled out from the table.

Mistake: I'm a fan of all periods of furniture and home décor but mixing too many can be overwhelming.
Suggestion: Choose only two periods in a room. For example — mix mid-century interior design with industrial Parisian chic. Rococo with ultra-modern. Eclectic is good, just don't overdo it. If you have different periods of furniture, perhaps stick to similar wood finishes.

Mistake: Matchy-matchy — every piece of furniture and soft goods in the room matches.
Suggestion: Add some whimsy, colors not in the same family as the upholstery. Try not to make your living areas look like they came off a showroom floor.

Mistake: Floor-length curtains that are too short. Hanging curtain rods right above the window.
Suggestion: Floor-length curtains should lightly puddle on the floor or at least touch the floor. Curtain rods should be placed near the ceiling to make the ceiling appear higher than it is.

Mistake: Only using overhead light in a room.
Suggestion: It's best to use multiple light sources in a room. Use accent lamps with low light for relaxing. Use dimmer switches to set the mood. Dining room light fixtures shouldn't hang too close to the ceiling. Aim for 30–36 inches above the table. Light switches should match the wall color.

Mistake: Art that is not hung correctly. For example, small art that is too high on the wall or large art that is too low on the wall.
Suggestion: Place art eight to ten inches above sofa or chairs. To help hang multiple pieces of art on one wall, use painter's tape to map out your space.

Mistake: Clutter and open storage.
Suggestion: If your objects don't spark joy, pass them on or donate. Try closed storage options for a more serene environment — especially in your entryway.

Mistake: Your open concept living space looks disjointed because you used different colors on your walls.
Suggestion: Try for a similar color palette in your open living spaces (not matchy-matchy). Your eye should seamlessly flow from living to dining to kitchen. Furniture finishes, doors and wood trim in the same family lends to a cohesive open look.

Mistake: An all-white room.
Suggestion: Add some contrast using color and textures in pillows and art so the room doesn't look like one big blur.

Mistake: Small rooms that have too many small accessories.
Suggestion: Surprisingly, adding a large vase in a small room will make the room appear larger.

Mistake: Not leaving enough clearance around furniture.
Suggestion: Leave space around your furniture. Your guests shouldn't be shimmying around furniture.

Mistake: Buying furniture and art without measuring the size you need.
Suggestion: Before hitting the shops, use cardboard, painter's tape or 3-D computer modeling to get an idea of the size of the piece you're looking for. Store your measurements in the note section in your phone.

Mistake: High-maintenance finishes and fabrics. Example: glass tables, glossy lacquer finishes, marble countertops, chairs and sofas with button tufted seats.
Suggestion: Granite countertops are a better choice because they are less likely to pick up stains from acidic liquids like coffee. Tufted seats accumulate crumbs and are hard to clean; also, they aren't very comfy. Tufting is fine on the back of chairs and sofas. Glass and lacquer finishes require constant maintenance.

Mistake: Worrying about making a mistake when it comes to home furnishings and décor.
Suggestion: We all make mistakes. Every mistake I've mentioned above I have made at one time or another. When it comes to your home, personal style trumps all. Don't be afraid to think outside the box. Frame Grandma's recipe, memorabilia or your favorite poem. Enjoy the journey, don't rush into filling your home with objects and furniture that aren't tailored to your lifestyle and personality. Stay away from trends in interior design—make your own trend. Your home environment should be a haven, a place to recharge your battery. A place where you feel calm and relief when you step in the door.

Elle's Guide to Common Vintage Jewelry and Clothing Mistakes and How to Fix Them

Mistake: Not cleaning vintage jewelry after purchasing it from thrift and vintage shops.
Suggestion: *Gently* wash using a mild soap and a soft toothbrush. Rinse in warm, not hot, water and set on a towel to dry.

Mistake: Storing vintage jewelry in plastic bags.
Suggestion: Store individual pieces in soft velvet or suede bags or in drawers with individual sections. I have an antique dental cabinet to store my small pieces.

Mistake: Keeping your vintage jewelry in your bathroom.
Suggestion: The humidity in bathrooms might cause the glue in your vintage pieces to weaken. Humidity is also an enemy of certain metals. Store items in a clean dry space. I store my necklaces on a 1930s ladder in my walk-in closet. And my pins in the aforementioned dental cabinet or soft cloth bags.

Mistake: Purchasing vintage or estate jewelry without checking for loose stones, protruding prongs or sloppy repairs.
Suggestion: Purchase a jeweler's loupe when buying vintage jewelry. Bring the piece into sunlight to check colors and clarity. If the piece is a bargain and still sings to you—flaws and all—stones can be glued and prongs can be bent with a tweezer to hug the stone.

Mistake: Putting on lotion or oil right before putting on jewelry.
Suggestion: Use hand lotion, body oil or perfume at least an hour before putting on your vintage jewelry.

Mistake: Letting your vintage fashions hang in a too-crowded closet.
Suggestion: Leave enough space between your clothing. Occasionally, spot clean or brush your garments to remove dust and dirt. Hang all fashion items with top button buttoned to keep the garment's shape.

Mistake: Wearing heavy pins or brooches on lightweight vintage garments.

Suggestion: Only wear lightweight jewelry pieces on fabrics like silk, linen, and cotton. Save heavier pieces for wool, jackets or blazers.

Mistake: Throwing vintage gloves, beaded and fabric clutches and scarves in a drawer.
Suggestion: Use acid-free tissue paper for wrapping your items.

Mistake: Buying online without asking if the seller lives in a smoke-free home.
Suggestion: This rings true from not only vintage clothing and handbags but also, as Meg will attest to, buying furniture from an online marketplace. Also be sure to ask where the items have been stored before buying. Musty basements, garages and sheds are conducive for humidity, dampness, mold and insects.

Wishing you great finds and a Happy Home! And remember, a modern home can meld perfectly with that little touch of Vintage. XO, Meg & Elle

About the Author

Kathleen Bridge is the national bestselling author of the Hamptons Home & Garden Mystery series and the By the Sea Mystery series. She started her writing career working at *The Michigan State University News* in East Lansing, Michigan. A member of Sisters in Crime and Mystery Writers of America, she is also the author and photographer of an antiques reference guide, *Lithographed Paper Toys, Books, and Games*. She teaches creative writing in addition to working as an antiques and vintage dealer. Kathleen blissfully lives on a barrier island in Florida. Readers can visit her on the web at www.kathleenbridge.com, on Facebook at www.facebook.com/kathleen.m.bridge, and on Instagram @authorkathleenbridge.

Made in United States
North Haven, CT
14 October 2024

58898727R00136